I0460881

Amelioration: A Change of Heart

L D Raylene

Published by L D Raylene, 2024.

For my family. As always . May we never give up on each other.

Special thanks to Felicia Sidharta. Thank you for your times to proofread and gave your honest feedback while working full time and taking care of your little cheeky toddler.

A tale is crafted from a puzzle of selected occurrences.

Prologue

Taking in the stunning view of the clear blue sky from the wall-to-wall window of a skyscraper office tower in Melbourne CBD had been her childhood dreams. The sight of the vast expanse of blue above the bustling city always filled her with a sense of wonder and joy. She aspired to become a prosperous entrepreneur, envisioning herself at the helm of a multi-million-dollar business and working from the most luxurious office within the company she built. Occasionally, her imagination ran high as she visualised herself gracefully sitting at a grand mahogany desk, delicately holding a cup and sipping her favourite Peppermint tea, letting the soothing aroma envelop her senses, and a gentle smile of fulfilment gracing her lips.

Currently standing in the middle of the massive office, her dream, in a way, had been realised.

Except for one problem.

This was not her office room. No fancy titles or big accomplishments whatsoever. She wasn't a business owner or in a high-ranking position at a company. She was just a regular admin girl.

After listening to her endless shudders for a few hours in the room, another silent prayer whispered in her heart, wishing this ordeal could come to an end soon. She gazed blankly at the only other presence in the room, watching him lay on the floor in a state of helplessness. His head was gently elevated, supported by a cushion she grabbed from the couch. His right leg was another part supported by another cushion, with the upper thigh knotted with a messy ribbon from his torn shirt sleeves. Seeing his poor shape intensified her fear as the cloth and the cushion soaked up more and more with his blood.

AMELIORATION: A CHANGE OF HEART

His eyes were closed, and his breathing sounded steady. It was hard to tell if he was sleeping or in distress. But he looked so calm and peaceful. What currently befell them was mind-blowing. Although he was the last man she would want to be stuck in a room with, the thought of him dying would be the last thing she had in mind. She hoped both of them could escape from this place unharmed.

Turning away from the miserable sight, her gaze returned to the skyscraper view outside the window. The beautiful sight brought her some comfort. Her lips drew a bittersweet smile, marvelling at the irony of life.

Ever since she graduated from college, she had dreamed of working in a multinational corporation. This dream inspired her to swiftly earn her degree at university. She landed her first dream job as a junior officer in business operations. Life continued to unfold beautifully with marriage to her high school sweetheart and the motherhood of a pair of gorgeous children. She was fortunate to work alongside a supportive line manager as his executive assistant before he retired.

Things turned out a bit patchy when she returned from her maternity leave. She had been assigned to different departments until she landed her current EA role with a man who was infamously known for his ruthless demands. It was supposed to be a temporary role filling in for the actual EA while she was on vacation for six weeks. However, the past month had been a real challenge for her.

The man who was lying possibly lifeless on the floor was the one who had tormented her. Just a little while ago, before they were in the current state, she had imagined being the one curled on the floor, weeping for her fate.

Until a gun unexpectedly exploded, releasing a deafening noise as the bullet penetrated the air, and he stumbled and fell to the ground.

Chaos ensued. A hysterical scream echoed through the air. The fire alarm blazed. The hallway outside the room became dark and full of smoke. Fear and shock washed over her. But witnessing his fall at her feet, her first instinct was to shut the door and lock it. Whatever that overtook her mind at that time, she had no idea. With all her might, she dragged his body away from the door.

His ugly cursing and growl reverberated in the room. Everything became blurry, and his voice was like a distant echo. Her brain was racing as her heart pounded hard, unable to wrap her head around what was happening. Then suddenly, a deep, dark, sinister male voice boomed from the central tower speaker. The office building had been hijacked. That was the last thing she could imagine working in such a prestigious place.

After the hijacker made his demands known, a heavy silence crept in. A wave of numbness washed over her, met with the grimace on his face as sweat sheathing on his forehead. Eventually, like a defeated beast, he grew quiet and rested his head with hazy eyes staring at the ceiling. She knew that was not a good sign. He seemed to be in a lot of pain and could even be on the brink of death.

Recalling the first aid course she was delegated to, she did her best to comfort him with whatever was available in the room. Although she was not anticipating any gratitude, she could tell he was too tired to express it even if he wanted to. Sitting quietly beside him, her gaze returned to the window. Her only wish was that they could come out from here. Staying positive, her family was her rock and motivation. They were the light at the end of the tunnel that she held onto tightly.

The clearing throat from the central speaker jolted her. His eyes snapped open from apparently only his peaceful sleep.

"Ladies and gentlemen, it's time to settle our scores!"

They exchanged curious glances, both pondering the words meaning.

"First of all, there is a man whom I want to meet. Mr Tyler Fraser! I'm pretty sure you're still alive. Open the door, and show us what you can do to save your company."

The hijacker talked about him. His lips curved into a bitter loop as if he had already anticipated it. He was an essential figure in the company. It would not be a surprise if the hijacker hunted him. He nodded at her, signalling her to open the door as instructed. She took another shuddering breath, unsure whether this would be a good idea. With full of hesitancy, she stood up and slowly made her way to the door.

She glanced another look at him before touching the door handle and met with his affirmative nod. However, her hand was left hovering in the air.

"He only wants me. He will let you go." His weak voice finally pierced the silence between them. "Besides, I believe you want me gone from your life."

His grin appeared on the corner of his lips. A wolfish smile that had been haunting her for the past weeks and always sent a disgusting churn in her stomach. The moment of what he almost did to her before this ordeal, flashed in her mind and ignited an ire in her chest. Yes, she wanted him gone from her life. But not by sending him to his demise.

His impatience was the answer to her doubt. He lurched forward, twisted the lock and flung open the door.

There he was, his potential murderer, standing outside with both arms on the chest and feet planted firmly on the ground. Dressed in a suit reminiscent of a soldier, the hijacker's tousled fringe fell slightly on his forehead as he tilted his head. His gaze landed on her first before he put on his fierce mask to glance at his prey.

"Are you alright, Amanda?"

She held her breath as her name was called. The person she saw as the hijacker made her question if her brain was playing tricks on her. However, his rich baritone voice was not foreign to her ear. His gentle voice was her routine morning short lullaby every time she stepped into the printing room on her office floor. He would greet her with his polite smile, and their friendly chit-chat for a couple of minutes followed. The same man now stood tall, with a tight jaw on his face and a weapon on his arm. It was like a nightmare she couldn't wake up from.

And yet, a lump in her throat wobbled as she found a way to breathe.

"Ben?"

Chapter One

The Past - *48 hours earlier*

C affeine. Caffeine. Caffeine.

That was the only word hanging in Amanda's head as she stepped into her work desk. The time showed 8 o'clock in the morning, and the office floor was only halfway full. From the half-opened double door of her new boss's office room, she let out a sigh of relief that she had beaten him in. In just a matter of minutes, Mr Tyler Fraser, the VP of Fraser & Co would enter his office and start to bestow her with a daily nightmare. What she needed to focus on now was getting a cup of his favourite latte on his desk before she could sip her own espresso.

Another long day, she thought. She filled in this role three weeks ago and had probably been working twelve hours daily. Fortunately, it was only a temporary role. But she did not recall Megan – the real Mr Fraser's EA warned her about his demanding boss. Perhaps it was her fault to trust Megan naively. Bitching around fellow EAs was common in a big corporate firm. No exception in this case. If she were underperforming, she would look bad, while Megan would shine. Besides, she should be aware when taking up this job, that her main role was to provide unwavering support to a high-profile person, the son of the founder.

Her heart questioned whether the sacrifices of her demanding job were truly worth it. The pay was bloody good, but her precious time with her family was irreplaceable. For at least six weeks, she had foreseen she could not see her children every day. Hamish and Isla were still in dreamland when she left for work and fast asleep by the time she got home. One thing she could cherish was watching their peaceful sleeping faces before crawling into her bed.

Amanda valued the importance of family. With her parents living far away in regional Victoria, without Sean's parents' help, none of them would have time to run the errands for the kids. She owed her in-laws a great deal. Whenever she felt like giving up, she reminded herself that this hectic time was only temporary. Hopefully, she would find a better work-life balance in her next role.

A gentle chime from her mobile phone caught her attention. Spinning her head around, she had not sighted any sign of Mr Fraser's appearance. Her fingers moved speedily to check her message—a text from Sean.

Bad News. I just received a redundancy announcement.

Amanda took a deep sigh. Sean worked as a technical engineer in a global automotive manufacturer for the past ten years. He already knew the ins and outs of the company and weathered a couple of restructurings in the past. But it never crossed their mind that this time it would be his turn.

Placing a quick glance at the clock, she still had a bit of time. No sign that her boss was coming, Amanda called her husband.

"What happened?" Her weak voice echoed as she shoved her side straight brown hair in dismay.

They had been married for eleven years. Sometimes it made her wonder whether their way of talking to each other became a bit too casual, lacking any hint of affection. They began their relationship as a friend before it escalated into romance. After the birth of two children within two years, they seemed to slip back into friend mode. Their conversations mostly revolved around kids' schedules, surviving household chores and work routines. Definitely, it was something they needed to work on.

Sean let out a deep sigh, mirroring her wary voice. "We had a town meeting this morning and it looks like my position is impacted by the changes. I've only got six weeks left here."

"Any chance you could potentially be redeployed?"

Though she could not physically see him, Amanda could visualize Sean shrugging his shoulder.

"No idea. I'll see if I can chat with some folks from different departments to see if any opportunities pop up."

"Do you see this was coming?"

"Kinda." Another deep sigh from Sean. "You've been so wrapped up in things lately. We haven't really had a chance to catch up."

His tone was filled with disappointment. Amanda closed her eyes briefly as a twinge of remorse hit her.

"I'm sorry. It's been hectic in the office." That was all she could say. Her eyes hawked around to ensure no one was within her earshot. "My new boss is horrible."

"For how long are you filling in for this role?"

"Six weeks. I'm just filling in for his EA who is on vacation."

"You're only in your third week."

Amanda chuckled at her husband's discouraging remark. "Right. And I'm dying."

"Hang in there. We only have six weeks to survive."

Amanda could not deny the reality of the situation. Once Sean was unemployed, and her career was up in the air, they would be left without any income. She had been fortunate so far, bouncing between different departments with only short breaks in between. At least it ensured the continuity of her income stream.

The chime of the lift door opening made her heart skip a bit. That could be Mr Tyler Fraser! Craning her neck to get a better view, her breath hitched at the sight of the formidable figure of her boss. Mr Tyler Fraser, currently sitting at the third for Fraser & Co's throne, made his way to his office room with his usual air of confidence. Perhaps that was how a leader was supposed to be, Amanda thought.

Apart from the unfriendly no-nonsense mask that he put on his face, in his mid-thirties, Amanda could not resist labelling him as awfully handsome. The girls who had been working on the same floor always seemed captivated by his presence. His dark suit was always immaculate, creaseless, glistening from luxurious brands. His dark brown hair perfectly complemented his deep lid brown eyes and eyebrows. He was always cleanly shaven most of the time, especially when there were meetings. Yet, when he showed up with a hint of stubble on his chiselled jaw, the whispers between the girls were even louder.

As a fresh face on the floor, Amanda hadn't had much time to form close connections. She only had time to exchange quick hellos with a couple of people whom she passed by on her way to her desk. How could she have time to speak with them, when most of her time was occupied with ceaseless demands from her boss?

Mr Tyler Fraser could be classified as an unreasonable demanding boss. Since her first day, Amanda shifted uncomfortably under the scrutinization of his eagle eyes. Her initial interview was with Megan, hence her first day was also marked the first encounter with Mr Fraser himself. The first few minutes of their meeting were full of his interrogation of her family life. Amanda was not offended by the questions. Building a rapport was as just as important as the job itself. However, the heat of his gaze on her sent a shiver down her nape.

As if he wanted to maul her.

She shook off the awkward feelings and reminded herself to stay professional. Man with power and position like Mr Fraser would tend to be intimidating. He handed her a long list of work to do, from preparing documents, sending emails and letters, travel arrangements, and meeting appointments, to taking care of his personal stuff, including organising his kids' school pick-up and getting birthday presents for his daughter's friend. It made her reminisce about the glorious time when she worked with her already retired wonderful favourite boss Mr Malcolm who never burdened her with his personal stuff. He was truly a rare find.

"I've got to go. My boss is here." Her quick whisper was responded to by a soft grunt by Sean. The word 'bye' was exchanged briskly, and then she hung up at the right time before Mr Fraser reached her desk.

"My office." He gestured his head to his office door.

Amanda restrained herself from rolling her eyes. No single morning greetings were even exchanged. She had accepted the fact that this would be a habit she had to endure for six weeks. She followed him to his room and closed the door behind her, anticipating he would begin ranting with the list of jobs he wanted her to do.

That was exactly what happened for the first twenty minutes of their meeting. Amanda could literally feel the adrenaline coursing through her veins as her brain switched on what she needed to prioritise. Nevertheless, she could not help but feel a bit queasy whenever she looked up. Unsure whether it was by coincidence or not, their eyes would clash, and her breathing became shaky to be the recipient of his hawking.

"I heard about the restructuring in your husband's company." His unexpected statement, though it sounded casual, caught her off guard, and brought their work topic into a sudden change.

Amanda blinked in confusion. He seemed to find her reaction amusing, with a small smirk playing on his lips.

"Um... How did you...?" she stuttered.

He seemed to anticipate what she was about to ask. "You must have forgotten who I am. Getting this kind of insider info is a piece of cake for me, especially when it involves one of my employees."

"Oh..." Her lips parted as she processed the news. Her thoughts raced, debating whether it was typical for an employer to be so well-informed. But instead of dwelling on it, she decided to push those thoughts aside and not overthink the situation.

"I suppose that means you will have to put in extra effort, Amanda. For your family. Your husband will be out of work soon." He continued with an unreadable facial expression that made Amanda swallow the lump in her throat. Thousands of questions swirling in her mind. What were those words supposed to mean? The crease on her brow did not go unnoticed by him. A slight smirk played on his lips..

Unsure whether she should respond to the comment, Amanda forced a timid smile. "Yeah, I guess so," she murmured.

Mr Fraser raised his eyebrows. "When was the last time you had a holiday?".

Amanda felt the question was meant to mock her. Though inevitably, she felt a hard pinch in her chest as the word holiday seemed had not reached her ear for ages. She could not even remember when she last took one. With the economic inflation and high mortgage interest rates, and she was in between jobs, she and Sean were focused on saving every penny for the kids' education and activities like music and sports. The anxiety over finances was always lurking in the back of her mind whenever she needed to spend.

With a sheepish smile, she shook her head. "I have no idea, Mr Fraser."

Mr Fraser leaned hard on his majestic leather seat as he threw his gaze to the window. The sky was cloudy since morning, and the forecast only mentioned showers throughout the day.

"Isn't it summer in Paris right now? Wouldn't you rather escape the wet winter here?"

The question only puzzled Amanda even more, and she perceived it as his poor jest. However, as her working brain squeezed in, she wondered whether this was a test of some sort. From the top of her head, she did not recall that Mr Fraser had any business trip schedule.

"I'm sorry, Mr Fraser. But I don't recall you are planning to go to Paris." She quickly wrote down her note. "Could you please tell me the dates you're going?"

An unnatural silence settled over the room instead. No sound from Mr Fraser. Amanda glanced up from her note, only to find Mr Fraser's unwavering stare at her. It made her nervously rub her sweaty palms on her work pants. His expression appeared dark and intense, possibly displeased that she had overlooked his schedule.

Amanda braced herself, swallowing hard. "I..I can get the details later on. You have a meeting coming up in fifteen minutes. Is there anything else you need in the meantime, Mr Fraser?"

She was unsure whether it was her imagination or not, Mr Fraser's face softened and a flash of a mischievous smile tugged at the corner of his lips.

"You forgot my coffee," he answered flatly.

Amanda cursed inwardly, visualising slapping her own forehead. Her hands gripped her pants as she berated her forgetfulness.. With a sheepish smile and murmured apology, she hurried over to the coffee machine tucked away in the corner of the room.

For the next couple of minutes, the room was filled with the gentle sounds of clinking coffee cups and saucers as she worked. Despite trying to stay focused on her task, she could feel the hair on her nape standing up, sensing the unceasing heat of Mr Fraser's eyes on her. She tried to push away the discomfort and directed her mind on her task, eagerly anticipating the moment when she could finally leave the room and take a deep breath.

She had to be proud that no single drop of the coffee spilled on the way to Mr Fraser's desk. Her hands were not shaking though they were perspired. But the moment she placed the cup on the desk, Mr

Fraser's hand immediately reached for it, causing friction between their hands.

Amanda's pure thought was assuming it was an accident. She pulled her hand away and tucked them behind her back. Somehow she expected a soft murmur of gratitude out of politeness. But there was nothing. Mr Fraser took the cup and sipped it, but his eyes never left her. Amanda could not wait to leave the room.

"I'll be at my desk if you need anything else, Mr Fraser." Then with a slight bow, she twirled away to be halted by the soft thud on the carpeted floor. Her head snapped around in reflex, searching for the source of the sound. Something fell, and her eyes caught an elegant black ballpoint rolling on the carpet for a mere second before it stopped just behind her shoes. Stepping back slightly, she bent down to pick it up.

A squeaking sound of Mr Fraser's chair echoed as Amanda could sense Mr Fraser also stepping out from his desk at the same time as the item in her hand. She straightened up her spine and twirled around to return the item to its owner but held her breath as her palm inevitably landed on the broad chest of Mr Fraser. His earthly masculine scents immediately invaded her senses.

Amanda's mind went blank for a second as such proximity was unexpected. Her first reaction was to move away, but to no avail, as his strong arms encircled her. Her heart skipped a beat, her lips parted, as she fell into the consuming gaze of Mr Fraser.

Amanda could not recall when the last time she was in a man's arms, specifically her husband's, especially with the hecticness in her life recently. It was a rarity to see her father as he lived far away in regional Victoria. The warm embrace became so foreign that it immediately prompted her to wriggle away. But when Mr Fraser squeezed tighter, it set off alarm bells in her head.

This is not right!

Mr Fraser seemed to have a great time watching her struggle. His lips curled in amusement, and his eyes sparkled with mischief. Their imbalance wrestle caused her to be pushed further until she was trapped between his herculean frame and the wall. Being his entertainment intensified her panic. However, her 165 cm petite figure was powerless compared to his 180 cm broad shoulder build.

"Let me go." She was almost out of breath, practically panting hard. She could feel Mr Fraser's face drawing near as his warm breath tickled her ear. Feeling a bit helpless, she stopped struggling for a moment to catch her breath.

"Don't worry, Amanda," he whispered. His voice was hoarse full of desire. "I can take care of you."

"Mr Fraser. I ..." She attempted to push him away, but he was still unmoved like a big rock pressing on her. "Please let me go."

"If you just follow my lead, everything will be okay."

Amanda's stomach churned with sickness as those words sunk in, intensifying her horror. The gut feeling that she had been ignoring turned out to be true. A wave of guilt and fear tightened her chest, sending a prick of tears in her eyes. She should have been more on guard. How could she be so naïve?

"I...I don't want this." She managed to say, mustering all her strength to fight back.

Her vision started to blur as her shoulder-length wavy French Roast hair fell messily around her face. Her whimper became louder as his rough palm kneaded her breast and his lips nibbled her neck. Her mind screamed to reject these advances. Her hands frantically tried to push him away, but it seemed the more she tried, it fuelled him to be stronger. Then, for one second, when she was on the verge of giving up, a sudden mobile ringtone broke them apart.

The splash of cold air on her face was like a breath of fresh air. Without looking back, she scampered towards the door. One pull of the door was fruitless as the door was locked. With sweaty trembling hands, she turned the key around and swung the door open.

She probably looked like a maniac as she dashed out of the room. But, once she was outside she was suddenly reminded where she was. To her surprise, most of the cubicles on the floor looked empty. Mr Fraser's office was slightly tucked away in the corner, with a heavy wide double timber door. Meanwhile, her desk was just outside his office in a little nook. Therefore, it would not be a surprise if no one noticed anything unusual or heard any commotion from inside.

She was standing in the middle of the floor for a moment with her whole body shaking. Glancing back at Mr Fraser's office, the door was tightly shut as if nothing had occurred. A few coworkers in distant cubicles were engrossed in their screens, oblivious with their headphones on. Not one person seemed to notice or acknowledge her presence, even though she stood there with messy hair and smeared makeup.. A wave of self-doubt crept into her mind, wondering if what she had was an illusion.

But she was sure she had not lost her sanity despite her recent work exhaustion. What Mr Fraser just did to her was undeniably real. She had become a potential sexual assault victim.

As if she was just being defeated, she took a deep breath and decided to fix herself in the restroom. Passing through the printing room, a gentle voice called her name. She stopped in her track and was met by a genuine friendly face that she desperately needed at this moment.

"Good morning, Amanda."

Ben – the building's facility staff- who had been working for the company for thirty years, smiled at her. The man was probably in his late sixties with white hair, a thin frame, and a slight hunch. His smile slowly faded as he took a closer look at her.

"Are you alright?"

Chapter Two

The Past.

Feeling like his leg was weighed down by heavy timber and sticky mud, Tyler felt helpless as he was immobile. A sharp scent of copper filled his nose as he struggled to open his eyes against the throbbing pain coursing through his body. After a couple of attempts, he finally managed to gaze up at the cream-white ceiling of his office. His mind slowly became clear as he recognised where he had been lying. A slight breeze of relief washed over him, knowing he was still living and breathing on Earth. The sight of a woman curled up on the floor a half meter from him, with her arms wrapped around her knees, was another solace he did not wish to let go of.

Amanda...

Shame and guilt flooded over him. What he had done to this woman was truly unforgivable, but in a strange twist of fate, she was the only person he could cling his life to at this moment. If he were to die today, he did not want to be alone.

Tyler had no idea what consumed him on the day he tried to overpower her. Women for passing pleasure were common in his life. He did not need to invite them, those women would come to him voluntarily. His marriage to the mother of his two children was merely a business arrangement. He was young and short-minded, attracted by the beauty his wife offered. Why did he need to reject the marriage arrangement when all the outcomes looked positive? Their business network expanded, wealth strengthened, they had perfect offspring, and they exhibited a beautiful picture of an ideal family. However, there was something that still left a hole in his heart.

A true meaning of a relationship.

As time went by, children grew up, things started to make more sense. Janine was a perfect wife and mother for the sake of vanity. However, they were too similar. Their strong head character, ambition and lifestyle. Too similar to the point they became predictable to each other. No one wanted to back down and always became the winner. Somehow, as if they had an unspoken agreement, Janine would find her own pleasure outside, and he was likewise. They had been great parents to their children, and they hid their secret affairs pretty well.

Tyler chose not to stick to one mistress. Why did he only invest in one when he had options for many? Sleeping with his EA Megan was strictly off-limit. She was too old for him, suited better to be his aunt. He valued her for her capability and constant subtle admonishment. But when Amanda Johnston stepped into his office as his temporary EA while Megan was away on vacation, something intrigued him.

Nothing was striking about Amanda's appearance. She dressed in old-fashioned business attire and presented herself in dull dark grey business pants and low heels. Her dark winding hair was cascaded down with a couple of pins on her side fringe. The make-up on her face was soft, too subtle in Tyler's opinion for most women who worked in the building. Even her pink lips looked dry and pale. However, there was an aura of purity in her mannerisms and speech as she moved through the room.

She appeared gentle and compliant, vulnerable and easily manipulated. And that was exactly what he did—exploiting her as much as possible with plenty of tasks and unreasonable demands. Sometimes when he caught the glistening tears in her almond-shaped eyes, a triumphant drum roll would beat in his chest. The desire to coerce her further got stronger and escalated into a lust to have her beneath him.

Physically beneath him, so he could be all over her, hearing her whimpering plea and moaning.

Tyler had a conviction that she would be easily tamed. Her dedication to work was unquestionable, but reading her weary facial expressions because of the work pressure and hecticness of her personal life, somehow, his gut feeling told him that her marriage was cold like his. All it would take was a crack in her emotion, and then one move from him would make her melt in his hand.

However, it seemed he had underestimated her.

Two days ago she demonstrated her resilience when he attempted to overpower her. The urgent call from the senior Mr Fraser, aka his father, helped her to escape. Growling in frustration, he had to calm himself from the heat in his core before returning his father's call. Afterwards, the endless back-to-back meetings and urgent interstate trips kept him separated from her physically. However, they kept communicating through phone calls and messages. He applauded her for maintaining professionalism, carrying on as if nothing had happened.

Or, that was a sign of her desperation to keep her job since her husband was soon on the edge of unemployment.

Tyler's chest expanded, feeling he had the upper hand. This morning when he stepped into the office, the sight of Amanda Johnston sent a hot swirl throughout his body. She avoided looking him directly in his eyes, and a hint of blush was on her pale cheeks. He lowered his face to hide his victorious grin.

"Don't you realise what I can give you?" he asked her.

They reviewed the agenda for the day as usual, and when she stood up to leave the room, he intercepted her, trapping her against the wall.

She shook her head and avoided his gaze. "I..I d'don't understand what you mean, Mr Fraser." Her gaze darted towards the door just a foot away. "I really need to get back to my desk and wrap up some work." But she could not budge as his hand leaned firmly to the wall, blocking her path.

Tyler was unsure whether he had to laugh or be mad with the pretence mask she put on. She was definitely not that naive and understood well what he was up to. The urge to tease her further was as strong as ever as he leaned closer to sniff her flowery scent that reminded him of baby powder. She froze up as he gently touched her cheek, closing her eyes and letting out a soft whimper.

She looked like a frightened kitten backed into a corner by a fierce bulldog. It gave him a sense of satisfaction.

He whispered in her ear as her shuddering breath touched his cheek. "You understand me perfectly, Amanda. I'm really fond of you. We can have fun together."

"I'm..." She turned her face away but stayed unmoved. "I'm married, Mr Fraser. This is inappropriate."

"Your husband doesn't have to find out. You need your job, do you?"

Her eyes blazed with anger as she shot him a look of disgust.

"You cannot make me do this," she hissed.

He could not figure out where her strength came from. She shoved his hand away and set herself free from his prison. With her head held high, she strode towards the door. But Tyler was not a man who could be easily deterred. With his long stride, he reached the door before her and blocked her way.

"Are you sure, Amanda? I would think you will be wiser," he smirked. It was rare for him to engage in this playful back-and-forth with women, but it was oddly satisfying.

"I am certain," she replied with trembling chin. He noticed her hands tightly clutching the side of her vintage business pants.

He arched his eyebrow with a slight twitch in his lips. "Are you sure you're willing to risk losing your job? Tsk..tsk..tsk, Amanda." He shook his head in mocking disbelief. "Think about your family - no income means no food on the table for your little ones. Why take such a risk when you could easily have peace of mind by doing me a favour?"

Tyler could feel the drumbeat on his chest as he witnessed the lump pass through Amanda's throat. Her face was full of hesitancy and fear, precisely like what he expected from the effect of his words.

"What...what do you want?" Her voice sounded weak, and he could tell she was on the edge of crying. "If you are asking me to be your sex slave.."

He quickly shook his head, placing a finger on his lips, hushing her to stop. "Those aren't very nice words to use, Amanda."

She pursed her lips, still eyeing him warily.

"As I mentioned before, we can have a good time together."

"But I don't want to have a good time with you, Mr Fraser! I'm here to work. " She gritted her teeth. "How dare you threaten me if I turn down your request?"

The growing frustration on Amanda's face only fuelled Tyler's smugness. He chuckled lightly as he reached for the door handle. He could win over any woman he desired, and the women would come to him voluntarily. Amanda Johnston would not be an exception. He had laid his offer on the table. Now all he had to do was wait for her to take the bait and come to him willingly. He opened the door and tilted his head playfully, daring her to take his challenge.

"The decision is yours, Amanda. Be wise."

The trepidation on her face only emboldened him further. He was certain she would give in soon.

Until the worst thing that probably ever happened in his life hit him.

A loud bang rang out, followed by a searing pain in his right thigh. Amanda's terrified scream resonated in the room. His vision began spinning as he collapsed to the floor. Just as he was trying to make sense of what was happening, Amanda shut the door and locked it frantically. Rushing to his side, she pulled him away from the door with a determined groan.

Chapter Three

The Past - *24 hours earlier*

The glowing crimson of the sunset peeking through the massive glass window by Amanda's office desk was the cue for her to pack up and head home. She had been so caught up in her work lately, that she hadn't even noticed nature's gentle reminder to take a break and go home. But after experiencing the malicious intention of Mr Tyler Fraser yesterday, she had been enduring the suffocation for staying in the office longer than she could stand.

Today ended up being a lucky day for her, as Mr Fraser had to take an urgent interstate business trip. She had been dragging her feet to get to the office in the morning. However, the short message from Tyler Fraser about his change of work agenda was like a light at the end of the tunnel, though she was fully aware that this was only a temporary reprieve. Nevertheless, she was determined to take one day at a time, dodging Mr Fraser as much as she could until she could find a new job soon, away from Fraser & Co.

There was a sense of achievement for completing most of the work with minimum interruption from Mr Fraser. She grabbed her handbag and quickly dashed to the lift, leaving the office with much lighter limbs. Her mind was full of the list of things she needed to prioritise for kids and, most importantly, to get a new job. Her chest was also inflated with the hope of having a glimpse of Sean. They did not have a chance to speak last night since he went out with Tom. Amanda figured her husband needed someone to listen to his worries about potentially losing his job soon, and Tom had always been his go-to guy since college. She understood that a good chat between men could be really beneficial.

The playful banter between her eleven-year-old Isla and nine-year-old Hamish greeted her like a sweet melody as she walked through the door. It felt like forever since she last made it home in time for dinner.

"Mummy!"

The wide smile and excited squeal, followed by their cuddle, were something Amanda yearned to treasure forever. Despite the anxiety of her work life, her children would be the source of her strength. She had a conviction that she would find a new job soon, away from the clutches of Mr Fraser.

"It's great to see you home early." Sean planted a light kiss on her cheek. Amanda shut her eyes for a moment, savouring the gentle brush of his stubble against her skin. She blinked to realise that it had been quite a while since they had such an intimacy. The thoughts of Tyler Fraser's aggressive advances suddenly sprang in, but she quickly dismissed it as a passing thought. Maybe her body just needed some affection from a man. But she reminded herself that only Sean, her loving husband and soulmate, could truly make her feel safe and loved.

"The advantage when the boss is away," she muttered with her mind muddled about whether she should share what happened in the office with Sean. Her husband deserved to know, and she just had to find the right time.

"Hope he's away for quite a while."

"Unfortunately, he's not," sighed Amanda. She also wished the same. "He's due back tomorrow."

The sound of Sean's exaggerated disappointed groan echoed in the room.

"How's work?" Amanda inquired, hoping to steer the conversation in a different direction. Work talk only reminded her of Mr Fraser. Besides, they were at the dining table, she just wanted to enjoy this rare family dinner moment. It was a special moment that she wanted to cherish. Her question about work out of sheer habit.

Sean shrugged his shoulder with downturn lips. "Nothing much. You know."

Yeah, of course, she knew! Amanda let out a quiet sigh and muttered a curse under her breath. Thankfully, Isla and Hamish kept up their lively chatter throughout dinner, saving her from any further stress. Once all the dirty dishes were stacked in the dishwasher, the children tugged in their bed, quietude finally slipped in. Amanda was looking forward to a relaxing bath and wished to have a meaningful moment with her husband.

She was completely undressed when Sean unexpectedly entered the ensuite. He looked taken aback but wordless.

Although she was now thirty-three years old, Amanda still felt great about her body. Her breast was still firm and slender after two years of breastfeeding. Some weight in her tummy due to her pregnancy had been shed over time, leaving only a few faint lines of post-natal cellulite. She thought this night could be a moment for them. They had not been intimate for quite a while, overwhelmed since the birth of their two children. Even until now, they were busy with work and kids' routines. Amanda believed a short weekend getaway would be just what they needed, and she was sure Sean's parents would be happy to help out with the grandkids. However, their recent work news only made the plan harder to be realised.

As Sean approached her, Amanda noticed a slight widening of his eyes before they quickly settled back to their usual state. There was something in his gaze that made Amanda's heart sink. Gone was the twinkle light in his eyes that she used to receive when they began their relationship. It became only a vacant stare. He moved closer to her, noticing the bathtub filled with warm water, and gently kissed her temple.

"Seems like you've had a long day. A nice warm bath will do wonders," he murmured as wrapping his arm around her waist. Her bare skin pricked against the thick layer of his flannelette shirt.

"Wouldn't you like to come along?" She snuggled into his neck. Even as she asked, she couldn't help but see him getting ready in his cozy flannel shirt, jeans, and puffy vest - his go-to winter outfit.

"Sorry, I have to head out now. Tom and the boys are waiting for me. We are going for a drink to catch up." He planted another kiss on the crown of her head before loosening his embrace, as if he couldn't wait to leave. "Josh will be there as well. He mentioned there might be some job openings in his office soon. Who knows, this could be my chance."

Amanda felt a big lump in her throat as she swallowed her disappointment. But she urged herself to cling unto him tighter. "Can't we stop worrying about that for tonight?" she asked, looking up as he glanced down. "I'm pretty sure we will find a new job soon. We still have some savings anyway to sustain us for a couple of months. We just need to be smart about it. Can't we just.." She was sure he understood what she meant. She lowered her face and buried it onto his chest, snuggling closer to him, wishing it would tempt him in a way. "Can't we just have tonight for ourselves?" Her whisper was filled with longing and desire.

Sean's lips twitched into a thin smile. "I miss you too, Amanda." He sniffed her hair. "But tonight might be my shot at landing a new job. Wouldn't it be great to find something quickly after being laid off? It would ease our minds about losing income for a while." He rubbed her forearms, soothing her. "I know we have some savings tucked away. Let's hold onto them for as long as possible, maybe for our next vacation. We shouldn't just let it drain away."

Amanda could feel a prick of tears at the corner of her eyes. But Sean could not see that as she buried her face into his chest deeper. He might find a hint of dampness on his shirt later. Sean gently pulled away from their hug and held her by the forearms so they could look at each other directly. He might not notice the traces of tears in her eyes, but her devastation reflected on her face.

Amanda could not figure out why she was feeling so down. The sting of rejection for intimacy in favour of hanging out with his friends was the main culprit. Though Sean had a valid reason, her heart seemed just to be broken into pieces.

"I got to go now." Sean's lips landed on her forehead. "Enjoy your bath. Don't wait for me, I'll be back late. But I'll see you tonight."

Amanda was unable to respond. A faint nod was her only acknowledgement. It seemed it was enough for Sean as he twirled and flew away without looking back anymore. The sight of his back disappearing behind the door left a wave of loneliness in her heart. She stood alone in her bathroom, unmoved for a long pregnant pause, only her shaky breath bouncing off the tile wall. Tears finally flowed down her cheek as she bit her lips to calm herself.

She did not get a chance to tell him about what Mr Fraser did to her. If she told him, would that stop him from going? But, perhaps it was wise not to let him know tonight. She promised that they would find time to talk about this together. Hopefully soon, once one of them secured a new job. In the meantime, she only needed to keep everything to herself.

• • • •

LOOKING AT THE TIME on his Rolex, Tyler finally understood why he had been yawning since he got into his car. Having Jack, his chauffeur behind the wheel was a big relief, as certainly he would not be able to focus his vision to drive in the late night hour. His flight touched down half an hour ago, and throughout the four-hour flight from Perth, he had been on his laptop, without any break. There was plenty of work he needed to catch up, and yet his body felt restless as his mind kept drifting to one person.

Amanda Johnston. His temporary personal assistant.

She was almost within his grasp. Until this damn urgent interstate meeting pulled him away from her. Yet a couple of emails and messages were still exchanged between them, strictly about work. He had to admire her ability to maintain professionalism between them. His fingers brushed his jaw as a smirk curled on his lips, picturing how relieved she must be to have a break from him.

Only for a couple of days.

He would be back tomorrow, and Tyler could not wait to see the apprehension in Amanda's round innocent eyes. He would begin his game again.

Sighting the grand massive Victorian steel gate as his car was approaching his mansion, Tyler felt a rejuvenation jolt throughout his body. His body ached for the comfort of his massive bed, but what excited him more was that tomorrow he would be able to play with his prey again.

The tranquillity enveloped him as he pushed open the massive wooden doors of his sprawling two-acre estate. The first thing that caught his eye as he made his way through the hallway was the beautiful family portrait hanging on the wall - a snapshot of himself, his wife, and their two teenage children, Aaron and Kylie, with their innocent smiles beaming back at him. Despite his cold marriage, the only reason he still came home every day was for them. The thought of peeking into their rooms and watching them sleep brought a sense of warmth to his heart. Eager to be near them, he skipped up the twirling stairs two steps at a time, eager to reach the top floor.

The soft glow of the corridor lights was the only illumination as he made his way through the east wing of the floor. Aaron's room was on the left side, while Kylie's room was on the opposite side. Tyler made sure to tread softly as he peeked into each room. The sight of the angelic sleeping of his children sent a twirl of warmth on his chest. He could probably look at them for hours if it were not for a soft thud coming from the west wing of the floor.

Tyler furrowed his brow and pondered the source of the sound. As far as he remembered, there were only library, study and music rooms in the west wing. There were a couple of guest rooms, but he was sure they were not having any visitors at this moment.

Unless he had an unannounced and uninvited guest.

Letting out an exasperated sigh, the last thing Tyler wanted after a long day was to deal with a thief in his house. He considered calling one of his butlers to go and have a look. But he might be overthinking and did not wish to overreact. Grabbing one of the first knick knacks on the console table that caught his eyes, he headed towards the source of the sound.

Another soft thud echoed. This time was much clearer to Tyler's ears, which convinced him that there was someone, and he was not just dreaming. The source of the sound came from the furthest door on that five-metre-long wing, one of the guest rooms. The closer he was to the door, he noticed a dim light seeping through. The soft thud persisted, accompanied by the soft moaning of a woman's voice.

Tyler slowly lowered down the ornament he was holding. He immediately recognised the woman's voice and could guess what had happened in the room before even opening the door. Taking a deep breath, between relieved and annoyed, he shoved his tousled hair and grasped the door handle to push it open.

The scene in front of Tyler was just as he had imagined. A couple on the bed, the man was lying back while the woman was on his top, without any layer of clothes on them. They were astonished to see his presence, stunned like a stone for a couple of seconds. Tyler shot them with a flinty stare, but the woman seemed to have recovered quickly from the interruption and responded with a twitch on her lips. Meanwhile, her male partner gently pushed her aside with panic spread over his face.

"Well, well, well...Tyler. You're too early."

Tyler gave his wife of fourteen years a knowing look and a small eye roll. The man beside her looked gobsmacked realising who Tyler was. He appeared much younger than Janine, with a boyish charm, and a big well well-toned muscled body. With a flick of Janine's head, she gestured for the young man to leave the room.

"Go. But don't make a sound," said Janine with a stern voice. The man nodded hesitantly, and quickly got himself dressed. He looked hesitant, like a scary kitten as he passed through Tyler to reach the door. However, Tyler did not even glance his way.

Silence pierced through for a moment while Tyler shut the door behind him. He could guess that they needed to talk, and obviously, they did not wish to let their children overhear them. Quietly Tyler felt relieved that his wife at least chose the furthest room to conduct her affair. However, it did not mean there was no chance she would not be caught red-handed. He found them easily. He was furious at the repercussions of her reckless action.

He darted his eyes at his wife with fury, but it was simply ignored by her. Janine simply gave her back on him as she leisurely dressed herself with her red laces nightgowns. It amazed Tyler for a blitz to realise that despite her figure being perfect and slender after giving birth to two children, no arousal within him.

"What the hell are you doing?" His angry hiss finally broke their silence.

Janine twirled around playfully and looked rather amused than guilty. "What?" She raised her eyebrows as a challenge.

"The kids are sleeping at the end of the other wing. They could possibly hear you. I don't care what you're doing, but we've agreed not to let the kids know."

Janine's brow creased. "What agreement? I don't remember we have such agreement."

Tyler wondered if he was someone who was into violence, he would probably strangle this gingerhead woman before him until she choked to death. Instead, he reminded himself to stay calm by clenching his fists.

What his wife said was partially true. They never had any written or verbal agreement about how they should conduct their ex-marital affair secretly away from their children's knowledge. However, he assumed they had a silent mutual understanding about it. It was not the first time Tyle was aware of what his wife was doing to find outside pleasure. Likewise, he was sure she knew what he did too.

"You know what I mean," he growled.

Janine's well-manicured fingers gracefully picked her half-finished wine glass that had been sitting on the side table, unaffected by her husband's furious eyes on her. "I honestly can't remember ever discussing or signing such an agreement."

Feeling half defeated, Tyler huffed. "Why are you doing this? Don't you care about our children anymore? Are you not worried about them seeing you with another man in our house?"

A false chuckling sound escaped Janine's throat. "It seems you're more worried if they find out." She turned to him with a mischievous twinkle in her eyes. "Aren't you?" she challenged while sipping her wine again.

Tyler's hands clutched tightly as his anger continued to rise. Janine understood well how protective he was over Aaron and Kylie. His children's happiness always comes first. Even though their relationship had grown distant, Tyler was determined to maintain a facade of indifference in front of the kids.

"What do you want?" He practically growled again as his blazing eyes never left his wife as if they could pin her immobile. However, Janine sat herself gracefully on the edge of the bed, ignoring the eagle eyes hawked on her. Instead, her corner lips curled as she had been waiting for this moment.

"I am tired of my acting as your children's good mother." Janine's voice pierced through the air.

The short statement was somehow like lightning bolted to Tyler's ear. He could hardly believe what he was hearing.

Understanding his wife's character, staying in their marriage to play as his perfect wife and their children's loving mother would be the only way to guarantee her lavish lifestyle, her vanity and her social status. He knew well his father-in-law eagerly wanted Foster & Co's powerful connection. Janine's father would not be pleased if his daughter severed their family connection.

Janine peeked over the rim of her wine glass when she continued, "Give me half of your asset, and then I'll be gone from your life."

Tyler narrowed his eyes. "Are you asking for a divorce?"

A small nod full of determination was a sufficient answer. "I am ready to start a new chapter. Kids are growing up. I think they are old enough to be given the truth about their parents."

Tyler scoffed, still in disbelief at what he heard. Janine's request seemed out of character. But when she requested to get half of his assets, he finally understood what his wife was trying to achieve. This was the reason they signed a pre-nuptial agreement. He knew if one day Janine would walk away from their marriage, she would not leave herself empty-handed.

Despite her high ambition, Tyler would not question Janine's dedication as a mother. Their children adored her, and never miss to celebrate Mother's Day with her during their primary school years. Things shifted gradually recently as teenage hormones began to take over, and the inner war between cool and uncool occupied their children's minds. And probably Tyler did not realise this earlier, but Janine probably had changed as well. Her motherly affection slowly diminished as she seemed engrossing herself with her own pursuit of life. Her small business as an event organiser began to bloom, thanks to the powerful connection she had as one of the daughters-in-law of Fraser & Co.

Tyler grew up in a household where love was scarce. Prenuptial and divorce were common terms for their empire family. Growing up as the youngest son of three, his parents had been separated since he was in grade six, but no official divorce papers were signed, for the sake of good vanity and publication. They would appear as a whole family in major occasions and events, however, there was no love and affection after they stepped out from the spotlights. All ex-marital secret affairs were conducted carefully, as much as possible, away from any pesky paparazzi. If any of them get caught, any effort would be made to brush it off, by displaying the pictures of perfect family, clear from the scandal.

Sometimes it made Tyler perplexed how ironically fantastic teamwork the Fraser clan had made, despite it was far from the true meaning of loving family.

But Janine's request for half of his assets was too much. Dissuaded by his pride and arrogance, he would not let his wife simply walk away from their marriage smoothly.

"You do realise what you're asking?" Tyler scoffed. "Severing ties with the Fraser family? Not being able to see your children anymore even when they grow up as adults and have kids? Are you sure that is wise?"

Having said that, Tyler was reminded that his grandparents from her mother's side were the only ones who genuinely cared for them. His dad sceptically commented that was because they were just old people, retired from the business world, worried if their allowances were cut and deserted to old folks' homes. While he could see some truth in his dad's words, he could not help but imagine himself growing old surrounded by his own grandchildren. He fondly remembered how his grandparents used to babysit them when they were kids, but their meetings became rare when he was growing up as his father wanted to toughen him up as one of Fraser's successors.

"It's not something that I am envisioning for my future," replied Janine cooly. "They will have nannies for their kids. They don't need me to interfere."

Tyler's face pinched with disgust. "Don't you care if they end up resenting you for leaving?"

"Well, I can be like your mother. Appearing when it's needed for publication." Janine flashed a cheeky smile. "If you allow me. We can specify that in the divorce paper. I can still play the role of a loving and caring mother for them. But I want my freedom. A freedom to manage my own money."

Tyler could feel the thunder brewing inside him as he attempted to restrain his anger. Janine obviously wanted to get the best of the two worlds. Her independence and her comfort as part of Fraser. A typical materialistic bitch that he usually encountered in his social life.

With a firm answer formed in his head, Tyler walked lazily towards his wife. Janine looked up at him, expecting him with her sweetest smile. His hand slowly lifted to brush her curled hair from her cheek and tugged it behind her ear. He studied her wife of fourteen years' face carefully and tried to recall the moment when he was captivated by her beautiful blue eyes. It seemed like ages ago, and he couldn't even pinpoint when his admiration had faded. What he saw now was just a pair of eyes hunger of the world, the same world that he had given to her throughout their marriage. Yet she craved more.

This was the woman that had mothered his children, but now she seemed more like a whore to him.

Slowly he lowered his head, and Janine craned her neck further so their lips touched. It had been a while since the last time they kissed. There was no old spark returned. Instead the image of his wife with another man that he witnessed earlier made his stomach churned.

"Janine.." He whispered as his breath touched her lips. Their lips were inches apart, teasing and tantalizing. His voice was full of restrained desire and seemed inviting as Janine reached up to draw him closer. Still unmoved from craning her neck, she kissed him deeper.

Tasting his wife's luscious lips, Tyler would have expected a sweet sensation in his core. But instead what he felt was only blandness. Feeling a wave of disgust as her tongue danced with his, a shiver ran down his spine. He did not immediately pull back, though. In a surprising turn, he let Janine take the lead and misled her with a soft moan from his throat.

Tyler could sense that his wife thought he had fallen for her seduction. Their lips finally parted. Her hazy blue eyes stared back at him, full of satisfaction. Tyler lifted his finger, caressing her cheek, closely observing the traces of youthful beauty on his wife's face.

"It's not going to happen," he whispered.

Her eyes blinked. The lustful in her countenance instantly faded. The crease formed on her forehead, partly hidden by her side fringe. Her luminous sparkling blue eyes darkened, as an ire slowly spread on her façade.

Tyler strengthened his spine without breaking his eyes on his wife's. An ironic feeling slipped in as he was fully convinced that Janine could read his mind well, as much as he could read her. They were so alike that Janine could easily decipher his thoughts, just as he could to hers. She knew exactly what he was thinking, but he was not ready to set her free just yet. After all, he had paved the way for her success in high society and was not about to let her go easily.

A sinister scoff curved on Janine's lips as she shook her head. " I have given you children," she muttered darkly.

It was a valid statement, but Tyler did not wish to acknowledge it. He was grateful for their precious children, he understood the incredible sacrifice a mother makes to bring a child into the world. But for a woman like Janine, having a child was merely for business.

"Then you still have a job," he replied nonchalantly, unaffected by the heat of restrained anger in his wife's tensed posture. "Watch your behaviour, or you might not have a chance at all."

Realising that she had been unsuccessful, Janine's face slightly loosened in defeat. A triumphant smirk sneaked on Tyler's lips. He knew he had the upper hand at this stage. He twirled and firmly stepped out of the room. As if he had eyes on his back, he was pretty sure that his wife would drown herself in her wine soon.

Chapter Four

The Present - *A Decade Later*

The rolling waves make a rumbling sound echoing through the clear pale sky. The strong wind blows, lifting the skirt of her white dress and tossing her shoulder-length hair around. Amanda stands firmly on the stone cliff, a few meters from the edge, soaking in the view of the vast greyish beach and ocean ahead. She is not quite sure how long she has been standing there, mesmerized by the giant wonder of nature.

The soothing sound of waves and seagulls instantly fills her with a sense of calm that she has been yearning for in her heart. It has been so long since she has had this kind of peaceful solitude. Maybe way back before her kids came along, before she met Sean, and before her heart was shattered by a painful divorce.

Despite all the recent chaos in her life, it is actually quite ironic that she finally has some time to herself. Supposedly she had let herself have this moment as her meditation during her turbulent time, perhaps it would salvage her marriage.

The fresh wounds of the failed marriage undeniably still linger deep in her heart. There are feelings of hurt, guilt, and regret that she cannot ignore. However, those are not the main reasons she decided to escape to the beautiful island of Bali. On the other hand, another more pressing reason brought her here.

Glancing around, she takes a deep breath and bites her bottom lips. After relieving some space to her mind earlier, her brain begins to active, focusing on how she can find a solution to a problem ahead of her.

"Isn't this place simply amazing?"

A gentle female voice echoes from behind. Without even looking, Amanda instantly recognises who it belongs to.

"You've picked the right place."

Her gaze falls on her fellow traveller.

As Elena takes a step to her side, her sky blue halter neck dress is gracefully fluttering in the wind, resembling a tail behind her. The beautiful Bali tie-dye motif batik design perfectly complements her fair complexion. Her blonde hair is styled in a bun, showcasing her elegant swan neck. The enthusiasm in her blue eyes shines brightly, reflecting her inner sparkle.

Amanda quietly admires the youthful look of her friend despite they are about the same age in their early forties. The fresh delightful smile on Elena's lips is not the picture Amanda would expect from a woman who also just went through a divorce.

"I wouldn't have chosen to come here if it wasn't for Isla," replies Amanda. Her voice sounds flat and bored. She shrugs her shoulder. "Although I must say, this place is pretty intriguing. I can't believe I've never been here before!"

Behind her sunnies, Amanda can guess that Elena is rolling her eyes as a chuckle forms on her lips.

"When was the last time you had a holiday?"

Amanda shakes her head, blushing as she admits, "I can't remember. All I know is that I've been putting away every penny I can for the mortgage and the kids."

"I guess you deserve this holiday."

Amanda darts her friend with a severe look. "But you know, we are here not for a holiday."

"Probably not you, but I am on holiday!" protests Elena. She twirls around, with both hands on her waist, admiring the cream-coloured buildings and traditional cone-shaped straw huts and gazebos at the other end of the cliff. "Look at this amazing resort! I can't wait to spend the next seven days in this place." Her hand pats her friend's shoulder. "Thanks for bringing me along on this trip!"

AMELIORATION: A CHANGE OF HEART

Amanda lets out a deep sigh, feeling a mix of annoyance and gratitude. It was her idea that led them here, all stemming from her concern for her daughter's safety. Maybe it was not the best move to keep tabs on her fully grown twenty-one-year-old daughter, who was at the resort for the company's teambuilding event. But after explaining her concerns to Elena, Amanda has convinced herself that she did the right thing.

"Have you spotted Isla? Or any of her colleagues?" Elena's palm on her forehead as she is throwing her gaze around.

Amanda checks the time on her mobile phone screen. "They should have arrived by now. Let's make sure we stay out of sight."

Elena tilts her head. "Are you saying you're going to spy on her? You're not going to reveal yourself?"

It is a question that makes Amanda shift uncomfortably. She has not had a chance to ponder it on their trip here. Elena was in high spirits all the way from Melbourne which made all their conversations kept distracting her. Her friend had been striking up conversations with every stranger they met on the plane, over-friendly greeting all the resort staff upon check-in, spreading her charm and energy.

Meanwhile, Amanda did not think anyone would want to be around her in her sullen mood. If it was not for Elena who dragged her to the nearby local market to get a low V-neck Bali batik dress she is wearing now, she would probably still wearing her spring cardigans despite the hot and humid weather greeted them the moment their plane landed.

"I don't feel like playing hide and seek on our holiday." Elena's protest voice returns. "I think you should tell her your concern, but at the same time, you also have to trust her judgement. She's a mature adult."

Amanda does not wish to argue, and she does not have the time anyway. The moment Elena finishes her sentence, her sight captures a figure that makes her breath involuntarily cease for a second. It's like a blast from the past playing out right before her eyes, leaving her momentarily paralysed.

Chapter Five

The Past

Waking up to the sight of the cream-pale white ceiling above him, he let out a gasp as panic washed over him. His heart started racing, and his breathing became fast and shallow. His mind was filled with fear of what might happen next. He felt immobilized, unable to move, reminiscent of the terrifying experience he had gone through. The intense pain in his body increased, causing sweat to trickle down his forehead.

Surrounded by nothing but silence, he could not even hear his own voice as his throat quivered with a groan. Countless unanswered questions raced through his mind, and his heart felt heavy with dread. It was clear he was nearing the end, a sign that his time on earth was coming to a close.

A warm squeeze on his hand made him hold his breath. Though he could not see who it was, the touch sent a glimmer of hope that he would hold onto dearly. The numbness in his body left him clueless if he had responded. He attempted to speak but was unsure whether there was any sound out from his throat.

"It's okay. I'm here."

The gentle voice was like the most melodious music he ever heard in his life. It filled his lungs with a sense of calm. Gradually, his mind cleared and, after a few blinks, he recognised his surroundings.

"I'm still here, Mr Fraser. Everything will be alright. Help is on the way."

Her gentle words were comforting, but Tyler could detect a hint of uncertainty in them. Yet, hearing Amanda's voice and feeling the warmth of her hand was like a breath of fresh air for his soul.

"I won't let him go until he gives us the money!"

The stern voice emanating from behind startled him. It alarmed him of the seriousness of their predicament.

"He's losing a lot of blood, Ben." Amanda's pleading voice followed. "You need to get help for him."

Despite feeling dizzy and his vision blurring, Tyler's mind started to clear. He could feel his own sweat chilling his skin, and the coldness of the room enveloping him, causing him to shiver.

The last thing he could remember before he fell into his state of unconsciousness was when he opened his office door, welcoming the hijacker into his office room. The horror on Amanda's face as she recognised the hunchback man with the soldier attire stood before them, sent goosebumps throughout his body. He was someone who had been working in the building for at least three decades but had never been under his radar, despite being on the same floor. When the man announced himself as a low-level staff working in the printing room, Tyler found his sarcastic smile was too sharp contrasting with his soft yet fully wrinkled pale face.

"Why are you worried about him, Amanda? After what he had done to you?" Ben's voice roared. "He coerced you to be his sex slave!"

Tyler swallowed hard. From his fuzzy sight, he could make out the pinch on Amanda's face. The words stung despite how true it was. The atmosphere in the room suddenly felt colder, and he could not help but whimper. However, when Amanda squeezed his hand, a rush of warmth spread through his body, calming his nerves.

A hush fell over the room briefly as the sound of footsteps on the office carpet gave Tyler a mental image of Ben pacing in frustration.

"If he dies, how will we get our money?" A nasal voice chimed in causing Tyler's senses to sharpen. Ben did not come alone. There was another man, which he guessed from his voice much younger than the old white hair hunchback skinny Ben. The man kept his mask on, only revealing his striking blue eyes and plump lips.

"We don't need to tell them if he dies," Ben responded. His tone was cold, sending shivers down Tyler's spine as Amanda's grip on his hand tightened. "After we leave this place, we can find a way to get rid of his body."

"You can't do that, Ben! How..how..." Amanda stuttered. "How are you going to walk away if he dies? They won't stop looking for you. And....and...Please don't do this, Ben."

"What do you think I should do, Amanda? You know how all these rich bastards treat us. I've given my heart and soul to this company for thirty years, all I want is a peaceful retirement. But then I'm manipulated and end up losing my job without any compensation!"

"But,...your manager is not Mr Fraser!"

"He's no different!"

"But..."Amanda sighed in defeat. "This is not right..."

From the heated conversation, Tyler began to piece together the reason behind Ben's action.

"How can I trust him?" Ben chuckled bitterly. "How can you trust him, Amanda? The moment we let him go, the police will catch me and I'll be spending the rest of my life in jail." He took a sharp intake of breath. "I want my money now. He can go free once I have my money and I'm safely out of here."

"But, how will he manage with his current state?"

"His family should be getting back to us soon. We have made contact with them since five hours ago."

Five hours ago? Tyler could feel his chest pounding hard. It had been a while. Where was his father? Did they know that he was here and bleeding? How much money did Ben ask?

"But we still hear nothing from them." Ben's sombre laughter pierced through his ear. "It seems they don't even care about you, Mr Fraser. We've informed them about your injury."

Tyler's heart sank at those words. He did wonder the same thing. Didn't his family care about him? His family clan had been wealthy for many years and generations. Was it so hard to meet Ben's monetary demand?

"How..." His lips tasted dry, and yet he tried to speak. "How much did you ask?"

"I did not ask for much, Mr Fraser. I am not that greedy," Ben replied with a bitter chuckle. "I simply asked for what was owed to me. It is only two hundred thousand dollars. It is nothing compared to your family's ten billion worth."

Tyler could not believe his hearing. *Two hundred thousand dollars?* And none of his family granted it immediately in exchange for his safety?

"Is this really worth it, Ben?" asked Amanda with a hoarse voice. "You will be accused of murder if Mr Fraser dies. If that's the only amount you need, I'm pretty sure Mr Fraser can accommodate that. You will be restored to your role. If you prefer to retire, you can get your redundancy pay. All you have to do is release him safely."

Ben's sarcastic laughter echoed. "After thirty years of dedication, I was accused of something that I did not do. They told me that I've stolen stuff from the company!" His scream filled with anger. "Can you believe that? I have never taken any single item from the company, not even a pencil!"

"There...." Tyler winced as a sharp pain pierced him as he tried to get up. Amanda stopped his move, and realisation hit him that his condition was getting worse. "There must be a misunderstanding?"

"Misunderstanding?" Ben repeated his words with a dejected shake of his head. "That was the exact word I used. They did not want to listen to me, and I was immediately escorted out of the building like a criminal. I did try to speak with someone in HR, but no one bothered to help me." He gave Amanda a sad look. "I remember you, Amanda. You might help me to speak with Mr Fraser, but I did remember when I found you looked flustered and dishevelled, dashing out from Mr Fraser's office. Though you did not tell me, I could guess what happened. He tried to assault you, am I right? How could you trust a bully like him? How will you ensure that he would not simply send me and my son to jail once he's out of this building?"

Tyler could feel his heart pounding, waiting in agony for Amanda's reply. He mustered up the last bit of his strength to turn his head and catch a glimpse of her expression, despite his vision being slightly obscured by sweat. Her lips were pursed. A deep crease was formed on her forehead. His eyes landed on where their hands loosely intertwined, and he could feel the moisture in her hand.

Their gazes locked momentarily. Her eyes were filled with a mist of anxious tears, but no sign of hatred. She had an opportunity to get back to him at this stage, kicking him or slapping him while he was defenceless. But instead, she chose to show compassion and spoke up on his behalf, trying to save him.

His chest felt constricted as guilt struck his heart. He had been selfishly taking advantage of her, bullying the oppressed ones like her and Ben. All because of his privilege as the son of Fraser & Co. And yet, as one of the executive directors in the company, despite he was trained in corporate negotiation and politics, it never crossed his mind how to apply this skill to someone who pointed a gun at him and shot him. This was a matter of life and death, and money even could not fix it.

"I really didn't mean for things to turn out this way," Ben continued. His voice became soft and almost like a whisper, full of sorrow and despair. "But if I don't do this, will I be heard? I only want to enjoy my retirement life. That's all I want." Tears welled up in his eyes. The young man walked over and comforted him, placing a hand on his shoulder. "I know this is all wrong, Amanda. I know I can't get away with this. With money or not, I will be hunted down and captured and sent to jail."

The room fell silent, almost as if the words were seeping into everyone's thoughts, including Tyler's. The words were true to reality, that probably no one, especially himself or any of the executive management would bother to care about the wellbeing of low-level staff like Ben. Ironically, this aggressive act served as a much-needed wake-up call.

Tyler had to admit the corporate culture in his family business was full of tyranny, in contrast to what has been presented to the public as a high-profile business that values the employees. Everyone was expected to perform to their best capability. Performance is measured solely by numbers. Competition is high to drive effectiveness and the best outcomes. It was not a surprise if an employee like Ben, whose job was simple and repetitive but done diligently with loyalty, had been overlooked. It had created dissatisfaction which prompted desperate action.

"Let us..." Amanda's shuddering breath broke the silence. "Let's focus on the future, Ben."

Despite his weak vision, Tyler finally noticed where Amanda's attention had been drawn. Her eyes had been staring at the gun in Ben's hand. In his anguish, Ben was talking animatedly, gesticulating with the weapon. It made Amanda nervous that he might accidentally let the gun explode and injure someone. But her next words made Tyler realise that her concern went deeper than that.

"Your effort is not gone wasted. You're right, Ben. If you don't do this, you won't be heard. Now, Mr Fraser is here, and he is listening. I'm pretty sure he will do something about it. Right, Mr Fraser?"

Tyler nodded his head, though he was unsure whether his head was moving "Yes." He tried to speak, though his voice sounded weak.

"Let us get help to treat his wound, Ben. Once he's recovered, he will help to get your money. And no one will put you in jail. Think about your son too. He still needs you."

At this point, Tyler began to pay attention to the young man standing behind Ben. The mask still covered his face, but his innocent blue eyes stood out. He appeared much younger than Tyler had initially thought. Amanda must have known about Ben's family better, hence she tried to knock on his conscience, wishing he would end this ordeal.

"Why do you still trust him, Amanda?" Ben flashed a dispirited smile. "After what he had done to you? How can we trust him?"

If Tyler were in Amanda's shoes, he'd likely ask the same question. He could see the grimace on her face that she tried to hide by lowering her head and glancing briefly at him. If he weren't in the midst of slowly losing blood, he might not be too keen on agreeing to such a request. He would make sure that Ben would not get away with this.

"He's dying, Ben," Amanda replied. "He still has family he wants to be with. What is the point for him to lie over two hundred thousand dollars?"

A valid point. It was another harsh reminder that the amount was insignificant for the price that he would pay to be alive and see his family again. Inevitably Tyler shut his eyes, washed by shame and self-loathing.

Another silence descended. The only sound that filled the air was the rhythmic ticking of the wall clock. Keeping his eyes shut, Tyler tried to focus on hearing the steady beat of his own heart, reassuring himself that he was still alive. He felt his strength waning and his eyelids growing heavy. The warmth of Amanda's hand in his hold somehow sent a serenity to his soul. The rhythm of his breathing slowly lulled him to deep sleep. A blissful quietitude embraced him to a peaceful dream.

Then a sudden loud thud jolted him awake.

His eyes snapped open, revealing an unfamiliar pale ceiling above him, starkly different from his office. The strong smell of disinfectant with undertones and artificial soap fragrance instantly struck his senses. Clenching his hand, he longed for Amanda's touch, but she was not there. As his eyes began to scan around, then he slowly figured out that he was in a hospital.

Chapter Six

The Present

Amanda does not see herself as a helicopter mother. As far as she remembers, she has always encouraged Hamish and Isla to be independent and responsible for their own choices. It does not mean she does not care about her children's life. She tries her best to be involved in their life even after they step into teenage and adult life.

The time they began to be off her radar was when the divorce happened two years ago. She was too consumed with her grief and resentment, burying herself in work, isolating herself from social life, wishing it would make her forget the pain. Both of her children also wished to give her some space, understanding that their mother, unlike them, was not accepting the separation.

As if just being slapped awake of what she had neglected what supposedly to be her responsibility as a mother, she immediately booked a flight ticket to Bali, for the sake of her daughter's safety. Her twenty-one-year-old daughter, who just completed her Bachelor degree three months ago, just landed herself a job that she described as her dream career. Amanda could not be happier for her when Isla broke the news.

Unless there is one problem.

Isla's new job is with Fraser & Co.

Fraser & Co. is a large multinational corporate firm. Based on Amanda's memory, and her knowledge, there were numerous teams and business units in the company. However, what alarms her is the fact Isla works closely with one of the sons of Fraser & Co, who will be the mentor in the graduate program on which Isla is enrolled. When Isla mentioned his name, it was like a bombshell had been dropped in her world, reminiscent of the shock she felt when she received the divorce request from Sean. Her mind was a cloud of confusion as she found herself completely speechless.

The news left her feeling completely overwhelmed, unsure of where to begin and how to react. Isla's luminous turquoise eyes were shimmering with excitement and enthusiasm, a picture of a young woman who was still green and unadulterated. Amanda did not wish to ruin her daughter's career hope, and she felt it was not wise to bring up her past. She reminded herself not to be hasty, and to think of a strategy to bring Isla to safety. But when Isla announced the company's team bonding to Bali for a week and dropped the name that Amanda wished she could erase from her memory, she knew she had to interfere.

And here she is now, and yet she still cannot make up her mind about how she will share her concern with Isla. Her anxiety heightened when her sight captured his presence. But her only reaction was pulling Elena to a hidden place, away from the bunch of sleek-attired people that she guessed as the Fraser & Co management team.

While being scurried away, grumbling words escaped from Elena's lips. Amanda could not blame her friend as she was literally dragging her without looking back.

"What the hell was that?" yells Elena once they reach their room, still catching her breath from their earlier mad dash through the crowds with no apology.

"Sorry.." Amanda manages to speak between her breaths. "I just ..."

She has not told any soul about what happened ten years ago in Fraser & Co. The hostage saga was on the media, but there was another story that she had kept to herself. That day she just wanted to be grateful as she managed to come out from the building unharmed, and reunited with her family. She was determined to leave anything related to Fraser & Co behind, buried them in the bottom pit of her past. Elena did not ask in specific the reason why she wanted to join Isla in Bali, as her friend was too excited about the journey to a paradise island.

"Can you fill me in on what's going on? You look like you've seen a ghost!" Elena is straightening her spine as her chest is still up and down from heaving. Both hands on her waist, she darts at Amanda with a stern look, demanding a nonsense answer.

Amanda is pursing her lips, averting her gaze, while her brain is scattered trying to find the right answer. "Nothing. It's just...I don't want Isla to see me yet."

Elena certainly does not buy it as she arches her eyebrow. "What is your real reason for coming here? I'm sure as far as I know you're not a control freak mother to your kids. Why the sudden concern for Isla? Is this her first time travelling overseas?"

Elena's guess gives an idea for Amanda instead. She nods affirmatively. "Yeah, that's one of the reasons. I am not trying to be controlling. But I am concerned that this is her first overseas trip. I just want to watch her from a distance. I don't want to embarrass her."

Elena's steep-arched eyebrow relaxes. "You probably shouldn't be too worried. She's already twenty-one. Jamie was only eighteen when he first went overseas to Bangkok with his friends. I get why you're concerned." She shrugs her shoulders. "But you have to trust them in a way."

Amanda nods but lowers her eyes, keeping her fingers crossed that her friend will not dig anything further.

"So, what shall we do tonight?" Elena throws herself into bed, with a content smile on her lips.

Amanda breathes a sigh of relief as the conversation shifts. "I read on the announcement board that the Fraser & Co team will have a dinner tonight in one of the restaurants. I suppose Isla will be there," she replies. Since their arrival, she's been exploring the resort and studying the map to figure out where everything is. She's already spotted a few announcements about Fraser & Co's upcoming activities.

Elena pops up her head with the support of her hands and gives her a curious look. "What is your plan?"

"Well...the whole restaurant is reserved for Fraser & Co only. I don't think they're allowing outsiders in. But, I scoped out the location. It is an outdoor restaurant, facing the beachside. It's quite open for everyone. So, probably I have a chance to see Isla from the distance."

Elena's eyes widen. "Wow! Are you planning to sneak into their event?"

"No, not sneaking in." Amanda represses her smirk at the notion of the idea. It sounds like she is a party crasher. "Just observing Isla from a distance."

"So, you're going to spy on her," groans Elena while rolling her eyes.

"I will show up when the time is right," states Amanda, but deep in her heart, she knows it will not happen anytime soon.

· · · ·

THE SOUND OF WAVES crashing serenades Amanda's stroll along the beachside. The illumination from the resort village fortunately is pretty bright, and from a distance of approximately a half kilometre away, Amanda can see the bunch of people lingering on the alfresco of the restaurant. She is pretty sure Isla will be among them, however, she has not been successful in spotting the slender lithe figure of her daughter.

Amanda is aware she probably needs to get closer. The restaurant's alfresco is big but the lighting is dim, giving off a jazzy vibe that matches the music from the band.. There are probably at least a hundred people, many of them look as young as Isla. And so far she has not spotted the only person who always makes her panic set off.

She has not been able to spot Isla either. Could that mean they are together?

Her heartbeat begins to race as her anxiety grows. Isla has been working at Fraser & Co for six months, and her daughter seems enjoying her job, always eager to share the stories from the office. How can she not be alarmed, when Isla starts to bring up her involvement in one of the projects with Aaron Fraser, the son of Tyler Fraser? Her daughter even showed some admiration for Aaron's father when there was once he paid a visit to the graduate program team.

Charismatic. That was the word used by Isla to describe Tyler Fraser. Her twenty-one-year-old daughter is young and naïve, easily charmed by man's persona. There is more about Tyler Fraser than what he presents himself. Probably only a handful of people from ten years ago could see his true self, and unfortunately, she was one of those handful people.

Taking a deep breath, wishing to fill some air into her lungs, Amanda focuses back to scan every single person in the restaurant alfresco within her sight. She blames herself for not having any binoculars. After straining her eyes for a good five minutes, her heart leaps when she recognises her daughter in one of her favourite flowery cocktail dresses.

Amanda fondly remembers the last time Isla wore the dress for her birthday a few weeks ago. As her mother, she has to admit how her daughter has blossomed into such a beautiful young woman. Her heart swells with pride. How she wished she could share this moment with Sean if he was still her husband. Perhaps she still could, because regardless, Sean is still Isla's father. It is a bittersweet to think about the future she and Sean once dreamed of - growing old together and watching their children with their own grandchildren. But those dreams have been shattered by their divorce.

Her breath is hitched when her eyes capture a tall broad-shoulder figure standing just next to Isla. Though the man has grown from the last time Amanda saw his picture on Mr Fraser's office desk, Aaron Fraser's distinctive curly ginger hair makes him stand out from the crowd. They are surrounded by some other people that Amanda guesses as Isla's work teammates, holding a glass in their hands, gleefully chatting.

Amanda's eyes are fixated on the figure of her daughter and Aaron, carefully analysing their body gestures. They seem at ease, but there is still an aura of formality as Isla looks at him attentively within a respectful distance while he is talking. Her demeanour mirrors their colleagues, with bright round blue eyes that Amanda can't quite decipher as admiration. She lets out a quiet sigh of relief, realising she may have been reading too much into their interactions.

Unfortunately, her consolation is only short-lived. The moment she notices another tall man, approaching the group, a loud thud hits her chest. Tyler Fraser still looks almost the same as ten years ago despite his son now as tall as him. Dressed in a short-sleeved tight shirt that flaunts his well-toned muscles, his brooding stern look induces a formal atmosphere. Isla and her colleagues immediately look slightly tense but break tentative smiles to welcome him.

Amanda's breathing becomes shaky. The presence of Tyler Fraser is always intimidating. Absentmindedly her fingers start to fiddle with her heart pendant necklace as she continuously stares at him. Suddenly, the feeling of getting caught red-handed of spying jolts her. She promptly hops behind the tropical plants' decorations around the alfresco, assuming it is enough to conceal her. Plus, the lighting where she's hiding is pretty dim. Hopefully, no one will notice her little game of hide-and-seek.

Momentarily distracted as she tries to get a better view of Isla, her eyes are scanning for Tyler and Isla's figures again. Her anxiety is ramping up. Within a minute, Tyler suddenly is standing next to Isla. What is horrifying her, is to see her daughter sheepishly talking with him with a shade of pink on her cheeks.

Amanda's world is suddenly spinning in circles. Her breathing becomes labour. What she fears the most is finally here. Her brain is quickly thinking hard about how she could bring Isla into safety.

She shuts her eyes in agony while pinching the bridge of her nose as a sudden sharp pain pierces her head. Before she knows it, her legs give out and she finds herself with her hands buried in the sand when she opens her eyes.

"Ma'am, are you alright?"

A dark complexion man gently takes hold of her arms, offering his support and aiding her in getting back on her feet. Her head is spinning hard and she is struggling to catch fresh air. Her vision is getting blurry as she is guided to sit down in one of the beach chairs.

The moment she is seated, and the man fans her with a drink tray, Amanda slowly gains consciousness. The man who is helping her is a waiter, and with his thick Balinese accent, constantly checks in on her well-being.

She is too weak to answer and quietly feels grateful when Elena shows up out of the blue. Her friend had been napping all afternoon, so she did not wish to wake her up and embarked on the spying by herself. Amanda cannot figure out how Elena always manages to show up at the perfect moment. Their unlikely friendship seems like her blessing in disguise.

"Are you alright, Amanda?" asks Elena as she presses her cheek with her palm. "Please get her a glass of water," she instructs the waiter, who quickly scurries off to fulfil the request.

Amanda gently shakes her head while leaning back in the chair. The soothing sound of crashing waves is a sweet music to her ears, while the fresh night air from the beach slowly fills her lungs.

"You look pale," comments Elena. "What happened?"

As if the answer will be left unanswered anyway, Elena does not press for an answer and the waiter returns with a glass of water. Letting the cold water flush through her throat feels like a burst of new energy for Amanda. Her dizziness starts to dissipate and she finally can breathe easily again.

"Would you like to see a doctor, ma'am?"?" asks the waiter kindly.

"No," replies Amanda. Her voice sounds weak to her ear, so she is unsure whether the waiter can hear her.

Just as she is about to repeat herself, a woman in Balinese kebaya and a man who appears to be another waiter join them. The three locals converse in their language, leaving Amanda and Elena puzzled.

The woman turns to them and asks, "Are you part of the Fraser group?"

Amanda swiftly shakes her head, causing a sharp surge of pain. She instantly wishes she had not been so honest as the man in front of her frowns.

"Sorry, this area is only for Fraser Group employees," he informs her.

That is the reason Amanda does not encounter any single soul on the beachside outside the restaurant alfresco. The signs clearly state that it is off-limits to anyone not affiliated with Fraser & Co, but of course, she ignores it.

The man has a security walkie-talkie in his hand, and he puts it closer to his mouth and begins to converse in the local language with the other party. Amanda glances at Elena who returns her look filled with panic.

Before she utters something to defend herself, a familiar voice comes from behind. Without turning her head, Amanda could guess the person behind her as Elena's facial reaction tells it all.

"Mum?"

If she had the strength to run away, she might have. But Amanda is feeling drained, and she knows she just has to face her daughter. She is not prepared for what she should say to Isla the reason she is here.

"What are you doing here, mum?" A puzzlement spreads over Isla's façade as she is standing in front of her mother. Her round blue eyes bounce from her mother's face and then to each person who is circling them. Her lips are parting when she recognises Elena.

"Elena? Is that you?"

"Hi, Isla." Elena waves. "Yes, it's me."

Isla's eyes widen, indicating her shock is deepened. "What are you...?" Her eyes go back and forth between her mother and Elena. "What are you...doing here with my mum?"

Amanda quietly swallows as Isla's question is valid. No one in her family would expect she would build an unlikely friendship with the ex-wife of her ex-husband's current partner.

Life is indeed unpredictably funny. When she was still with Sean, her conversation with Elena was limited to a friendly exchange of greetings at their friends' gatherings. Their husband at that time were best friends, but Amanda did not think she would click well with Elena, and it seemed Elena thought likewise. Elena is a true cheerful extrovert, who seems never to be afraid to put herself out there, in contrast to herself who is more reserved.

But after the divorce, just because of one coincidence they bumped into each other in a café and started chatting more often. Amanda quietly had to be grateful for their unexpected encounter. It was a rough day for her, she was a lost zombie in a chaotic world. The divorce shook the ideal world that she had been striving for. Elena probably noticed her gloomy appearance and invited her to have a chat. For someone who had been on the same boat, and received the same blow because of what their husbands did, they instantly felt connected.

"We are on holiday!" Elena exclaims jovially, throwing her hands up in the air. "You see, we've been needing a break for ages. I've always dreamed of visiting Bali, and your mum mentioned you'd be here for work. What a small world that we ended up in the same resort. Great place, isn't it?"

Amanda quietly compliments her friend's swift response but is uncertain about the last part. There are numerous lovely resorts in Bali, and Isla can probably tell that Amanda chose this place intentionally.

"Right," murmurs Isla. There are still traces of shock on her face. "When did you arrive?"

"Yesterday."

"Today."

Amanda shuts her eyes as her answer clashes with Elena. She mentally scolds herself for opening her mouth too soon. Isla narrows her eyes at them suspiciously.

"Well, doesn't matter!" Elena waves her hand dismissively. "Your mum is unwell, Isla. She almost fainted."

The diversion of the topic is probably working as Isla's face instantly switches from shock to concern. She jumps closer to her mother. "Are you alright, mum?"

"I'm alright, sweetheart. I guess I'm still not used to this humid weather."

"So, is she with you?" The security man interrupts as he gives a severe look at Isla. Amanda's neck tense up as the tension in the air remains palpable.

"Yes, she is," replies Isla.

"Are you part of the Fraser group?"

"She's Miss Williams." The kebaya dress staff member pipes in. "She's the liaison officer for the Fraser group."

"Alright," mumbles the security man as he is still eyeing Amanda suspiciously. "We have closed this area for the Fraser group only."

Amanda swallows nervously while exchanging glances with Elena, realising they may be seen as trespassers.

"So, do you need a doctor, ma'am?"

Amanda restrains herself from rolling her eyes. It is clear that since the security guard found them, he has been scrutinizing their every move. She can not blame him as he is only doing his job.

"I'm fine, thank you."

The security man is not pushing any more questions, but the repeating beeping sounds from his walkie-talkie while he talks are creating a commotion and drawing people's attention to the alfresco. A couple of people are passing by and asking Isla what is happening, to which Isla responds casually. Amanda, who was lounging half-heartedly, suddenly sits up, hoping to put an end to the continuous questioning from onlookers. But her heart skips a beat when she recognises a tall silhouette approaching.

"Is everything there alright, Isla?"

His voice is deep and carries a sense of authority, instantly triggering a memory from Amanda's past. The loud sound of the waves in the background only adds to her anxiety as she holds onto her batik dress tightly, as if expecting a bear to appear. Whether it is only her imagination, it seems everyone holding their breath seeing his presence.

As he slowly makes his way towards her, his face emerges from the darkness, revealing his striking dark brown eyes that glisten in the dim light of the garden lanterns. When his gaze meets hers, his eyes widen slightly and his lips part in surprise.

Amanda cannot interpret his facial expression. As if comprehension finally dawns on him, there is a ghost of a smile on his face as a slight twitch curved on his corner lips. It is a devilish grin that instantly sends a chill down her spine.

Standing confidently with his thumb casually tucked in his jeans pocket, he gazes at her intently, oblivious to the curious onlookers around them. Amanda barely has time to calm the thundering of her heart before he speaks, his voice blending with the crashing waves in the background.

"Hello, Amanda. It's lovely to see you here."

Chapter Seven

The Past – *three months after*

A piece of a cherry petal on his knee and the gentle afternoon breeze mixed with twenty-degree sunshine created a lovely scene of Melbourne's spring season. Sitting outside his an-acre mansion's well-manicured garden, which was fully bloomed with colourful leaves of the spring was something that Tyler had to be grateful for. Lifting up his head to the clear blue sky reminded him of the contrast of the cloudy sky he witnessed three months ago from his wall-to-wall office window.

The season had shifted, transitioning from the cold of winter to the warmth of spring. As time went by, he couldn't shake off the memory of the frightening hostage situation that left him with a bullet wound in his leg. The pain from that incident still lingered, a reminder of the ordeal he had endured. Despite undergoing numerous therapies for a month, he was still confined to his wheelchair. He had been working from home, with lots of assistance from his personal assistant – Megan.

Not Amanda.

The moment he finally gained consciousness, he found himself alone in the hospital. His mind immediately flew to Amanda, and the hijacker Ben. But he did not learn much about their whereabouts until a month later.

The HR director of Fraser & Co informed him that Amanda had left the company since the incident, was uncontactable and believed had moved interstate. Meanwhile, Ben was serving time in prison. Apart from that, all business resumed as usual. The media covered the news as their hot selling point for a couple of weeks, then the story eventually faded away.

Tyler was determined to focus on his recovery. He was only in his mid-thirties, and there was no way he would let himself be forever bound in a wheelchair. The best surgeon and therapies were engaged to ensure his full recovery. Despite he received top-notch treatment, he could not shake the feeling of loneliness that lingered in his heart. Only this time, he felt lonelier than ever.

Aaron and Kylie visited him regularly in the hospital, and they were his source of strength. But never he had Janine visiting him, or making any single call for him. Instead, she flew to Paris immediately after the incident.

He was prepared for his wife's lack of attention, but was it really so unreasonable to hope for a little bit of love and care from his parents and siblings? Most of his family only visited him once when he was in hospital. But his father, as far as he remembered, only had one video call with him since the incident. Every time they had a chance to talk, it always revolved around business matters. Acquisition. Merger. Buying. Selling. Project Deal. It felt like money was the only thing that mattered. A sense of being overlooked crept into his heart.

Two hundred thousand dollars. That was the only amount Ben wanted. In his desperate effort to get his well-deserved money, he ended up in jail instead. And yet, Tyler felt powerless and numb as he had no idea how to act upon it.

The sound of footsteps hitting the brick pavement broke his reverie. His hands slide the wheel in his chair in response. Twirling his wheelchair had become his new skill since he was discharged from the hospital. Within a second, he had positioned himself sideways, so he could see his visitor. Initially, he thought it might be Megan. However, his lips parted as a tall broad-shoulder figure, much like his own, strolled towards him.

"Dad..." Tyler was even unsure if his voice was carried away by the wind and reached his father's ear. The senior Mr Fraser strolled towards him, both hands resting on his immaculate business pants, wearing a matching dark blue tie and creaseless blazer. They shared the same dark brown eyes, but his father's angled thick eyebrow showed his strong authority character. The slight hill on his tummy was a mixed indication of ageing and overconsumption of beers over business meetings. A twitch formed on his corner lips as his dark eyes lowered to look at his son.

"Hey, son. It's great to see you making progress!" John Fraser spoke in his usual gruff and stern tone. Tyler could not sense any hint of affection instilled in it.

"I am still in my wheelchair," muttered Tyler flatly.

"I am pretty sure you will be walking soon," replied John lightly, unaffected by the grumpy response. "I've heard you've been working hard in therapy every day."

Tyler remained silent, feeling like his father's words were more of a command than a comforting pat on the back.

"I believe you heard many things," he muttered again as he looked away, uninterested in what he perceived as insincere concern.

Tyler was pretty sure the next words from his father would be about work. In the past, he never bothered how their tone of conversation was always business-like. Chitchat or even light jokes in the family were rare. It seemed like every minute was counted as money. They do a Christmas party as a family, but it usually ends up like a big gala dinner where all acquaintances are invited. The loneliness that struck him in the hospital was like an eye-opener of how cold their family relationship was.

"I suppose you know where your wife is." The reverberation of John's voice pulled Tyler back to the present. As much as he tried to get rid of his negative thoughts, the wound was still raw in his heart. His father's words made him turn to face him again. A frown on John's face made Tyler immediately guess where the conversation was heading.

"Of course, I know," he replied.

"I know currently you cannot travel, but don't you think you should do something about it?"

"What do you think I should do?" Tyler lifted his chin, showing his defiance.

An ire slowly spread on John's face. "Are you going to let her ruin our family?"

Tyler had expected such a question. The man in front of him was his father. A man who had educated him since he was little on the importance of family. But there was more than that. It was not about the relationship, but it was about the face value. The substance of what others perceived about them.

"Is that all you care about? Our family reputation?"

John's eyes widened as he huffed. "What's gotten into you, son? Of course, you know what I mean."

Tyler was totally aware of it. Janine's actions were bound to stir up some gossip. Perhaps now his wife spending time with her lover openly under the spotlight of paparazzi. It was Janine's sweet little revenge on him. She even did not care if their children saw the news. Perhaps their children had grown much more mature than Tyler had thought. He could sense Kylie was hesitant to mention the whereabouts of her mother, while Aaron always deflected the topic by bubbling about his school. The pretence was not to upset him while he was not in good shape.

"Are you going to let her ruin us?" John pushed the question again as he stood tall before his son with a pout on his face. "She's taking advantage of our good reputation for her own benefit."

"Good on her," blurted Tyler. He was even surprised with his own words and as a consequence, he was gifted with a sharp glare from his father. He averted his gaze, pretending not to see it, though John took out his hands from his pocket in a sudden move that Tyler thought his father was about to punch him. He was taken aback by his own negative thoughts.

How resentful he was now towards his father, as far as Tyler remember, his father never hit him or his brother. How could he had time to hit them, when he did not even have time to be with them?

"What's gotten into you, son?" John shook his head, frustrated. "I know you just experienced a terrible ordeal recently. You see, your wife even is not here for you. What an ungrateful slutch, she is!"

How true his father's words were, Tyler could not blame Janine. Perhaps he deserved it.

"You were not there for me, either, Dad." His voice was cold as he glanced at the old man before him. His father's face turned from irritation to bewilderment as he continued, "You only care about your business."

What Tyler witnessed afterwards was something that he had to admire from a man who had run a family empire for the past two decades. John's frown deepened, his body tense, hands clenching and unclenching, chest heaving with each breath. A flare of anger in his nostrils as he tried to restrain himself. Tyler clenched his own palm, anticipating if his dad would pull him up and strangle him.

However, a few minutes later, John's expression became softened as he averted his gaze away for a glimpse before he looked back at his son. The flame in his eyes slowly dampened.

"Why are you speaking like this? You know I do care about you. What do you think is the reason I call almost every day?" His voice was barely a whisper.

"You are always talking about business all the time," Tyler responded. He became fully aware the tightness in his chest intensified. He could not wait to squeeze them out. "You never bother to ask what I felt after the ordeal. You did not even bother that I was almost bleeding to death at that time. You did not try to save me! After five hours, you did not give in to the request of the guy who shot me!"

John looked perplexed. "Why should I give in to his demand?"

"He only asked for two hundred thousand dollars, Dad!"

Tyler could not help it. He raised his voice and somehow like a rock just being lifted on his chest, his scream at the very person he had hidden his bitterness out of respect, finally made him breathe. Still, it was the question that had been haunting him since he was awake lying in the hospital bed. Why did his father away on business trips, leaving him in limbo, and questioning his decision?

John chuckled while shaking his head as if he were mocking him. "Son, it's not about the money."

Tyler narrowed his eyes. "It's not?"

"It's about the principle of the matter. He is a troubled employee. He stole from the company."

"But he had been working for us for thirty years. "

"Precisely! He had been stealing from us all this time."

Tyler looked at his father with a sceptical gaze. A deep crease formed on his forehead as he tried to comprehend this new piece of information. A twinge of uncertainty made him question if he had underestimated the situation. However, being groomed as one of the future leaders at Fraser & Co, he knew the importance of being critical and playing devil's advocate when necessary.

"Do you have any evidence?"

John waved his hands. " "That's what HR told me. They fired him for stealing from inventories, which explains why things kept disappearing during a stocktake."

Tyler did not simply buy it. "Why did he only ask for two hundred thousand dollars? He said that was all the amount he should get if he got retrenched during the restructuring."

John lifted his shoulder as his both hands spread on his side, did not look convincing. "I don't know, son."

"How much did he actually steal?"

John shook his head as he lowered his eyes, and a pinch expression spread on his face. "I don't know the detail, son. I don't feel the need to know. What he did was absolutely wrong. The fact he shot you to ask for money was another example of his poor character."

"He was frustrated. He was dismissed unfairly," argued Tyler with a firm tone.

"Come on, son." John raised his hand dismissively. "Why are we arguing over someone else? He's just an old low-level employee."

The disrespectful words aimed at Ben only fuelled Tyler's anger.

"I was shot. I was almost bleeding to death!" He gritted his teeth as he darted his father with a dark expression. "Don't you care if I die?"

John huffed showing his growing frustration over their conversation. "You're being dramatic, son."

"And yet you're .." Tyler quickly interrupted. "You only concerned about keeping your two hundred thousand dollars from him."

"He doesn't deserve it!" John was so worked up, waving his hands around and his eyes popping out. "Besides, I have everything under control! Our bodyguards plus the police worked well together. We came at the right time to save you all!"

Tyler did ask his brother how he got into the hospital after that ordeal. Sam had explained that the police managed to barge into their office when Ben and his son off guard. Fortunately, there was no shooting saga because immediately Ben's gun was seized. The medical team worked in a flash to bring the unconscious state of him to the hospital.

Amanda was also taken to the hospital for a check-up, but she left on the same night despite the doctor's advice to keep her overnight. She said she just wanted to go home and see her family.

And since then, nothing heard from her except her resignation letter to leave her role earlier than expected.

John's gruffy angry voice pierced through the wind, scattering a few cherry petals over them. The spring breeze kept swirling around as silence descended upon them. They were unmoved, staring at each other with heavy heaves on their chest, none wished to utter the first words.

Tyler took a shuddering breath as he took in his father's figure. John still stood tall before him, as if the heated argument they just had was only one of many little business battles he usually had. His face was impassive, despite the crease between his thick brows stayed. But Tyler could not see any trace of regrets or remorse over this argument. The ups and downs that his father had gone through had forged him into a steel, far from a human with feelings. It made him come to the realisation of how distant their father and son relationship.

Feeling half defeated over the argument, thinking it was pointless to continue it as his father would justify his decision from every possible angle, Tyler spun his wheelchair around, giving his back. If his father would like to bring work matter at this second, *this* would be his answer. Looked childish as it was, he was officially still recovering and needed a break.

"Son..."

"I am feeling tired, Dad." Tyler purposedly began to slide his wheel. "I'll head to my room for rest." He paused for a second, giving his father a chance to say something, though, in his little heart, John Fraser would not do it. Quietly he felt relieved that his father did not try to stop him either. He wheeled his chair towards the house with an indescribable heavy heart.

• • • •

AMELIORATION: A CHANGE OF HEART

THE RED SUNSET PEEKED through the window forcing Tyler to pinch open his eyes. He had taken quite a long nap for a few hours after his father's visit, feeling completely drained from the devastation of the day. He probably had fallen asleep after doing something that he never had since he was twelve years old when his mother chose to live in a separate house.

Shedding his tears.

Just when he least expected it, his phone started ringing and he saw it was a video call from the last person he thought would reach out. He could not help but laugh at the irony of the situation. It seemed like today was going to be one of those days. After an unpleasant visit from his father, his estranged wife finally decided to reach out at just the right moment.

"Hellow there..." Janine was practically purred as her face popped up on the screen. Her wavy hair was dishevelled despite her flawless make-up. Tyler could catch a glimpse of a black bra stripe on her shoulder, guessing that she was in her underwear. Her rosy cheeks suggested she may have been enjoying a few drinks. Tyler wondered whether his wife had called his number by accident. But he repressed his smirk as she still recognised him.

"How are you there, Tyler?" She squeaked followed by her giggle. "Are your feet feeling like they've turned into wheels?"

Now Tyler understood that the purpose of the call was to mock him. Though there was a little spark of annoyance with the joke, this kind of conversation somehow had been a habit almost throughout their marital relationship. Drunken Janine would be hard to control, but Tyler could not help smiling at himself, remembering the time when both of them drank together in the early years of their relationship. It was funny how alike they were.

However, the ordeal might have changed his life perspective. The hard conversation with his father this afternoon was another painful revelation that he had to accept. It made him question whether he could continue to live under the name of Fraser & Co. He almost lost his life, and he was grateful that he survived. Life is short, and you only have one chance to live. Is it worth living circled by the sarcasm and little revenge over a strong desire to pursue power and win?

"Thank you for asking, Janine," Tyler replied nonchalantly. "How are you there? It looks like you're having a blast over there."

"I am!" Her ear-piercing laughter echoed, causing Tyler to cringe a bit. " "Have you been keeping up with the news? I've become even more famous!"

"Yes, you certainly have!" Tyler joined the laughter with a hint of sarcasm. "I can see exactly what you're up to."

Janine's laughter grew even louder. "I hope you're enjoying the show from your wheelchair!" She raised her glass of wine towards the screen.

If he wanted to win over this revenge game, Tyler knew he could. He still had the upper hand. As much as Janine wanted her freedom, she knew she could not live without maintaining her current glamorous lifestyle. But he was tired of playing this game. He just wanted to focus his energy on the people he cared for and genuinely cared for him in return. His children. Quietly he felt grateful, that Aaron and Kylie were young enough to be moulded and guided in the right direction. He did not wish to have his children grow up being bitter like he was now.

"Does it make you happy?" he asked.

"Anything that annoys you is happiness for me, Tyler," she replied with a victorious smirk on her corner lips as she was sipping her wine.

"Are you aware of the mistake you're making?"

The smile on Janine's face instantly vanished. A slight crease formed between her tapered eyebrows. Tyler repressed his smile as he finally caught her attention.

"My father read your news," stated Tyler. "I am absolutely fine with what you're doing, Janine. But it doesn't mean with the man who holds the highest power in Fraser & Co. You're still using Fraser's money."

Janine's face became darkened as her bosoms heaved up and down, either caused by the remaining excitement fuelled by the alcohol, or by the severity of Tyler's statement. "What did he ask you to do?"

"Of course, he wants me to handle you."

"So, you're going to divorce me?"

"Maybe."

Tyler observed his wife's reaction. Janine's face slightly beamed at the thought of her freedom. However, she must be fully aware that was not the only thing she desired. The frown on her face deepened as she slightly tilted her head to look at the screen from the corner of her eyes suspiciously, anticipating the 'but' word.

Tyler felt his chest swell with contentment as he lounged in his comfy spot, resting his head against his soft pillow while observing the hesitation on Janine's face. "Ending our marriage is a clear decision to make. Are you positive that's what you truly desire?"

A lump went through her throat. Her voice grew softer with each word "You know what I want, Tyler."

He knew exactly what she wanted. But Tyler would keep his carrot just out of reach until he heard those magic words from Janine, revealing who was truly in control.

Suddenly, he realised the parallels between this moment and a past incident with Amanda in the office, where he had used his power to intimidate her. A flash of Amanda's frightening face, when he cornered and harassed her in the office, was playing before his eyes. It was a familiar rush of power, a trait that seemed to run in his family. The thrill of wielding power over others for his own satisfaction. His mind tried to rationalise his actions with Janine, but a sense of unease crept in as he remembered how Amanda had helped him despite his past behaviour towards her.

But Janine was not Amanda. If she were, perhaps he would...

"You'll get your freedom, Janine." He averted his gaze from the screen as his mind turned distant for a mere second, contemplating on which coin side weighted him more. He had been brought up to live with plenty of choices, all due to the power that Fraser & Co. bestowed on him. Now he could make the decision. A right one. For a better future that probably he actually wanted.

"And..?" Janine's arch eyebrow on the screen sent a disgusted churn in his stomach. The twinkle in her emerald eyes was a display of her greediness. Surely Janine was fully aware, that her freedom would not come without a price, but she was more than ready to fight for it.

"You know I won't stay silent, Tyler," she continued as if she could read his mind. "I know you are a great father to Aaron and Kylie, and I'm pretty sure you're aware of how this would affect them."

Despite how true those threatening words were, Tyler's blood was boiling. Janine had turned herself from a loving mother into a greedy woman. She even addressed her own children as if belonged to a stranger's children.

"I'm pretty sure you will not leave this matter alone, Janine. You can get ..." Tyler took a deep breath. "Half of my assets." He could see Janine's face light up with excitement. "With conditions."

The word 'conditions' did not seem to deter Janine as she flashed a satisfied smirk on her face. "What conditions?"

"Don't get too ahead of yourself, Janine." Tyler rubbed his jaw, a habit that he would do in the meeting to assert his authority. "It might not be as smooth sailing as you think. Until you fulfil all the conditions, the official paper will not be signed."

Janine's cheerful expression gradually turned sombre as she nervously chewed on her lips. Meanwhile, Tyler's smirking face filled the screen, his corner lips turned up in a cocky manner.

"How many conditions are there?" asked Janine as she seemed just to realise what she had missed to take into account.

Tyler lifted the three of his middle fingers. "Three. And your first will begin now."

"And the other two?"

"It will happen in my own time."

The scowl on Janine's face deepened as Tyler openly flashed his victorious grin.

"Half of my assets, Janine. Think carefully how that will make lots of difference for your freedom."

Realising that she would be at his mercy anyway, as Mrs Fraser or not, Janine turned her face away from the screen. Her chest rose up and down as she pursed her lips before she took a moment to collect herself and turned back to the screen.

"What is the first condition?"

Tyler could not help but be impressed by his wife's drive and determination. Janine had made herself climb up pretty well from her ordinary life coming from middle-income families, into the ladder of high-class society. The fire of ambition in those pair of emerald eyes inflamed more and more with the increasing accumulation of her ages and wealth.

However, Tyler was sure that his first condition would make her jaw drop.

"Beg. Just beg, Janine."

Just as he suspected, Janine's eyes widened and anger began to flush her cheeks. Her lips were tightly pursed, and her whole body tensed as the vein on her elegant neck bulged.

One thing that Tyler now could understand about the problem of having lots of power was the emergence of pride. Due to pride,

John Fraser hesitated to fulfil Ben's simple request, even if it meant risking his son's life. Pride can lead to a downfall indeed.

Janine had every right to feel proud of how well she had positioned herself in her current situation. The pride that it seemed had changed her into an arrogant woman as if she did not need anyone, not even her own family. Tyler might lose half of his assets to this greedy woman, but those assets would not be something that he could bring to the grave, should he die because of Ben's gunshot. He was confident he still had the capability of building up his wealth again for his future. Therefore, it did not bother him at all if Janine could build her own empire on his money. The thrill of watching her bow down on him was far more rewarding.

There was only silence descended upon them for a couple of minutes as Tyler darted a hard stare at the screen, waiting for what he had demanded. After it seemed like an eternity, Janine stood up from the sofa that she had been leaning on throughout the video call. She carefully placed her glass of wine on a nearby console table, her lean figure clad in a stylish black dress. She flicked away her side brown wavey hair as a lump went through her throat. She lowered herself to one knee and looked directly at the screen, mustering the courage to speak up. In a soft voice, she hesitantly murmured words that felt foreign on her tongue, with a look of discomfort crossing her face.

"Tyler Fraser, I beg you. Please."

Chapter Eight

The Present

What Tyler could remember after the gunshot, his vision was blank white as his body shivered, fighting the chillness and the excruciating pain in his leg. But in one moment, a gentle squeeze on his hand sent a spiral of warmth to his lungs, as Amanda's face started to come into view. She looked like an angel with a halo over her dark hair. Her smile was tentative, a mixture of relief and anxiety as their eyes met. At that moment, Tyler knew if he had to die, he would leave in peace. Because at least Amanda had forgiven him.

But now standing before her again, after a decade since the incident, what he finds is different from what he has expected. Dressed in a simple casual light blue Bali batik beach dress, she has a similar length of hair with small pins on her side fringe, which reminds him when the first time she reported her first day of work in his office. However this time, she exudes confidence, a far cry from the scary kitten and sheepish Amanda ten years ago. She used to avoid direct staring at him. But this time, the same woman is standing firmly on her feet, with a lifted chin. Her grey eyes are looking at him squarely with pout lips. Her arms are crossed, inadvertently drawing attention to her ample bosom and the hint of cleavage peeking out from her low-cut dress. Tyler can imagine, though they are hidden, her fists are clenched tightly.

She is far from thrilled to see him. And he fully understands the reason.

And yet, in the past, Tyler would not let himself be intimidated by such an unwelcome aura. He was the man who always got what he wanted, and he had the power to make it happen. That was exactly what he did to Amanda ten years ago, and he enjoyed every second of witnessing her countenance start to crumble under his pressure. He would push up to the point she would finally give in. Unfortunately, the moment never came because of the incident, which Tyler should vexed about. Surprisingly, he felt grateful that Ben's attack took place instead.

And this time, having a sight of fierce Amanda, he could feel the heat of her indignation radiating from her body language. Instead of being his usual cheeky self, trying to tackle it with his charm and power, an odd feeling struck him. He is not scared of her. But he wants to take care of her feelings.

"Hi, Tyler. This is my mum. Have you two met before?" Isla's gleeful voice pierces through the invisible intense eyes trances between him and Amanda. Tyler blinked, glancing around to each of the people around him, and noticing that some of them are the hotel staff.

"Good evening, Mr Fraser," The man with the walkie-talkie nods at him respectfully. "We found these two ladies on the beachside. We thought they were trespassing by accident. But it turns out they are related to Miss Williams." He gestures towards Amanda and the other lady, who Tyler does not recognise, but it does not mean he is not familiar with her.

He is a resourceful man. When he, by coincidence, read Isla Williams' personal info from the HR team and stumbled upon the name of the emergency contact, he initially thought Amanda Johnston was just a common name. However, as her memory still stuck in his head, the urge to dig deeper was strong. For the past six months, he was well informed about Amanda's movement, including her friendship with Elena Taylor. He had expected *this* very moment that he finally meet her again face to face. It was just much sooner than he had anticipated.

"We are not trespassing!" protests Elena.

"It's just a misunderstanding," Isla interrupts with a wince.

Sensing that he should make a word to settle the commotion, Tyler lifts up his hand. "It's alright, Wayan. Thanks for checking. All good here."

Wayan nods his head again. "Sure, Mr Fraser. Do you need us to call a doctor?"

Tyler tilts his head, brows furrowed. "Doctor?"

"This lady..."

"My mother.." Isla adds in quickly. Tyler's eyes bounce between her and Wayan, confused.

"She almost fainted," Wayan explains.

Tyler's lips part as his heart races. He darts a concerned look at Amanda, but she is not thrilled. Still, with a pout on her face, she snaps, "I'm fine!"

Tyler can not help but search her eyes intensely. "Are you sure?"

Seemingly annoyed instead of flattered, Amanda rolls her eyes. "I should probably head back to my room," she says with a slight huff. But then she catches Isla's eye and her expression softens. "I apologise for interrupting your work event, my dear. That wasn't my intention. I'll go back to my room, and we can talk later." She shoots a quick, determined look towards her daughter's boss. "We definitely need to have a chat soon."

Isla nervously follows her gaze and agrees, "Sure, Mum, tomorrow morning sounds good. We might be working late tonight."

With the woman who has plagued his thoughts for ten years about to leave, Tyler scrambles to speak up. He has been waiting for her.

"You should come with us, Amanda!"

His words immediately draw all eyes on him. He ignores Wayan and the other staff as they nod at him and take their leave, realising their presence is not needed anymore. Amanda's almond shape eyes widen as her lips slash into a thin line, obviously taken aback by his invitation.

"Tonight is not a work event. It's merely an ice-breaking session for everyone. You and your friend here.." Tyler flashes his charming grin at Elena which she returns with her sweet smile and battling eyelashes. "..are welcome to join in as well. Unless..." He can see Amanda's fiery eyes are not diminished yet. "... you are already engaged with something else tonight."

"We are not," Elena replies enthusiastically. Her smile instantly drops as she receives a poke of elbow from Amanda. She scowls for a second before throwing another congenial smile at Tyler. "We will be delighted to join in."

"That's awesome!" But Tyler is aware that Elena's answer is insufficient until Amanda says a word. It's Amanda he truly wants, not Elena. Despite the tension between them is palpable to everyone, his eyes are inevitably on her thin pink lips, that like last time, soft moist, unpolished with lipstick. He used to have some pretty intense thoughts about what he'd like to do with those lips. However, as his eyes are up to meet hers, his heart sinks. The flicker of the lantern light in her captivating grey eyes tells him all he needs to know - she despises him. Without understanding why, his chest becomes tightened.

A momentary silence descends as all eyes are now landed on Amanda. She blinks, realising everyone is waiting for her answer. Her lips move silently a few times before she takes a deep breath and finally speaks.

Tyler holds his breath, anticipating the words uttered as he holds his gaze at her. When their eyes meet, he sees the same determination in her gaze from when she rejected his advances before. And he knows that her answer will mean that the game is on.

· · · ·

AMANDA'S MIND IS FULL of battle. Standing before the man who bullied her a decade ago, anger boils in her veins and heat slowly creeps to her cheek. She has tasted the ups and downs of life, which has taught her how she should stand up for herself and her loved ones. This time Tyler Fraser might be looking for his new victim, and Amanda will not let this man come any closer to her beloved daughter. She is not afraid of him anymore, because she is not the same quite young woman ten years ago.

If it is not for Elena's excitement to join in the Fraser & Co's party, Amanda will choose to retreat to her room. She needs time to form a plan, or maybe in precise words, the right words to deliver to Isla about the truth of Tyler Fraser. She has to be prepared how to convince her daughter if Isla does not believe her. However, as everyone is still waiting for her final word, her brain is racing quickly. Joining the party might not be a bad idea, after all. She can pay close attention to Isla, ensuring that Tyler keeps his hands to himself.

However, there is something niggling at the back of her mind. She does not wish to embarrass Isla if she cannot control herself. She might slap Tyler Fraser if he goes overboard. Tyler Fraser whom she knew was capable of causing a scene, she did not doubt that. He is the one who upheld the highest power here anyway. No one would dare to question him.

Probably her motherly protective instinct is much stronger than she thought. Breathing in deeply, as if gathering her strength for a battle, she darts her eyes at the very man that she would fight against for the safety of her family. With her chin lifted high, she accepts the offer to join in the party.

The mirth in Tyler's eyes causes her to clench her fist. He sees right through her, and his eyes are laughing at her. The same amusing set pair of eyes that looked down at her when he cornered her in his office room a decade ago. Though her heart is slightly trembling, having Isla's safety in mind, she steels herself to be brave.

"So, how do you know each other?" asks Elena when they are settled down after taking drinks from the bar.

Amanda helps herself with a mocktail and does not wish to let herself be swayed by alcohol at this moment. The divorce has made her drink more than usual, but she is sober most of the time. The mission for Isla is set firmly in her mind. Whenever there is a chance, she will position herself to stand like Isla's bodyguard, distancing her daughter from Tyler Fraser.

The question prompts her to take a quiet sip of her drink, her mind racing to find the perfect response. Yet, the question is not just for her.

"Amanda worked for Fraser & Co before," Tyler replies.

Isla's mouth is falling open as her daughter gives her an incredulous look. "Seriously, mum? Why didn't you tell me?"

That is actually a harder question for her to answer. She gulps her drink again while wracking her brain for an answer.

To her surprise, this time Tyler let her answer. He sips his drink while watching her. Her pulse is speeding as she interprets his hidden smile behind his glass as mocking her.

"It was a while back," she finally makes a sound as she gives a solemn look to her daughter. "You were still in primary school back then."

Isla's eyes are still widened in disbelief. "But you never mentioned it to me."

"Well,..I have worked in multiple places in the past. I had a brief stint at Fraser & Co as a temporary employee. When you mentioned that you work there, it rang a bell and I remembered that I had been there before, probably just for a few weeks."

"But Mr Fraser still remembers you," Elena says with a smile, reaching out her hand towards Tyler, and raising an eyebrow playfully. "That's impressive! You must be a very attentive employer."

The word 'attentive' is like a rock thud on Amanda's chest. The blitz from the past inevitably makes her wince. Her eyes glance sideways to Tyler who seems unfazed as he takes a sip from his beer bottle.

"First of all, please call me Tyler." He flashes his grin after his Adam apple bobbed with the drinks. "Amanda was one of my capable personal assistants. Her leaving was a loss to the company."

Amanda cannot deny Tyler's words send a chill to her nape as she inwardly shudders. Every word uttered by him only reminds her of the distress that he had put her on.

"Why did you end up leaving?" asks Elena, tilting her head with curiosity.

"That was when Sean landed a job in Brisbane," Amanda replies. She quietly compliments herself for giving a coherent answer. Despite the media frenzy surrounding the hostage situation, the company chose not to disclose the names of those involved. Sean was the only one to whom she had confided the full story, and they agreed to keep it between themselves and felt unnecessary to tell the children. Because the most important thing was that she was safe.

"Ah, right." Elena nods as she comprehends the timeline mentioned.

"Oh, mum." Isla shakes her head in disbelief. "You worked as Tyler's personal assistant and you don't remember him?"

Amanda lowers her head as she chuckles dryly. However, her heart seems to cease for a beat when Isla continues speaking while glancing at her big boss with an admiration gaze. "He must be one of your best employers, and you don't remember him?"

Her grip on her glass is tightened as she purses her lips. Isla's laughter echoes crisply against the noise from the upbeat music background that accompanies the event. Amanda averts her gaze to the crowd circling in the middle of the room, hoping her daughter does not notice the tears welling up in her eyes. Her chest tightens as she quietly takes a shuddering breath.

She never told a single soul about that particular past. It was a distressing time that she wished she could erase from her memory. How every fibre of her being hoped to prevent history from repeating itself, especially with her daughter. Yet, her worst fear is unfolding before her. How much at this time she wishes she could drag Isla away and share the truth about her and Tyler Fraser.

"It's been ten years, Isla," Tyler's deep voice chimes in. "I don't blame your mother if she does not remember when you mentioned Fraser & Co."

Amanda quietly is taken aback that it seems Tyler is trying to help her.

Isla smiles sheepishly. "Yeah, right. I can't remember much about our time in Brisbane, too. We were there only for a year, right, mum?"

Amanda gives a weak nod. It was a year of another tough moment she had to endure. On the bright side, it did help her cope a little better with the trauma from Ben's frightening experience with a gun. However, it was also the year she started to drift apart from Sean. Now she finally comprehends her husband's insistence on returning to Melbourne.

"Alright, I have to go, mum." Isla puts down her beer bottle on the table as she pushes her chair and stands up. "I have to lead the program for tonight."

Amanda realises her daughter is still working and isn't sure how to feel - relieved to be spared more questions or be concerned for Isla.

Isla taps her shoulder lightly "Are you sure you're alright, mum?"

Amanda quickly flashes her reassuring smile. "Of course, I'm well, love. Don't worry about me."

Isla takes her leave, and before Amanda recovers herself, Elena unexpectedly stands up too.

"I'm going to grab more drinks," Elena announces, prompting a curious glance from Amanda. However, Amanda is aware that Elena is a good drinker. The moment they sat down, Elena had gulped probably more than half of the bottle. Amanda can't help but wonder if her friend is just thirsty or if she simply loves her drinks. That leads to another question in her mind whether her friend is already drunk. But seeing Elena pushing out her chair firmly and walking away towards the bar without any sign of tipsyness, Amanda quietly feels relieved that her friend seems to know her limits.

Then she turns her head, to find Tyler is unmoved from his seat. His gaze has been holding onto her, watching her. In the past, Amanda would probably be intimidated by his dark consuming eyes. But this time, she has a tough mission in her mind and she will not let herself be cowed by him anymore.

The sound of people cheering from the stage breaks their trances. Isla jumps to the stage, grabs a microphone, introduces herself and starts her casual speech. It is impossible for Amanda not to feel her heart swell with pride as she watches her daughter shining on stage. Her daughter is a picture of a vibrant, enthusiastic young lady, who looks more than ready to soar in her career as a leader.

"She is incredible. You must be so proud of her."

Tyler's resonant voice lingers in Amanda's thoughts. Turning back at him, Amanda cannot discern the meaning of the twitch on his corner lips. Is he scheming something that she has been afraid of? She does not wish to jump to conclusions too quickly, though she will find the right time to speak with Isla, to convince her to leave Fraser & Co.

"She is," she murmurs.

Amanda hopes Elena will return soon. Instead, her friend is leaning on the bar, holding a bottle of beer with the company of a man, probably about their age with half of his hair turning white. From the distance, she cannot make out his face, but his tall stature suggests he is pretty cute. Giggling inwardly, Amanda has to salute Elena's talent for having a good time.

"He's one of our project managers. His name is Chris." Tyler supplies the information before Amanda even has to ask. "His wife passed away two years ago due to cancer. He had two grown-up daughters, living in State currently. It's the first time I see him enjoying himself chatting with a woman. He's a nice guy, I think they might really hit it off."

Amanda is close to bursting into laughter. Is Tyler Fraser playing the role of matchmaker for his employee? That is truly unexpected to her. She chuckles rather sardonically.

But Tyler does not seem phased by her reaction.

"I heard about your divorce, which means Elena's divorce too," he says. "I am sorry to hear that."

Amanda cocks her head to the side in surprise, struggling to trust her own ears. Is the apology delivered to mock her? She stares at the man before her, his brown eyes are shining like twinkling jewels. No sign of mirth. Instead, those eyes are looking at her gently, expressing genuine sympathy.

"How do you know that?" She blurts the question as her eyebrows draw together. Has Isla been speaking a lot of her personal life to Tyler? The thought of it makes her chest tight because if it is true, that means they work close together in the office.

Tyler's Adam apple bobs as he looks slightly uncomfortable with the question. "Well, Isla told me about her parents' divorce and how it's been affecting you. She shared details about how the divorce happened."

Amanda quietly takes a shuddering breath to calm her pounding heart. "It seems Isla confides in you a lot."

"Please don't be upset with her. She is worried about you."

Amanda's head begins to spin, but she remains determined to stay put. "Are you still one of the directors, Mr Fraser?" she asks. Amanda recalls when she was the personal assistant of Tyler Fraser, most of his meetings were only between the leadership team. He would not be bothered to speak with someone lower than his status. Back then there was no graduate program yet. So, she wonders if that was the reason for the change.

"I am." Tyler furrows his brow and seems taken aback by the question. "Why?"

"I am surprised that you have time to speak with graduate students," Amanda remarks without any hesitancy. "It's unusual for someone in your position."

Tyler's laughter roars against the energetic jazz music from the live stage performance. The dance floor is a lively scene with everyone showcasing their best moves. Amanda spots Isla dancing with a bottle in hand, chatting with a group of young ladies who are likely in the same graduate program as her.

"Things now change, Amanda. Fraser & Co has had a massive transformation throughout the past decade. I actually came up with the idea for our graduate programs, so we can recruit the most talented individuals to our company. I am not the one who runs the program, it is the HR team. But I do like to pop in once in a while to check how our young future leaders have been progressing."

His eyes fly to where Isla is. Amanda follows his eyes' direction and her heart flutters to see the fond smile on his lips.

"Isla is one of our bright employees, I must say. It's impossible not to notice how she thrives in her role."

Amanda purses her lips to hear the compliment. But her eyes never stray from his face as she tries to interpret his every mimic, whether there is something that she needs to read between his lines.

His head turns back at her. "She must have inherited your diligent and persevering spirit. She's young and beautiful. A bright future lies ahead for her."

Though most of his words sound like genuine praises, Amanda cannot shake the feeling of unease creeping down her spine. Perhaps it's just her scepticism, especially considering their rocky history. She senses there might be more to Tyler's words.

"It seems you have a special plan set for her." Amanda licks her lips, realising that she is trying to dig deeper. Probably it is a bit bold, but it is her fierce mother instinct that pushes her.

Tyler tilts his head at her with a twitch on his corner lips. "I do. She's a valuable employee. I will not let the competitor snatch her up without a fight."

Amanda can feel her blood starting to simmer, and the heat slowly creeping up to her neck. She can sense her worst fears unfolding right before her eyes. Their eyes are locked for a moment as if they are sizing up each other. But Amanda will not be the first one to back down.

"What is your plan, Mr Fraser? I am her mother, and I will not let you repeat what you did to me last time." She is practically seething as she speaks through her tightly clenched teeth. Clenching her fist tight, Tyler returns it with a solemn calm look.

"Do you actually want to hear it, Amanda?" He arches his eyebrow, and Amanda knows that he is placing down a challenge to her. "First of all, please stop calling me Mr Fraser. Just call me Tyler."

Amanda restrains herself from speaking any word, as she bit her lips to remind herself to remain calm. Whatever it is, as much as she wishes she could give the man before her a punch, she will not let herself lose her cool. She is not the same naive young woman from ten years ago.

"Secondly..." Tyler stretches out his hand and opens his palm before her eyes. "Shall we have a dance?"

• • • •

HER RESPONSE AMAZES him.

Without a second of hesitation, Amanda takes his hand, eyes staring hard at him without blinking. She stands up and twirls herself gracefully, letting the tail of her batik dress brush his leg, following his lead to the centre of the venue that has been transformed into a dancing floor.

In a heartwarming display of teamwork, experienced employees step up to lead the way and encourage the newer, shyer ones to join in, making sure the dance floor stays lively. Some of the staff have come with their partners, which is allowed under the company's policy, adding even more fun to the mix. From his peripheral view, Tyler captures the sight of Isla with Aaron and other colleagues, dancing as a group. Her eyes widened with mirth when she saw them.

Feeling Amanda's hands in his triggers the memory of Ben's gun hostage. Her warm gentle hands were his source of strength, the ones that he would cling his life onto at that cold lonely time. He has been yearning for those same hands for the past ten years. Each of her fingers is thin, with mediocre manicured fingernails, which is clearly the sign she does it herself instead of by a professional. Yet, her skin is so soft, tempting him to gently rub it against his own. He could spend an entire night lost in this simple activity.

Having the privilege of being so close at this moment is a treasure Tyler yearns to preserve for eternity. She has been a distant dream for the past ten years, but now he finds himself intoxicated by her sweet, flowery fragrance. His gaze lingers on every detail of her face - the untouched, natural brown eyebrows, the dark almond eyes free of makeup, the delicate straight nose, the pale pink lips, and the smooth cheeks with faint wrinkles. Every fibre of his being longs to kiss each feature, for she is effortlessly beautiful in her own right. He yearns to touch her like a precious jewel, treating her with the care and delicacy she deserves.

However, he reminds himself despite this woman now in his arms, swaying with him perfectly in tune with the jazz acoustics rendition of Whitney Houston's 'I Wanna Dance with Somebody', he discerns the suspicious look in her eyes. Yet he cannot resist taking in a deep breath, savouring this moment, feeling the warmth of her body against him as the lyrics of the song verbalise his mind.

Clock strikes upon the hour
And the sun begins to fade
Still enough time to figure out
How to chase my blues away
I've done alright up 'till now
It's the light of day that shows me how
And when the night falls, loneliness calls
I wanna dance with somebody.
I wanna feel the heat with somebody.
Yeah, I wanna dance with somebody.
Somebody who loves me.

"So, what is your plan for Isla?" Amanda's voice breaks his reverie. She swallows hard before the question is out of her mouth. They have been dancing with no words uttered for a while moving in sync with the music. She seems cannot be held in suspense anymore.

"Plenty," Tyler replies.

He never averts his gaze from her, fixated on every move she makes. The palm of her right hand, still clasped in his, trembles slightly, leaving a trail of moisture in its wake. A pang of remorse unexpectedly grips him as he senses her inner turmoil. Their past is tainted with a blend of disrespect and aggression. He cannot be offended if she interprets his words in a negative light.

"How long are you planning to stay in Bali?" he asks, hoping to steer the conversation in a different direction. It will not happen immediately, of course. She lowers her eyes for a brief before steeling herself to look at him squarely.

"It is not your business," she mutters.

Her cold reply does not deter him from smiling. Tyler knows he holds the upper hand in their situation, which makes him feel tall.

However, at the same time, a conscience-stricken feeling also slips in. He does not wish to toy around with her anxious feelings over Isla, but he also does not want her to simply go away. He has been anticipating her presence, sooner or later, since he found out about her family relationship with Isla.

Her presence here in Bali is, in a way, perfect! It is not the first time he has been visiting the infamous paradise island of Indonesia. The last time he was here a year ago, he was standing on the gorgeous Kuta beach, clenching in and out his hands, imagining her by his side so he could hold her hand once more.

"You are here because of Isla. And because I am here, too," he states. The way Amanda purses her lips is enticing, and he can not help but glance at them again. He must find a way soon how he can nibble on that sensual part of her body. "You are worried that I might treat her like I did to you last time." His heart skips a beat as she sends him a fiery glare. But he will not be Tyler Fraser if he is simply back down. "So, you are here to protect her. That means you'll be sticking around as long as I am."

"I am going to speak with Isla," she hisses. "I am going to tell her who you truly are."

"Do you think she will take your word for it?"

" I am her mother."

"Who has not been talking to her since the divorce two years ago?"

A shade of pain reflected on her face. Another guilt-ridden feeling strikes.

He's been uncovering so much about her tough divorce from Isla without even trying too hard. It all just came up during a few laid-back chats. Isla is so chill and open, not afraid to share her struggles. The story of her parents' divorce just naturally came up in conversation, making her seem wise beyond her years.

"You shut her out," he points out, delivering another blow. Amanda's eyes begin to burn with intensity.

She shakes her head as her breath quickens. "You know nothing about us."

He arches his eyebrow. "Do you think so?"

The song comes to an end. She quickly removes her hand from his grip, pulling herself away from his arm. But Tyler sneakily puts his hand on her small back, guiding her close on their way back to their seats, though it is pretty obvious that she just wants to break away from him.

"Have you been here before?"

His question makes her turn to him rather abruptly. The crease on her forehead indicates that she is baffled by how calm and collected he is after their unpleasant conversation. Her pinch expression compliments a disgusted look she shoots at him.

But Tyler has been facing similar reactions for half of his life. Amanda has been blinded by their dark past, and he knows he has to work hard to show his new self.

"I think you should chill a bit, Amanda. Isla will think likewise too. If you simply just drag her now and bring up our past, she will think you are simply mad. After two years of isolating yourself from anyone, including your own children, your story will not make any sense to her."

He slips his hands into his pocket, watching her chest rise up and down. She is obviously trying to calm herself down, realising how his words are true to the core.

"Come with me tomorrow," he continues.

She blinks in surprise.

"If you feel you need to be your daughter's bodyguard, then you must keep an eye on me, right?" His corner lips twitch into a smirk. "I'll show you around. You will love this place."

The incredulity on her face runs deep. Tyler can't help but enjoy it, like he's giving her a nice shock. He is a changed man, far from the hideous man a decade ago that she knew. And he is eager to prove it to her.

Sensing that someone is approaching them, he takes a step backward. He can hear her deep breath as she composes herself before Isla and Elena land themselves in front of them.

"How is it going, mum?" Isla rubs her mother's arm gently. "I hope you're having a good time."

From his peripheral view, Tyler can see Amanda has calmed down and managed a faint smile, though it looks vague in his opinion.

"I am," she replies. "But I think I'm ready to call it a night. I'll head back to my room now." She turns to him with a slight nod. "Thank you for the dance, Mr Fraser."

Tyler has to admire the serenity reflected on her face. The flame in her eyes may have dissipated, but the severity of her gaze at him remains.

"You're welcome, Amanda." He gently takes her small hand, and plants a light kiss on it. Her eyes widen for a brief before she frowns. "Please call me Tyler."

"I think I'll call it a night, too," says Elena. Her eyebrows bounce with amusement at Tyler's gentlemanly gesture. She sticks out her hand, teasing him for a farewell kiss. Tyler and Isla chuckle lightly. Tyler has to admit that he likes Elena's outgoing personality, and without hesitation, his gentle kiss also lands on her hand.

"Good night, ladies."

"Good night, Tyler. Bye, love." Elena returns the greeting while giving Isla a smooch. Amanda does the same to her daughter, but her goodbye murmur to Tyler is almost unheard as she strolls away without looking back anymore.

Tyler quietly takes a deep breath as he watches the silhouette of the woman that he obsesses slowly fade into the night.

· · · ·

THE JOURNEY TO THE hotel room is only filled with deafening silence. No one utters any word. The only sounds are the chirping of grasshoppers and the rhythm of their footsteps.

Their room is situated on the west wing, about a kilometre away from where the Fraser & Co employees are staying in the east wing. They decided to book a shared hotel room while most of the employees, including Isla, opted for the cottage villa accommodation. That is the reason their accommodation is far from each other.

The distance does bother Amanda initially. She hopes she can pay closer attention to what Isla is doing with Tyler Fraser. The night is still young, time only shows nine o'clock local time, though it means midnight Melbourne time. She should have stayed longer at the party, ensuring Isla's safety. But the conversation that she had earlier with Tyler makes her heart feel heavy. She does not feel she has the strength to stick around anymore.

You shut her out.

Those words keep resonating in her head. Each word pokes into her heart until it bleeds. What has she done? Has she been so consumed by the pain of the divorce that she unintentionally neglected her own children?

The last two years since the divorce have been a tough time for her. Not only had she buried herself with work as an operations manager in a non-profit organisation, but she had been keeping her distance from everyone. She did not mean to ignore her children. Isla was in her first year of university and Hamish just finished his VCE. They have accepted the news with more grace than she has. No one blamed her or Sean. She realises she takes longer to move on. In fact, she has not fully moved on until now.

Family events like Easter and Christmas become painful, especially when Hamish and Isla spend special time with their father and his new partner. She would run to her parents' house, waiting for the children to join her afterwards in their grandparents' house. Until now, she never thought things would change. She has no idea when she finally has the courage to see Sean with his new partner, and openly accept them, like what Hamish and Isla wish.

She tries to self-retrospect. Despite isolating herself from social life since the divorce, she has been trying to stay in touch with their children. She has to admit that most of their conversations are only short chitchat, on the surface but no deep talks, and probably only happen once every fortnight. She thinks that her children have grown up and are busy with their own lives. She does not want to be overbearing or intrude too much. It never crossed her mind that her good intentions could be understood as ignorance.

As they finally reach their room, she quietly breathes in deeply before pushing the door open and plopping down on the sofa. Resting her head on the soft cushion, she closes her eyes, hoping it will help ease her agony.

"Are you alright?"

Elena's voice reminds her that she is not alone. She has been lost in thought, unaware her friend is on her side all this while, watching her crumpled face in silence. Elena plops down on the sofa next to her.

"There's something more between you and Tyler Fraser, isn't it?"

Amanda takes another heavy breath, bracing herself for a difficult conversation.

"I remember the timelines when you left Fraser & Co."

Elena's statement prompts her to snap open her eyes. Raking her fingers across her fringe, Amanda turns her head to her friend who gives her a solemn look.

"Tom told me. Well, of course, because Sean told him. You and Tyler were in the gun hostage saga in Fraser & Co. at that time. That was the reason there was no argument from your side when Tom found a job in Brisbane for Sean. Sean told him that you definitely needed a change at that time."

Unable to repress her dry bitter chuckle as Tom's name comes up, Amanda shakes her head.

"What else does Tom know?" she asks. She should have known that no secret between the two mates. "Did you tell anyone else?"

Elena shakes her head firmly. "No. Tom warned me not to. The media also did not mention any of your names." She reaches out to soothe Amanda's arm. "It must have been really tough for you back then."

"It was," Amanda sighs. She is glad it has been a decade ago. Time heals the trauma bit by bit. At least she did not have lots of nightmares about it. She did meet with a psychologist a couple of times in the first year after the incident.

"Tyler owes you, correct? I heard you saved his life."

Amanda chuckles bitterly. "Not really. You know how we were saved."

Elena nods. "Yes, I remember. It was in the newspaper."

Silence falls momentarily, only heavy breaths are heard in the room. Elena stands up and opens the minibar. She takes out two bottles of beer and passes one to her friend, who welcomes it without any word. The cold drinks are probably what they need to accompany their talks tonight.

Amanda does not remember being a big drinker when she was younger. She did not let herself fall into alcohol when the divorce happened. But after she begins seeing Elena often for a couple of catch-ups about eight months ago, she starts to drink more, happily taking whatever drinks Elena offers.

"So, what is going on between you and Tyler apart that both of you were trapped together in the hostage saga?" Elena asks the question again, indicating her curiosity needs to be fed soon. "The way he looks at you tonight..." She clucks her tongue. "I think he falls hard on you."

If Elena is not talking about Tyler Fraser, probably Amanda will be flattered to hear someone is interested in her at her ripe age of forty-three. However, with the unpleasant past she has with Tyler, the words make her blood boil.

The way Tyler looks at her tonight only reminds her of the stressful moment she had to suffer under his scrutinisation. He almost looked like he was ready to maul her most of the time. Tonight was no different, but an outsider who is unaware of Tyler Fraser's true nature will interpret it like a love-struck.

"You were his personal assistant. Did you have an affair with him?"

The question only inflicts her rage. Not because Elena's guess is far from the truth. But the word 'affair' only reminds Amanda of the true reason for her marriage divorce.

"I never strayed during my marriage," she mutters darkly. "I was devoted to my family. The persons who have the affairs are our husbands back then." And her heart aches as the bitter memory of the past returns. It was unthinkable how Sean and Tom's affairs had happened for almost a decade.

"I know you still can't accept what Sean and Tom did," Elena sighs. "But it already happened. Why is it so hard for you to move on?"

Amanda turns to her friend dumbfounded. "How can you be okay with this? They have been doing this behind our back for nearly a decade." The heat of fury starts to creep to her neck as her eyes bulge out. "They were cheating while we were working hard for our children and our marriage!"

A flood of bitterness from the past comes rushing into Amanda's mind. She tried everything to get her husband's attention - arranging a babysitter for date nights and buying new lingerie in hopes of sparking intimacy. All those efforts were gone astray and only made her look dumb. Because Sean was no longer in love with her anymore. His heart belonged to someone else. But her husband had tortured her with false affection, forcing her to reluctantly accept that their young love had turned into a mere commitment for their children. She went from being a lustful needy wife, into a simply dutiful mother, feeling lost in transformation. However, when he finally announced the divorce, the pain that had been inflicted had been intensely deep. She had been deceived far too long, that she could not see a way out of the hurt. It has transformed her into someone unrecognisable to herself.

"It's important to remember that they were struggling, too," Elena's consoling words break in as if wishing it would subdue her anger. "They did not mean to hurt us. They were trying to understand themselves too. Same-gender relationship was still a taboo back then. Can you imagine if Sean told his parents when they were still alive? It would have been even harder. You know it was not easy for them to simply open up because of the family and society expectations."

Amanda cannot help but scoff again. Elena's words are partially true. Many times she tries to put herself in Sean and Tom's shoes. Perhaps she would be able to accept it better if Sean opened up to her earlier about his circumstances, rather than trying to cover it up. However, things already happened, and no one could change it.

"Did you actually sense it?" Amanda may have asked her friend this question before, but she could not remember Elena's response.

Elena's head gently moves from side to side as she tightens her lips. "Between yes and no. But Tom still..." She grimaces. "We still had sex..."

Amanda lets out a soft gasp and her face goes tense.

"Sometimes," Elena quickly adds on, then closes her eyes as if a huge storm just passed by seeing Amanda's expression soften. "But we haven't had that in years before the divorce."

Amanda scoffs as she shakes her head in disbelief. "I was just trying to be proactive for our marriage, but Sean always shut me down. And then, out of nowhere, he drops the bombshell of divorce." Inevitably, tears start to prick her eyes, as the old wound resurfaces. How could she have missed the signs? She had naively thought Sean's vague avoidance was because of work stress. They had been working hard to save every penny for the house mortgage and the children's education. It never occurred to her that there could be another woman involved.

Indeed, there was no other woman.

She snorts, laughing at herself. The third wheel was no other than his best mate.

"I must look stupid." Her voice is just above a whisper, dripped with anguish.

"Please don't say that, Amanda." Elena reaches out and pulls her into a comforting hug. "You're not silly at all. Everything happens for a reason, trust me."

Amanda cannot contain her tears anymore as she starts to sob in her friend's arms. It is not the first time she found solace in Elena's embrace, and the habit seems will stay for a while.

"You have to admit, Sean and Tom are great fathers to our children," whispers Elena as she gently soothes her friend's small back. "That is why I can overlook their faults. If the children can accept them, I am accepting them too for the sake of the children. I am confident, you will be able to do the same too. You have been a great mother to Hamish and Isla."

A great mother.

The word sounds ironic to Amanda's ear as Tyler's words about what she did to Isla resonate back in her head.

You shut her out.

As she gently shakes her head, her hair lightly brushes against Elena's small chest. "I don't think I am a good mother," she murmurs.

"Never doubt yourself," Elena reprimands her, giving her a reassuring tap on the shoulder. "Remember how amazing Isla was earlier when she delivered that speech to her colleagues? You've been the strong pillar that has given her the confidence to be who she is today. You've made sacrifices for your family. Don't let the beautiful memories you've built be tarnished because you can't forgive the past and their father."

Amanda is quiet as she has nothing to say. Elena's words make her think. Reflecting. How sensible those words are. She claims herself as a devoted mother, and yet she cannot overlook Sean's sins against her, despite the silent pleas from her children. In the first year after the divorce, Hamish and Isla have been trying to reach out to her, wishing she would let go of the matter, and they could be together in one room as a family despite the changes. However, she declined their requests repeatedly, which made them slowly retreat to trying again. That is probably the meaning of Tyler's words that she had shut her kids out from her life.

"I understand that things take time, Amanda," Elena's comforting tone breaks the silence in the room.

Amanda straightens herself up, rubs the remaining tears from her cheeks, and sips her drink again. Probably sensing that she is calming down, Elena continues, "I am not saying you have to be happy for Sean and Tom, but they have found each other. Your time will come, too." With a knowing look, she playfully suggests, "Who knows, maybe this Tyler Fraser will be the one for you." She finishes with a mischievous grin on her lips.

As soon as the name of Tyler Fraser is mentioned again, Amanda rolls her eyes in annoyance. Apart from Ben's terrifying ordeal, Tyler Fraser was another past trauma that she would rather forget. Recalling how his rough hands disrespectfully touched her, inflames her fury. How helpless she was at that time, only makes her beat herself more.

"Could we not bring up his name again, please?'," she groans.

Not detecting her frustration, Elena pushes on. "Why? For his age, he's bloody hot!" She pronounces the last word with hard punctuation. "Even more attractive than his son."

"More than your Chris?" Amanda arches her eyebrow, attempting to lighten the mood by returning the tease.

Elena bursts into laughter, instantly changing the vibe in the room. Amanda wonders whether they will receive a complaint call soon from other guests. Seeing her friend's cheerful demeanour, quietly she feels grateful that she is here with this amazing woman. Her earlier meltdown instantly feels like a distant memory.

"Well, I had a great time with Chris." Elena smiles sheepishly. Her face turns severe again afterwards. "But come on, Amanda. Why can't you consider Tyler? He must be admiring you after what you did to save him from the hostage saga."

"I did not save him," Amanda protests. "I just tried to talk Ben down." She takes a deep sigh as Ben's name is on her lips. "I feel bad for Ben. All he wanted was the money he was owed if he got laid off. It was only two hundred thousand dollars. But none of the Fraser family granted it. Tyler did not keep his promise, either. He was supposed to give the money once we were out. But it never happened."

Elena pauses, her eyebrows furrowing as she drifts into thought. "I guess if Ben did have the money, the police would not let him get away as well."

Amanda nods weakly as she agrees with the theory. "Yes, you're probably right."

"You can't entirely blame it on Tyler."

Amanda shakes her head as she huffs, "He could have done something."

Elena lets out a long sigh, placing her bottle down and crossing her arms. "I still think you should give Tyler a chance."

Amanda finishes her drink straight from the bottle, getting a bit annoyed that her friend is still insisting. Remembering Tyler's warning that Isla may not just take her side over his, only adds fuel to her fire. It seems that even Elena may not believe her if she spills the truth about Tyler Fraser. Tyler has a way of using his wealth to charm and deceive, masking his true self.

She tilts her head to her friends with a pinching frustrated face. "Don't you understand why I rushed you to get here?"

Elena blinks before slowly shaking her head, indicating her uncertainty. "You said you are worried about Isla."

"That's correct. I am worried about Isla. I am worried that Tyler might do something to her."

Elena frowns. "What do you mean?"

Amanda takes another big swallow of her drink before she places down her bottle and shuts her eyes. This is the moment she finally must tell a soul about her past with Tyler Fraser. There is no point to hide it anymore. There is no Sean anymore in her life. He probably does not care anyway. Everyone needs to know what Tyler was like a decade ago. He was simply a monster.

She opens her eyes and stares at her friend squarely in the eyes. Elena bites her lips, clutching to the heart pendant of her white gold necklace, anticipating the next words.

"Tyler is not as charming as you, Isla, or everyone believes," she firmly declares. Her energy seems about to drain soon once she utters the truth. Elena does not make a sound, giving her rapt attention, knowing she has not finished her sentence yet. The crease between her brows is deepened while waiting in suspense.

Amanda is looking up to the ceiling, shutting her eyes as if asking for strength from the almighty God above to say the words. It is unbelievable that she has kept this secret for such a long time. Many times she held her tongue when there was an opportunity to tell Sean for the least. But she did not do it. The secret was pushed to the side, swept under the bottom of her mind, buried deep to be forgotten. But no matter how hard she tries to forget, it always resurfaces. And now Isla is in the middle of this entangled past. She must do something before her daughter falls into the same trauma.

Quietly taking a shuddering breath as if it will give her the strength she needs, Amanda finally turns to her friend who is still patiently waiting. Elena's face looks comforting as if telling her that whatever it is, everything will be alright. Forcing a weak smile, she finally speaks up.

"He sexually assaulted me."

Chapter Nine

The Present

The morning sunshine peeks through the window curtain reminds Tyler that a new day has arrived. Despite he has been lying on his massive bed in his villa for probably eight hours ago, his mind is restless. He still lives in disbelief that last night finally he met Amanda. It felt like a dream, but he knew it was real. The warmth tingling of her soft hand in his lingers in his mind, and he cannot wait to feel it again soon.

He shuts his eyes for a brief second, reminding himself that he has to be patient. Last night was only the beginning. The journey to prove himself to her is still a long way ahead.

Pushing himself out of the bed, he jumps into the shower and refreshes himself with the cold water on his head. Fortunately, last night he made the wise choice to stay sober and decided to immediately return to his room after the event concluded. Since Amanda had already left, he did not feel like sticking around for too long either. Plus, there was a dedicated team to run the work event. Aaron was also around to supervise. He did not feel his presence was needed.

He could not sleep well either way. Feeling like a teenager having a crush, he has to admit he wants to see Amanda soon. He hopes she is still in Bali, and he is confident she will. He can sense how his words about Isla might have piqued her curiosity. The fierce love of a mother is obviously shone from her expression.

Pleased with his appearance reflected in the mirror, he strides towards the door. The sound of birds chirping, and a thin layer of morning mist accompanies his stroll towards the hotel restaurant a kilometre away. A couple of local staff nod their head respectfully with greeting murmurs seeing his presence. He returns the greetings politely while inhaling the fresh crisp morning air, feeling rejuvenated despite his lack of sleep.

As he steps into the restaurant that hosts the international buffet breakfast, he is greeted by the lively clattering of plates and silverware. The place is bustling with Fraser & Co. staff, and it does not take long for him to spot Isla sitting with her colleagues. The moment their eyes lock, her face lights up and she wastes no time in pushing her chair back and making her way over to him with a big smile.

Tyler cannot deny the fatherly affection he has towards this young lady. Isla is probably about the same age as his own daughter – Kylie, who prefers to run her own fashion design company rather than join Fraser & Co business empire. Tyler supports his daughter's decision, as he can see clearly where Kylie's talent has been inherited from. Isla's presence in Fraser & Co is like a little consolation for him where he can spread his fatherly love towards a daughter.

"Good morning," Isla greets him. As if it is natural, without hesitation Tyler's arm opens wide for her. His palm lands gently on her forearm as he places a light peck on her temple.

"Good morning," he murmurs as he pushes her gently within his arm's length, so he can have a good look at her face that has been concealed with soft touch make-up. "You don't look tired at all. What time did you guys wrap up last night?"

"Around one in the morning," Isla replies with a sheepish smile. "We had a blast."

"Did Aaron stay up with you?" Tyler scans the crowd, trying to spot his son among the sea of employees in Fraser & Co's navy blue polo uniform.

"No, he turned in about midnight. Jason, Marley and Claire stayed with me. So, all went well," reports Isla.

Tyler nods in satisfaction as his eyes are still roaming around, still unsuccessful in finding his son. Isla is probably able to read his mind.

When her lips are parting, about to utter a word, suddenly her eyes capture something behind Tyler. He turns around, and instantly his heart leaps, a happy drumroll on his chest.

The sight in front of him is like a bolt of energy running through his whole body. He straightens up his spine, keeping his lips close while his eyes stare at the object before him, registering the presence of Amanda in his mind, ensuring that he is not dreaming. She looks stunning in a light blue V-neck maxi beach dress, letting the pale skin of her cleavage sneak out, partly covered by her long wavey brown hair. Returning his stare in equal intensity, she tilts her head slightly as her eyes bounce between him and Isla.

Tyler barely manages to contain a grin that's threatening to show on his lips. Amanda caught a glimpse of him and Isla earlier, and it is clear she's not thrilled about it. This would definitely give him more leverage to convince her to stay a little longer.

"Good morning, Dad." Aaron who has been standing beside Amanda, waving his hand at him. Tyler blinks as he just notices his son's presence, who seems to come over with Amanda. Elena slowly pops in as well from behind. "I bumped into Amanda and Elena in the lobby, so I invited them to join us for breakfast," Aaron explains.

Tyler knows he owes his son to this. "Sounds terrific to me. Good morning, ladies."

Amanda and Elena murmur a greeting back. Isla moves forward to land a peck on her mother, and soon afterwards, Tyler cannot think of any great moment he will enjoy for today than sitting on at the same table with Amanda, accompanied by the faint sound of waves crashing and pale blue sky on the beachside.

"Remember how you promised to show us around today?" Elena flashes a mischievous grin at him while she thrusts her fork into the sausage on her plate.

"Absolutely! " Tyler replies while sipping his juice. "Come join us for our adventure today."

"Yeah, Mum!" Isla exclaims eagerly. Her bright turquoise eyes shining with excitement. "We're going to hop on a bus to Ubud, a beautiful spot near the mountains. We can either go river rafting for some adventure or cycle leisurely around the village."

"Sounds exciting," Elena responds with her mouth full of her sausage.

"So, what will you choose, Isla?" Amanda asks. There is a crease between her brows as she looks at her daughter.

"Definitely river rafting, Mum," Isla replies without hesitation.

"Let's go cycling instead," Elena suggests. "I think we're getting a bit too old for adrenaline activities like river rafting. What do you reckon, Amanda?"

Amanda nods weakly.

At this, Tyler knows he has to play his cards well.

"Have you thought about who you want in your boat, Isla?" He asks, glancing at Amanda, who perks up at his question.

"I have no idea yet. Do you want to join me?"

"Absolutely! I think it'll be more fun with just two people in the boat, plus the captain. You'll feel the bumps and shakes more."

"Yeah, that sounds exciting! Let's go for a grade three route for more challenges and obstacles," laughs Isla.

Even though he is not making eye contact with Amanda, Tyler can sense she is bewildered. Her lips are about to open as her hand lifts to tap on Isla's shoulder. However, before she has a chance, Aaron pops in to announce that it is time for them to leave.

The journey to the Ubud takes about an hour. Tyler is inwardly groaning that he does not have a chance to pull Amanda to sit close to him on the bus. Instead, Isla and Jason from the HR team take the seats next to him as they begin to speak. He sneaks a glance to where Amanda is sitting. She just a couple of seats behind them, sits together with Elena. They seem to fall into a deep conversation as the scowl on her face tells it all. He suspects that she is probably unhappy with how close he is with Isla. Even though it means Amanda will keep hovering around them, an uneasiness also slips in causing her to be upset.

He wants to see her smile, something he rarely witnesses in real life, only in his dreams. He is partially to be blamed for this.

He had oppressed her.

Suddenly, something strikes his mind. Is he unwittingly repeating his past mistakes? Is he unknowingly taking advantage of her once more? He struggles to find an answer.

The rest of the trip is filled with a talk surrounding work and the company's performance. Tyler is quietly relieved that it helps to ease his guilt-ridden mind in a way. While the group is being divided between those going for rafting, and those for cycling, he spots Amanda standing alone in between, looking undecided. He follows her eye line of direction where Elena is. A small smile formed on his corner lips as he watches Elena seem enjoying herself with Chris. The couple is checking on the bikes that they are going to choose for their cycling trip.

"Aren't you going for cycling?"

His question jolts her. She turns her face at him with apprehension all over her face. Tyler is tempted to touch her forearm to soothe her. But he knows one impulsive act might ruin the rest of his chance.

"I...," she stutters, clearly still indecisive as her eyes bounce between Elena, and the group of young people whom Isla is gleefully chatting with.

Tyler is already on his bather and holding a life jacket that will soon cover his bare chest. Amanda's eyes land on his half-naked body before she meets his eyes again. He represses his smirk, realising that she is checking on his well-toned muscle, something he is proud of for his age. However, it is not a lustful desire shone from her eyes. She glances at Isla who is still standing in the background, animatedly talking with her colleagues.

"I've changed my mind." Her eyes are back firmly on him. "I want to join your rafting trip and be on your boat."

Tyler feels the excitement of the winning drumroll coursing through him. Everything is going according to his plan. He has to admire her determination, though she winces at a squealing roar from the first group of boats released to the river. Her eyes show a hint of wariness, and he can read that this type of activity is not her cup of tea.

"Are you sure?" His question is meant to tease her, unable to hide a mischievous grin on his lips. He lowers his head slightly, but probably she sees it as the flame in her eyes returns.

"Of course, I'm sure. As long as you're not the one steering the boat, I am good."

She brushes his shoulder in the process of approaching the captain of the boat and getting her life jacket. The captain, a friendly local man, points her to the changing room to put on a wetsuit. She nods in agreement but leans in to whisper something in his ear, whatever it is Tyler has no idea, but he has a gut feeling that she is telling the man not to let him get into the boat before she returns. Tyler has to turn around slightly to hide his victorious grin.

While he is waiting for her return, Isla taps his shoulder. A child-like excitement shone from her bright eyes.

"Is my mum coming for the rafting?" she asks in disbelief.

Tyler shrugs his shoulder. "That's what she told me."

"That's unbelievable!" laughs Isla. "What did you tell her?"

"Nothing. She was torn between rafting and cycling, then she suddenly decided on rafting."

"Well then, I'll hop on James' boat." Isla twirls around and swings herself to the riverbank, where James is having a safety brief with one of the boat captains. Amanda returns at the right time watching her daughter enthusiastically waving and squealing with joy as her boat starts to glide into the river.

It is a scene that makes Tyler cannot contain his laughter again.

"Isn't that Isla?" Amanda tilts her head, perplexed.

"Yes, it is," Tyler replies lightly as he grips her elbows gently to the riverbank where their boat captain is waiting and begins to conduct a safety brief. Isla seems to have chosen the worst time to make a quick exit. He is worried that Amanda will change her mind, now that her daughter is safely away from him. While his heart is pounding, anticipating that she will back off, he purposely puts his rapt attention on the briefing. Quietly he's taken aback that Amanda also listens to the brief attentively with no sign of interrupting or retreating. Within five minutes, their boat joins the herd of other fifty boats on the river.

"Have you done this before?" he asks while quietly taking a relieved breath the moment Amanda hops into the boat.

"Nope."

"Are you feeling scared?"

Without answering, she looks around for something to hold onto. There is not much space to have a chat anyway. As soon as their boat hits the river, they are tossed from all directions. What amazes him is not a single squeak escaped from her lips. A couple of times he sneaks a glance at her, finding her stiff expression. Her eyes sternly focus on what's ahead as her hands turn white, gripping tightly to the paddle boat. She acts promptly for every command given by the boat captain.

As their boat glides down the calm stream, Tyler can't help but search for her face. Amanda lets out a deep breath, a faint smile of relief playing on her lips as she gazes up at the sky. The morning sunshine creates a silver halo around her helmet, giving her a serene glow that Tyler wishes he could freeze in time.

"How are you there?" he asks.

Somehow Tyler is relieved as she replies, "I'm alright."

Their boat drifts past a floating market, where an elderly lady offers them drinks. Amanda politely declines with a shake of her head, her eyes lighting up as someone from another boat waves at them.

Tyler smiles to recognise that it is Isla and James on the boat not far from them. Amanda waves back with a wide smile drawn on her face. It is an admirable ability how she composes herself and hides her fear pretty well when she needs to.

"The steep waterfall is ahead, mum!" Isla yells from the distance. Her voice echoes through the quiet valley they are in. "Be prepared!"

Amanda gives her thumbs up to the sky with a straight spine. The moment Isla's boat sails away, Tyler cannot help but chuckle seeing how quickly the colour on Amanda's face drains as she deflates on her seat.

"You'll be fine," he winks reassuringly. "You've been brave."

And he truly means every word.

Amanda was the person who held his hand while they were under the gunpoint of a desperate man. As she held his hand, her fear palpable through the moisture on her palm, it was she who bravely tried to reason with Ben. Beneath her delicate petite appearance, her unwavering inner strength and will are beyond doubt.

The boat rocks back and forth as it navigates through the strong currents once more, eventually reaching the imposing waterfalls. The captain warns them to embrace themselves. Whether it is unintentional or not, the warning comes with a delay. Tyler barely has time to catch his breath before the boat shoots up into the air.

Tyler believes he has screamed from the top of his lungs, in harmony with Amanda's horrified squeals. It felt like their boat was soaring through the air for a brief three seconds, leaving him breathless.

Once their boat splashes back on the water, swaying through the quiet stream, his laughter roars. And what makes his lungs expand more is to see Amanda laugh with him.

She laughs hard.

Wholeheartedly.

With glistening relieved tears in her eyes.

Tyler cannot tear his gaze away from her.

This is the precious moment that he has been waiting for.

• • • •

DIPPING HER FINGERS in the water while letting their boat roam slowly along the quiet river stream towards the edge of the river banks, a calamity fills Amanda's mind. The heart-stopping experience she just had is mind-blowing, like a weight lifted off her heart. It feels like it has been ages since she felt this alive. The smile on her face is hard to contain. However, when she becomes aware of her existence to be sitting in the same boat with Tyler Fraser, who openly stares at her, she lowers her head, wishing to hide the warmth on her cheek. The captain's voice announcing the end of their rafting journey is her saviour, as it is a clue that they can leave the boat.

Transitioning from the wobbly boat to stable ground has been quite challenging. Amanda tries to catch her balance, but still she needs help. As if understanding her struggle, Tyler extends his strong arm for her to catch, so she can jump off the boat. Murmuring her thank you, she averts her eyes as her heart is trembling under his intense gaze.

This time, something feels different. She cannot quite put her finger on it. It was not like in the past as if he wanted to maul her. His dark-coloured eyes are gentle, and his face seems kinder, sending a tranquil breeze to her heart.

Taken aback by her own thoughts, Amanda immediately looks around to search for Isla. It is not hard to find her daughter. Isla's jovial voice rings out above the crowd, totally still buzzing from the thrilling experiences. A pride and content feeling easily slips into her heart, witnessing her own daughter. She quietly congratulates herself for keeping her daughter away from Tyler Fraser.

Her mind flies to Elena. She joins the rafting, totally unprepared. But Elena decides not to be on her side at this instance. She cannot blame her friend, who has shown an obvious reluctance for rafting. But after the truth about Tyler Fraser that she shared with Elena last night, Amanda wishes her friend would support her no matter what.

Earlier on the bus, they had a little argument. Amanda has to partially agree with Elena's opinion that she should trust Isla to have a better judgement. Dangerous man in the world is not Tyler Fraser alone. Isla is no longer a little girl. Her daughter has grown up and she, as her mother, cannot keep sheltering her. However, Amanda is determined if she can be there to protect her daughter, then she will not miss the chance, even though that means she has to join in the activity that scares the hell out of her.

The activity concludes with a buffet lunch in a restaurant located on the top of the hill, overlooking the same river that they just had the rafting. Amanda feels refreshed once she is back in her dry clothes, and the spice fragrance of the local food triggers the grumble in her tummy. She is not good with spicy food in general, but she does not want her tongue to miss the dancing of tasting the local food. After taking some rice and a famous Balinese satay, a gentle touch on her elbow makes her gasp. Not because she is in shock, but more because of the person who stands behind him.

His earthwood scent strikes her senses, and Amanda has to admit that the appearance of Tyler Fraser is always immaculate. Nothing has changed despite a decade has passed. Even his faint line of five o'clock shadow still adds to his allure. Amanda catches a couple of female tourists doing a double-take as they pass by him. It is Tyler's trait that makes her ponder whether Isla might fall for him as well regardless of the significant age gap.

The thought only makes her heart beat faster. She must find a way to speak with her daughter.

"Come, join us on the balcony." Tyler is pointing to a cozy spot in the restaurant where they can take in the beautiful views of the rice terrace and surrounding hills. Amanda does not have a chance to respond, but somehow, Tyler's palm on her small back is guiding her way. As she sits down, she realises she was kind of swept away by Tyler's actions, almost like she was under a spell.

Fortunately for Amanda, Tyler gets caught up in a conversation with some managers from Fraser & Co. Her smile becomes wide when Elena and Chris join her table.

"How was the rafting?" asks Elena as she places her plate on the table and starts digging in. "Mmm... I'm so hungry. This jasmine rice is delicious. I could just eat this all day."

"The rafting was amazing," Amanda replies, repressing her smile at how Elena tugs in as if she has not been eating for days. "How was your cycling?"

"Fantastic!" Elena exclaims with a mouthful of food. "The scenery is gorgeous. I can't believe I cycled all morning."

"That explains why you're starving," Chris jokes, prompting a light laugh from Amanda.

In a quick motion, Elena raises an eyebrow at her friend, noting with a smile, "You seem happy."

Surprised by the comment, Amanda tilts her head and mirrors Elena's expression with a puzzled frown. "What do you mean?

Elena gestures animatedly, not realizing she is waving her fork and spoon in the process. "Oh, nothing. But it looks like you had a blast rafting. I was worried you'd be scared."

Laughing, Amanda agrees, "I was worried too, but it turned out to be so much fun!"

Elena gives a little tilt of her head and raises her eyebrow. "Who's keeping you company on the boat?"

Amanda breathes a sigh of relief before answering, just as Chris leaves them to get some drinks. But then he is held up by a colleague for a chat.

"With Tyler, of course. Who else? I need to keep him away from Isla."

"Is Isla also on the boat?"

Amanda shakes her head. "No, she decided to join her friend instead." Speaking of her daughter, automatically her eyes scan around, trying to find Isla. But she cannot locate her daughter. She did not spot her in the changing room either.

"So, what is happening?" asks Elena, her curiosity still piqued.

"I'm not sure. I guess the thrill makes me feel..." Amanda shrugs. "Free." She chuckles while scooping the rice into her mouth. Reflecting back on the experience, she does not mind repeating it. It makes her realise that it has been a while since she has done that kind of adrenaline rush activity.

"Good on you," says Elena, showing off her white teeth as she munches on a prawn cracker." You should definitely do this more often!"

The words send a realisation on Amanda's head. Indeed, she has not been having vacation for a while. Before the divorce time, she was the main organiser for all family trips, carefully balancing time and money to make sure they could afford to go away at least once a year, even if it was just to a neighbouring state. The divorce had ruined her mood to organise a trip, though her parents have been encouraging her to go somewhere. This impromptu trip is unplanned, but it becomes her first trip after the divorce.

Probably it is true. Having a change of life scene is refreshing, breaking away from the boredom of routines. She should have done this sooner. Ironically, this trip happens because of Tyler Fraser's presence in her daughter's life which she wishes to prevent.

Thinking about Tyler and Isla again, her eyes wander around the room once more. Isla is still nowhere to be found, but she does spot Tyler chatting with some of the Fraser & Co employees. At least he is not anywhere close to Isla. But still, Amanda begins to worry and think about finishing her lunch soon and finding her daughter. However, before she cleans up her plate, Isla suddenly jumps in from behind, circling her arms around her shoulder. Amanda gasps in surprise but smiles in relief at the same time.

"Hello, Mum," Isla giggles, waving a rectangular card in front of Amanda. "Look what I've got."

Amanda squints her eyes as the card is held up close to her face. It does not take long for her to realise that it is a piece of photo. There are three people in the photo, all in the same uniforms, the life jacket and helmet from the earlier rafting adventure. The helmet makes it hard to see the face of each person. But upon closer examination, Amanda cannot help but burst into laughter seeing herself in the picture.

The picture must have been taken when they were in the infamous jaw-dropping steep waterfall. Her eyes were wide, her mouth was agape. She looks totally horrified in that three-second moment. Tyler looks in shock as well. On the other hand, the only person who looks smugly brave as he points his finger directly at the camera is no other than the boat captain who probably does this every day.

"You look absolutely petrified!" laughs Elena as she peeks into the picture.

"But it was so much fun, Mum! I'm glad you did it," exclaims Isla.

Amanda nods in agreement in the remainder of her laughter. "Can I keep the picture?" she asks.

"Of course! I got this for you." Isla places the picture on her mother's hand. But Amanda notices there is another piece of photo. Isla looks around, craning her neck. "There he is. This one is for Tyler." And before Amanda manages to utter a word, Isla skips away. Amanda watches as Isla's lithe figure approaches Tyler, who is sitting with a couple of senior management staff. Without any hesitation that she might be interrupting, Isla jumps on Tyler's side and waves him the picture. In an instant, a roar of laughter erupts before the picture is passed around between the group. Some of them might have asked who the woman in the boat with him is, and Isla seems the one who answers the question, as she turns her head to her mother, the group's eyes fall on Amanda.

Being conscious that she has been watched, Amanda flashes a timid smile. But what really bothers her is seeing how close Isla is getting to Tyler. She watches as her daughter interacts with her boss, keeping a respectful distance. Isla pulls up a chair next to Tyler and he gently touches her forearm, inviting her to join in the conversation. As they all chat, Isla seems at ease, and at one point, she rests her hands on Tyler's arms.

Like a rock sitting on her chest, Amanda quietly takes a shuddering breath. She wonders whether she is thinking it too much, but she is determined that Isla needs to know who Tyler really is.

· · · ·

THROUGH CHRIS, AMANDA is informed about the schedule for the rest of the afternoon. There is an hour break time for all Fraser & Co employees to have a rest before they resume for a conference. She feels this can be a good time for her to finally speak with Isla. As if her prayer is answered straight away, or probably Isla can read her mind, Amanda is surprised when Isla comes to her room. Elena is fortunately having another quality time with Chris, so they can have a peaceful time of mother and daughter together.

"I am checking out what your room looks like," says Isla gleefully as Amanda opens the door and lets her in. Her eyes eagerly roam around, taking in all the details of the room. "The room is pretty good," she remarks, flopping down on the sofa by the window with a view of the beach. "What a lovely view from here!"

If Amanda had a choice, she probably would not choose this beach-view room. The price is higher than what she is willing to pay. But for the sake of being in the same hotel property with Fraser & Co, only this room is the one available.

She turns on the kettle, planning to make her a cup of tea, something that hopefully makes her calm and relaxed. "Would you like some tea, Isla?" The question automatically comes out from her lips, but she knows her daughter is not a big fan of tea. For a twenty-one-year-old young lady, probably drinking tea only for old people.

"No, thanks, Mum." Isla opens the mini-bar instead. "I prefer a cold drink in this humid weather. How are you finding Bali so far, Mum?"

The question is a subtle hint to Amanda, suggesting that Isla is trying to figure out the reason she is in this place.

"Good. It's a beautiful place," Amanda quietly replies.

Isla takes a sip of her Coke and flops back onto the sofa with a grin. "Looks like you're enjoying your time here so far," she teases. "I still can't believe you went rafting!"

"Yeah." Amanda sheepishly nods. For a moment she lets herself focus on dipping the teabag into the cup that is filled with hot water, while her brain is working hard on how to formulate the right words. "How about you, Isla?"

"Of course, I am having a blast!" Isla replies enthusiastically.

"Are you getting along well with your colleagues? How is it going sharing the villa?"

"I'm sharing the villa with Tanya and Sarah, and we make a great team as the main committee for this event. It's so convenient being in the same villa for our discussions."

Once she's happy her English breakfast tea is rich enough, Amanda pulls out the tea bag. Carrying the cup and the saucer carefully, she joins her daughter on the sofa.

"You must be tired," she murmurs.

"Yeah. A bit. But I have a great fun."

Amanda turns to her daughter and studies her for a moment. Isla has always been a vibrant and engaged student, diving into a multitude of college activities. From music concerts to drama musicals, swimming carnival to chess club, Amanda knows her daughter is capable of leadership management. Her career prospects are going to be good no matter what.

"Do you think you'd enjoy working at Fraser & Co?" She swallows after blurting out the question.

As she expects, Isla straight away answers without hesitation. "Yeah, of course." Her daughter shoots her an odd look. "Why are you asking, Mum?"

"Because..." Amanda shuts her eyes for a brief, letting out a sigh. "Because I did not have a great experience working in Fraser & Co."

"Why not?" Isla furrows her brow. "You worked with Tyler, didn't you? Isn't he a great boss? His current personal assistant, Megan, has been working for him for twelve years. It's a shame she can't make it to the event today because of family obligations. But Tyler seems to manage just fine without her. He's very hands-on with his schedule." She suddenly beams as her big round eyes twinkle. "Isn't he handsome, mum? Was he as charming back then when you worked with him?"

Amanda has a feeling that their conversation is going to be difficult.

"Yeah, he's handsome," she replies softly. "When I worked with him, he was quite demanding. I often had to stay late to finish my work."

"Really?" Isla looks puzzled. "Megan never has an overtime. She always leaves the office at five o'clock on the dot, even when Tyler is still around. Megan even proclaims that she is lucky to be Tyler's personal assistant. He's the best boss ever."

Isla's statement makes Amanda ponder whether they are talking about the same Tyler Fraser. "Do you work closely with him? Like, do you have daily meetings with him?"

"No, I actually work more closely with Aaron on our current project. But my desk is on the same floor as Tyler's office, so I do chat with him and Megan quite often."

Hearing Tyler's son's name is mentioned, Amanda starts to think that she might have missed something. "Is Aaron married?"

"He's already engaged." Isla sips her drink with a twitch on her lips. "Come on, mum. Do you think I am interested in him? He's not my type."

Amanda shakes her head. "No." But married or unmarried, in a relationship or single, Aaron still shares the same blood with Tyler. An apple will not be far from the tree. "That is not what I meant, Isla."

Isla arches her eyebrow as she sips her drink again. A brief silence hangs in the air as Amanda tries to figure out the best way to express her true thoughts.

"It's been a while since we had a heart-to-heart like this, Mum," Isla's voice quietly pierces in. She repositioned herself to face her mother, resting her chin on her arms as she leaned on the sofa. Her round turquoise eyes remind Amanda how young and beautiful she is like a little girl. "I'm glad you're here for a holiday. You have not been on holiday for a long time, haven't you? You seem much more at ease."

Amanda takes a quiet, shuddering breath as she reflects on her past. Most of her life has been dedicated to the family, and this is the first time she is on holiday after the divorce. It is completely unplanned but gives her a breath of fresh air in a new country. It also highlights how she's been suffocating herself with the bitterness of the divorce.

"I am not actually here for a holiday," she quietly murmurs. Isla is unmoved from her position, listening to her attentively. "But you're right. I feel much more relaxed. I guess it's good to break from the routine sometimes."

"That's true, mum. You should do this more often," Isla smiles. "It's funny that you ended up choosing the same place as my work event. Whose idea was it to come here? Yours or Elena's?"

Amanda takes a deep breath, feeling the moment has come to share the real reason for her visit. "My idea. Because I need to speak to you."

Isla squishes her eyebrows together as she lifts her head. "You come here to speak to me?"

Amanda nods weakly. "You mentioned something about this event during our last phone call. That's why I knew I had to come see you."

"Why?"

Amanda shuts her eyes briefly before bracing herself to look at her daughter in the eyes. " I have some concerns about you working for Fraser & Co. As I have mentioned before, my experience working there wasn't the best, especially with Tyler Fraser."

Isla's lips part in response, but Amanda can tell that she is listening. Giving her daughter a pointed look, she continues, "Tyler is not as you think. During my time as his personal assistant, he was a demanding boss."

"Right." Isla nods her head in acknowledgement, still with squished eyebrows. "You mentioned that before."

"It's just not that." Amanda sips her tea and sighs, letting the suspense for a couple of minutes. Isla is waiting patiently, staying unmoved.

"He groped me."

The words escape Amanda's lips as she exhales deeply.

Isla's eyebrows shoot up. "By accident?"

"No." Amanda shakes her head vehemently. "On purpose. He..." She braces herself to look Isla in the eyes, feeling a twinge of shame. It happened a decade ago, but she cannot help the feeling that she is partly to be blamed for letting it happen. "He demanded that I sleep with him, or else I would lose my job. And I couldn't afford to lose my job then, because your father was just being retrenched."

Though finally she has said what she has been struggling to say to her daughter, much to Amanda's disappointment, there is no comfort to be found. Witnessing the shock on Isla's face, she could not shake the feeling that she had just shattered the image of her daughter's idol.

For a moment, Isla was rendered speechless as she seemed to be processing the news. Setting her teacup down on the console table, Amanda reached out and gently touched her daughter's arm.

"I know it's hard for you to believe. I can see how much you admire him."

As if jolted from a dream, Isla snaps, "Are you absolutely certain we are talking about the same person? I can't imagine Tyler behaving that way. He is always so polite and respectful, not just to me but to all of his staff! Many staff are singing praises about him."

"I am not sure, Isla. But that's how he was when I worked for him."

Amanda is contemplating whether it is necessary to share about Ben's gun hostage saga. However, what Ben did was for other reasons, and not because of Tyler's sexual harassment of her.

"I understand this story is hard to believe," she continues. "But I need to let you know." She darts Isla with a stern look that she usually does to demand obedience from her daughter. "You must leave Fraser & Co."

The reaction from her daughter is not exactly what Amanda has expected. While she expected some pushback, she did not think she would get such a decisive response right away.

Isla shakes her head vigorously, looking at her mother with wide eyes. She jumps off the sofa, shooting her mother a puzzled look "No! I'm not going to quit my job because of this!" Probably realising the stun on her mother's face as she speaks, she quickly clarifies, "It's not because I don't believe you, Mum. But, quitting my job is not the answer. I love this job! I love working at Fraser & Co. I don't have any trouble working with Aaron, Tyler, or any of my colleagues. I don't see any reason why I have to quit."

Amanda insists, "But this is for your own safety! For a peace of mind. Tyler has a bad past history. I don't want you to end up like me."

Isla raises her hand confidently. "No, I won't! I am pretty sure Tyler will not do such a thing."

Amanda quickly interrupts, hoping to offer a stronger reason. "You can find another job in another reputable company. You're smart and capable. I am confident you can build up a career in another workplace."

"It's not about that, Mum." Isla's chest rises and down as she heaves a heavy sigh.

The revelation hits Amanda hard, feeling like a sharp blow to her heart. Isla's decision to stay with Fraser & Co despite this dark truth makes Amanda consider the strong bond between Isla and Tyler. Has she underestimated their connection? Or is it possible that their relationship runs deeper than she realised?

Reluctantly, Amanda cannot help but voice her doubts, narrowing her eyes at Isla. "Then, why?"

Isla responds with an eye roll and a frustrated wave of her hand, "Well, Mum. It's not I don't believe you."

Amanda doubts those words are true from her daughter's heart. She can sense despite Isla disagreeing with her at this stage, her daughter may be trying to spare her feelings.

"I don't want to simply run away. I know this kind of thing could happen in any corporate office. What I can see now, no one is going to hurt me, especially Tyler."

Amanda shakes her head. The fact her daughter is questioning her story is vexing her. Though she tries to remind herself to be wise and calm, rather than being defensive, she cannot help but blurt out. "How about Aaron?"

Isla responds with an exasperated exhale. "What about him? What do you think, Mum? That he might be like his dad? Is that what you mean?"

"They are Fraser," mutters Amanda. Then she realises that she sounds biased and sarcastic. But she cannot help it with the past that she had. Is it wrong to make such a negative perception? But she decides to press on. "They are people with power, Isla." Her voice is chilling, even to her own ear. "They can do whatever they want as they like it. They...." The reason for Ben's attack swamps her mind. The culture in the company was rather toxic at that time, and Tyler was simply one of the people who abused the privilege he had. "They are *that* kind of people. You are still young and naïve, new to corporate politics. You don't know yet. But things can get ugly if you are not careful."

As Amanda ends her words, awkward silence descends. Isla remains motionless, staring at her with a bewildered expression. Amanda slowly stands up from her seat and reaches out to grab her daughter's forearm. But before their skin touches, Isla takes a step back, avoiding the contact. Then something in the way Isla looks at her, it's indescribable. It sends an odd rather uncomfortable feeling to her heart. Is her daughter repulsed by her?

"Looks like you've said what you needed to say," Isla's voice finally breaks the silence. "I guess that means you can go now."

The words hit Amanda's soul like a bolt of lightning. She becomes stiff as she wonders whether she has heard it correctly. Her mouth is agape as Isla gives her a cold stare.

"What..?" She is too speechless to even form a sentence. They just had a good time together this morning. But in an instant, her daughter wishes her to disappear from her sight. All because she brings up the past truth of Tyler Fraser. Her intention is to protect her daughter, but now Isla stands against her because of the man who hurt her. How ironic the circumstance becomes, her face falls as she stares vacantly at the floor, as if the ultimate disappointment swallowed her to the earth.

"I should head back to my room now," Isla continues. "The conference is about to begin." She tosses her empty can drink into the bin, and strides towards the door. Just as she reaches for the handle, she suddenly pauses and looks back at her mother.

Amanda lifts her head expectantly, thinking her daughter might apologise. It is not because she is demanding one, but she only hopes, though there is a slim chance, that Isla can understand and acknowledge her concern. However, Isla's next words only make her heart sink even deeper.

"I thought you had changed, Mum," Isla says quietly. "But you're still the same. Since the divorce, you've been bitter. You can't seem to be happy for Dad and Tom. And now it feels like you can't be happy for me either."

"Isla, no..." Amanda tries to stop her, but it's too late. Obviously, Isla does not want to hear her anymore as she dashes herself out, disappearing behind the door in the blink of an eye, leaving her alone, like a statue - completely devastated.

• • • •

GLANCING DOWN AT HIS wrist, Tyler cannot help but grimace as he realises how fast time is slipping away. His phone chat with his father lasted longer than he thought, and now he is running late for the conference. Hurriedly making his way to the elevator, he feels like he just hit the jackpot when he jumps into the empty lift and presses the button for the ground floor. As he waits for the doors to open, his mind drifts to thoughts of Amanda.

He regrets not having sufficient time to be with her during lunch. Sadly, this is still a business trip and he is not officially on vacation. Naturally, it will be challenging for him to spend time with the woman who has lingered in his dreams for a decade. He longs for them to sit down peacefully and have a meaningful conversation. He desires her to perceive him in a new perspective.

As if his prayer is answered instantly, the moment the lift door opens, the sight before him causes his heart to skip a beat. His eagle eyes quickly identify the slender figure of Amanda walking towards the lobby. All he can see is her back and her wavy hair bouncing with each step. Yet Tyler is absolutely certain that the woman in the stunning dark blue dress is the one he desires.

Strolling a mere meter behind her, Amanda appears blissfully unaware of his presence. For a fleeting moment, Tyler simply desires to etch her graceful silhouette into his memory, marvelling at the elegant sway of her steps. However, as his gaze falls upon the oversized cabin luggage trailing behind her, realisation dawns upon him - she is departing. She reaches the lobby and hands out her key room.

"You're leaving?"

She jumps at the sound of his voice and twirls around, and the moment she recognises him, her expression twists into a frown.

"Yes, I'm leaving, Mr. Fraser," she replies with tight lips and a lifted chin. "You must be laughing at me."

Tyler furrows his brow. "What do you mean?"

Amanda stays silent. The seriousness in her gaze eventually makes him realise the implication of her words.

"You told Isla."

Amanda remains silent, but Tyler is well aware of the truth. Taking a quiet breath, his mind races as he contemplates how the conversation unfolded. Isla is now privy to his dark past, the ugly version of himself that he regrets for his lifetime. He is prepared for the past to be revealed one day to the young lady whom he begins to care for like his own daughter. He accepts the possibility that Isla may despise him. However, he is determined to show his worth and will not give up

With Isla still in the conference and Amanda leaving her daughter behind, along with her sarcastic remarks towards him, Tyler has a good feeling that the conversation between mother and daughter went in his favour.

Tyler narrows his eyes. "What did Isla say?" he asks carefully.

Amanda scoffs, a sardonic smile playing on her lips. "She trusts you more than she trusts me. Isn't that what you want?"

Tyler's heart pounds with excitement as a triumphant drumroll echoes in his chest. His lips are parting as his eyes light up. But witnessing a deepening scowl on Amanda's face, uneasiness takes over as he has laughed over her disappointment.

Amanda shoots him a death stare. The burning flame in her grey eyes intensifies as she takes a menacing step closer. Despite her height only reaching his chin, he can feel her breath fanning on his neck.

"I warn you, Tyler Fraser," she hisses with a sharp tone. "If you lay a finger on Isla, I will make sure ..." She swallows hard. Her eyes blink as if she is trying to formulate the right words. Clearly, she never made a threat before. "I will kill you if I have to. You will regret it for the rest of your life."

Tyler attempts to suppress his grin, aware that she would be even more upset if he starts laughing. Her chest heaves up and down, her fist tightly clenched. The rage inside her is at its peak. He desires to comfort her by wrapping her in his arms and reassuring her that everything will be okay. However, he understands that this gesture will only escalate her anger.

"What could I possibly regret if I die in your hands?" He playfully mocks her, noting her slightly jumbled words born from frustration. Hoping to bring a smile to her face, he watches as she blinks in surprise, shooting him an irritated glance before stepping back.

It seems she thought he was making fun of her. He straightens his spine and tries to straighten his face as well.

"So, you're going to simply leave?" he asks. How he hopes she will stay. He knows he has to throw another strategic dice, though he hates that he has to use Isla as the tool.

"Isla doesn't want me here," she mutters, looking totally dejected.

"She probably doesn't mean it."

Amanda waves her hand dismissively. "Anyway, this is a work event. I don't want to disturb her work."

Tyler is racking his brain, trying to figure out how to make her feel better. What is his next move to get closer to her and break through her defences? As she starts twirling around and wheeling her luggage, he knows he must act fast. However, Tyler feels good fortune is on his side again, as Elena and Chris suddenly appear.

It is obvious that Elena has no idea that her friend is leaving. She is bewildered when she sees Amanda and her luggage.

"Are you leaving? Now? What's going on?"

Amanda simply shakes her head, indicating she is not ready to talk about it yet. Elena grabs her forearms, searching her face, and probably can see the glistening tears in her friend's eyes. Though Amanda is not facing him, Tyler can see how she rubs her eyes with the back of her hand.

"Alright. I'll go with you," says Elena.

"You don't have to." Amanda glances at Chris uneasily. "I can go by myself."

Elena insists, "No, we came here together so we'll leave together. Do you want to wait for me here or in the room?"

"I'll wait here," replies Amanda with a nod towards the chairs in the lobby.

Elena nods and dashes away determinedly. Chris seems confused and smiles sheepishly at Tyler as he is caught red-handed for missing the conference. Tyler only rolls his eyes and gestures for Chris to follow Elena. It also gives him an opportunity to speak with Amanda alone, as he has figured out his next plan.

"So, do you want me to stay away from Isla, right?"

Amanda turns at him again. The anger in her eyes remains as the pout on her face returns. She does not reply but only gives him a dirty look.

Tyler will not let himself be intimidated. His lips draw a solemn smile. "Like I told you before, Isla is one of our best employees. I have plenty of plans for her career. There is a big project coming up in Brisbane next month, and I'm pretty sure she will be excited to be part of it. If she accepts it, she will be assigned there for a couple of months."

As he speaks, Amanda's expression starts to soften. However, the frown remains as she anticipates his next words.

"That means she will be away from me if that gives you peace of mind."

A momentary silence falls. Tyler watches the woman before her intensely, as she does similar things, as if they are sizing each other up.

Unable to contain the suspense any longer, Amanda arches her eyebrow. "But?"

Tyler represses his smile. In Amanda's mind, Tyler Fraser whom she knew would not do good things for free. Although he feels a slight twinge of offence at her assumption, he understands where she is coming from, which he cannot blame her for. He takes this as an opportunity to be able to hover in her life.

"There is no 'but', Amanda."

"That's impossible."

"Well..." Tyler shuts his eyes as the itch to put his conditions getting stronger. His only wish is the opportunity to spend time with her. "I am going on a two weeks holiday soon. I haven't taken a break in a year. Maybe you'd like to join me?"

Amanda scoffs. "I knew it!" She gritted her teeth at him. "You're never going to change!"

The sarcastic words cut deep, but Tyler manages to muster a smile. "I'm guessing you need a break too, right? This doesn't really count as a vacation since you're leaving early."

Amanda shakes her head. "Don't be too optimistic that I will agree with this!"

Tyler already knew she wouldn't immediately say yes, but he was prepared for that.

"You don't need to answer this now. You can wait until Isla is already in Brisbane. But of course, if I don't hear anything from you, I can simply call her back to Melbourne."

As he has expected, Amanda glowers at him. She strides toward him, pointing her finger at his face. "You! You..." Her anger leaves her speechless, her chest heaving with emotion.

Tyler stays rooted in his place, watching her with a stoic expression as she slowly retreats. She starts pacing back and forth, visibly attempting to control her anger. Inwardly, he despises the fact that he must resort to such tactics. Threatening her, coercing her like what he did to her in the past. But, if he does not do this, will Amanda even give him a chance?

A brief silence descends once again, but Tyler is determined not to delay any further. From his peripheral view, he catches Elena and Chris emerging from the lift, signalling Amanda's imminent departure. He is eager for her to be aware that his offer is still on the table, requiring only a quick 'yes' from her

"Things have changed, Amanda." His voice breaks their silence. She lifts her eyes at him, looking slightly calmer from her short breathing exercise. "You are divorced. I am, too. Basically, we are just two single people, trying to have fun together. I do not see the problem with it."

"You are the problem, Mr Fraser," she mutters darkly.

The words cut deep into his heart like a sharp blade. She despises him, and it's completely justified. He longs to shake her awake, to show her the new him. But he cannot blame her - he has not proven himself genuine yet.

"I won't hurt you," he says weakly, almost like a whisper. But he knows she can hear him, as her lips parts, taken aback by his words. "Please, come with me." With that, he twirls around without looking back anymore, before Elena and Chris land at Amanda's side.

Chapter Ten

The Present

Tossing her car keys onto the kitchen table, Amanda eagerly anticipates a hot shower and a cozy rest in her bed. The five-hour plane ride from Denpasar, Bali to Melbourne has finally come to an end, bringing her immense relief. It was an overnight flight, leaving her exhausted from the cramped economy seat. Yet, she must be thankful that she had company for the long journey.

Elena stood by her the whole way, despite her friend's attempt to convince her to change accommodations for another night in Bali. Amanda hates to be the spoiler, but the trip is unplanned anyway. She prefers to be in Melbourne soon and returns to her routine, which has been her soothing ointment whenever she feels not herself. She encouraged her friend not to follow her, especially Elena seemed had a great time with Chris. But her friend was true to her words, keeping on her side until they touched down in Melbourne and parted ways with their parked cars at the airport.

Nothing much was uttered despite they had plenty of time to have a chat while waiting at the airport. Luck seemed to be on her side, as the next plane had two available seats for them. She went quiet most of the time, though finally, she opened up on her conversation with Isla.

"She's clearly enjoying her time at that company," Elena commented as she was referring to Isla. "Like I said, she's an adult now. She can take care of herself."

"I'm having a hard time understanding why she did not consider my concern. I know the thing with Tyler Fraser was a decade ago. But it doesn't mean the history will not be repeated." Amanda vented her frustration. "If this is about her career, she can have it in other companies. Fraser & Co is not the only and the ultimate great company she can work with. It seems to me she does not believe my story."

"What you said it's true." Obviously, Elena tried to console her. "The history may repeat itself, but not necessarily at Fraser & Co. She might have it if she moves to another company. I guess that's where her points are coming from."

"But she's choosing Tyler over me, choosing the man who has bullied me. And now she works with that hideous man quite closely. How can I not be concerned?"

"Well..." Elena hesitated, shaking her head from side to side. "I think she didn't mean to choose him over you. She just wasn't ready to leave the company yet. I've seen her interactions with Tyler, and they seem like regular friends."

Amanda could sense where Elena was siding at. Her friend bit her lips, giving her an innocent look, hoping her words would not cause any harm. But Amanda could see right through her.

"It's just a matter of time," Amanda muttered. "Tyler will reveal his true self one day." She shut her eyes in agony, feeling a surge of pain as memories of Tyler's actions resurfaced, causing her anger to rise. "I do not want that to happen to Isla."

Elena's gentle hands on her forearms pulled her back from the past, for which she was grateful.

"Don't worry too much, Amanda. I'm confident Isla is capable of looking after herself. I'm sure she's taken your advice into consideration. Plus, isn't she attending a self-defense class?"

Amanda chuckled rather dryly. Having a self-defence class is not a guarantee that Isla will be protected. Trauma can leave a lasting impact and create deep wounds, just like Amanda has experienced.

Amanda understands that Elena was only trying to help her see that things are not as bleak as she thought. Isla is a mature adult, who can manage on her own. This is probably what is called a mother's curse, constantly fretting over her children.

Taking a deep sigh, she strips off all her clothes and enters the shower box, letting the warm water flush her until her muddled mind finally clears. Stepping out of the bathroom, her whole muscles seem loosened, she cannot wait to lie down soon on her bed and catch her overdue sleep. However, when her head just touches the pillow, her mobile phone rings. Looking at the caller, she decides to answer it.

It is Hamish. If it were not for Tyler's accusation that she had cut Isla out of her life for the past two years, she would ignore this call. You shut her out. Tyler's words continue to plague her thoughts, stirring up her guilty conscience, and she is determined not to repeat her past mistakes.

"Hey, Mom!" Hamish's smiling face and tousled curls appear on her screen. "How's it going?" He squints, taking in the background on his mother's screen. "Are you at home?"

Amanda finds herself sitting up and leaning on her unique silver metallic curve bedhead before picking up the call. She is surprised that Hamish can recognise it, but then she notices that her pillowhead cover is the soft pink flower he gave her for Christmas.

"Yeah, I'm home."

"I thought you were in Bali! Isla texted me yesterday that you were at her work event, and even knew her big boss."

One thing that Amanda has to be grateful about her children, is that Isla and Hamish get along pretty well together. They seem to message each other more often than they do with her. She feels guilty for realising she has been too absorbed in her own world and neglecting her children.

"Yeah, I just got back." She cannot restrain her yawning. "I literally arrived this morning after an overnight flight."

"Right." The shock on Hamish's face still remains. "Why are you coming back so quickly?"

It appears that Isla has not disclosed the uncomfortable conversation with her mother, and Amanda is undecided on whether to share it with Hamish.

"I did not really plan the trip. I have to go back to work tomorrow," she lies.

"Right." Hamish nods, yet the crease on his forehead still stays. "So, how was your short trip?"

"Good." Like a revelation hit her, Amanda is conscious that she consistently responds curtly to her children's genuine questions about her wellbeing. She ponders on when it started - most likely post-divorce, during her lonely moments grappling with deep disappointment over her ex-husband. Trying to keep their conversation flowing, she quickly adds, "What's up with you?"

"I'm great. Busy with work as usual. But all good. I am calling because I thought you were in Bali. Isla mentioned you went for rafting." He laughs. "I can't imagine you did that. Did you have fun, mum?"

"Very much," Amanda chuckles. "I will show you my picture, to see how petrified I was."

Hamish's laughter bounces off the screen. Something seems to strike his mind because his face turns to be serious when his laughter subsides. "You claimed you did not plan the trip. But why were you there?"

Amanda wracks her brain to deflect the question. "Elena asked me to go with her. She wanted to have a getaway."

"Elena? Tom's ex-wife? Jamie's mum?" Hamish. clearly perturbed, gives her an incredulous look.

Amanda cannot help but suppress a laugh inside. Hamish's response mirrors Isla's when her daughter caught her and Elena in Bali. It is clear that her children did not anticipate the surprising bond between her and Elena.

"Yep, that's Elena," Amanda confirms.

Hamish's eyes widen and his lips begin to form a smile. "Wow, that's...amazing! I didn't expect..."

Her son's unfinished words make Amanda furrow her brow. "What's on your mind?"

"Well, Mum." Hamish shrugs with a sheepish smile. "I'm glad you're making a friend. And I'm glad that's Elena, who is someone from Tom's life. I mean...." Probably noticing his mother's stunned expression, he swallows hard. "In the past, you tended to steer clear of anyone connected to Dad and Tom. I'm glad that..." His adam apple moves nervously. "I'm glad that you start to open up."

Those words hit Amanda hard, reminding her of the pain she has been trying to push past since her divorce. Avoiding Sean and Tom has been her way of coping, but she realises now she has unintentionally been closing herself off from her children as well. Hamish has been truthfully blunt with his own thoughts, a trait that she recognises in her son very well.

As tears well up in her eyes, she quickly blinks them away, hoping Hamish does not notice. She puts on a weak smile, trying to hide the emotions that threaten to overflow.

"What's up with you?" She tries to steer the conversation in a different direction to ease any tension, noticing Hamish's nervousness as he looks around everywhere but at her.

"I'm...I'm well."

His stuttering answer makes Amanda realise that she has asked the same question a minute earlier.

"Are you..." She racks her brain for a new topic. "Any exciting things coming up?"

Her question strikes a chord. Hamish's lips break into an excited smile which instantly melts away their awkwardness.

"Yes! I'm going for hiking!" Hamish replies enthusiastically.

But Amanda does not share an equal enthusiasm. She never knows that her son has an interest in outdoor activities. Similarly to his father Hamish is not a sports player or outdoor enthusiast. He's pretty good in technical academics and prefers to play music and board games. As far as Amanda remembers, Hamish used to complain after returning from school camping.

Noticing the confusion on his mother's face, Hamish laughs. "My new hobby, Mum. I join this hiking club. It seems fun. I did a short hike once, and I liked it. So, this time I'm going for a longer hiking trip."

"Are you joining because of ...." Amanda arches her eyebrow as her lips curve into a mischievous grin. "..someone?"

The question hits its mark as Hamish is blushing. To see a young man like him smitten with someone is simply beautiful. It reminds Amanda of when she and Sean just started their relationship in college. They were young and naïve, but the feelings they had towards each other were pure. She has no idea when Sean began to develop different feelings toward her and his best mate. Probably she was too naïve.

"So, where are you going?" Amanda asks to spare her son any embarrassment.

"Mount Feathertop. I'm so excited about it."

Amanda has no idea where the place is, but hearing the word 'mountain', it seems the place must be wildly nature. Hamish can read the concern on her face.

"Don't worry, Mum. I'll be hiking with a group of experienced hikers."

"When are you leaving?"

"Next month."

Amanda glances at the small table calendar that she got from her favourite charity organisation. The paperboard calendar is simple, but pretty handy for her to keep track of the days and months.

"Your birthday is coming, too," she murmurs.

Hamish nods in agreement. "Yes, I'll be back in two weeks before my birthday. And speaking of my birthday..." He smiles sheepishly. "Dad is organising a birthday bash for me. I'd love for you to be there, Mum."

The request that she has been dreadful about since the divorce has resurfaced. Unsure of whether to feel grateful for her son's persistence, she is struck by uncomfortable emotions as she grapples with the fresh wounds of the divorce. Facing Sean and Tom with courage seems daunting, and she struggles with the idea of disappointing her own son. Elena's advice to accept reality for the children's sake echoes in her mind.

"I ..." she quietly takes a sigh while glancing at Hamish, who eagerly awaits her response. His pleading eyes and hesitant smile tug at her heartstrings, but she struggles to give a definitive answer. "I'll have a look at my calendar first. I'll let you know once you're back from your hike. In the meantime, stay safe and enjoy yourself."

Noticing his mother skirting around the topic, Hamish simply nods in understanding. Even though no words are exchanged, Amanda can see the disappointment written all over his face, and it pains her, even though she cannot do anything about it.

"I'm sorry but I'm tired, Hamish." She is mustering a fake yawn and feigning sluggish eyes. "I had an overnight flight last night, and you know, you could not get enough sleep on the plane."

"Sure, mum," Hamish responds lightly. "Have a good rest."

"Thanks, sweetie. Enjoy your hike."

"I will!"

Once the phone is hung up, Amanda slides down, lying flat on her bed. Exhaustion and devastation are absolutely not a good combination. She chooses to let herself drift off to sleep, wishing when she wakes up, she can have a better spirit.

Chapter Eleven

The Past

The panoramic view from the expansive office window was always Tyler's cherished retreat. It provided a sanctuary for his thoughts to flow freely, aiding in the resolution of pressing business matters and obstacles. This particular instance was no exception, as he had just overcome a perplexing puzzle. A sense of contentment washed over him, evident by the gentle smile that graced his lips. While anticipating a call from the old Mr Fraser soon, a glimpse of the past came into his mind.

A year ago, within these very walls and likely upon this very spot, he lay on the ground, half-conscious, battling the agony of a gunshot wound to his leg. Amanda clasped his hand tightly, yet her gaze drifted emptily towards the window. Unspoken words hung heavy in the air, conveying her shared fear of the uncertain future, a future fraught with imminent danger from a faceless figure lurking outside.

That day could be their last day on the earth.

Taking a deep breath, Tyler felt relieved that things turned out better than he expected. Both of them were safe from the danger. Though now he had no idea where Amanda was, he promised himself he would find her one day. He had not got a chance to say 'thank you' for keeping on his side, despite the assault he had done to her.

If he was a changed man, probably he was. Determination was his personal trait, something that his father and mother had been complimenting him on since little. The things with Amanda were something he had to sort out one day.

The gentle ring of his Cisco desk phone brought a big grin to his face. He made his way over to his desk, still favouring his leg from the gunshot injury, and answered the call.

137

"Tyler, your father is on line one." Megan's voice came through the other end.

"Thanks, Megan. I'll take it."

After a brief beep, the familiar deep voice of John Fraser filled the line. "Tyler!"

Whenever his father called him in that high-pitched tone, Tyler would usually prepare himself for a lecture. He figured he must have done something that his father didn't fully approve of. And he was right - he had indeed done something that would surprise his father.

"I heard you let go of one of our talented employees!"

No warm greetings, whatsoever, or probably just a light question on how he was, but Tyler was used to it. Despite he expressed his disappointment over his father's handling of the hostage situation, his father remained unchanged. Sometimes, the reprimanding tone in his father's voice made Tyler wonder if his father truly cared for him.

"Yes, Dad, I have," Tyler replied casually, plopping down in his chair and leaning back. "He's very talented indeed! He stole from the company for at least five hundred million dollars."

"Are you absolutely certain? Is there any proof backing up your claim?"

"Good question, Dad. I remember asking you the same thing when you found out that Ben, the guy who shot me and held me hostage last year, stole money from the company. Do you recall what you said back then, Dad?" His sarcasm was clear, with a hint of regret creeping in despite his victorious smile.

"Tyler! What nonsense are you talking about? I don't understand!"

Tyler could sense the increasing agitation in his father's voice.

"It's exactly a year ago, Dad. That I was shot, and taken as a hostage for a minimal amount of two hundred thousand dollars.

Today is my celebration of finally finding out the truth about the person who is actually responsible for Ben's actions."

There was no voice from the other end. Tyler believed his father was in a state of bewilderment. All he could hear was the sound of his father's heavy breathing for a few moments.

"I understand you may still feel some resentment towards me," John Fraser's voice quietly piped in.

"It's not that I'm resenting you, dad." Tyler closed his eyes, scolding himself internally. In reality, he did resent his father's decision. It was one of the reasons he was determined to get to the bottom of the problem. He just did not like using harsh words when all he wanted to do was uncover the truth. Maybe his hurt ran even deeper than he realised. "I just want to find out the real issues of why Ben did not get his retrenchment entitlement."

"Why are you so concerned about that guy? He's the one who shot you."

"Yes, but he did it out of frustration. He did not mean to harm me. The person to be blamed is the one who put him in his misery. He has been a loyal good employee but he was dismissed unfairly."

"My goodness, son!" groaned John Fraser. "Are you out of your mind? Why are you wasting your time on this?!"

Tyler could not help but raise his voice. "I am not wasting my time, Dad. I found the truth! The truth that will save our company's next potentially five hundred million dollars. Your so-called capable employee, one of your trusted people, had been smuggling the company's money!" He took a deep inhale to calm himself but quickly continued before his father cut him off. "The evidence is already on your desk. Don't you see the red folder on your desk?"

He hand-delivered those files to his father's office earlier today, anticipating his father's return from his business trip in Europe. The office was locked afterward as per his instructions to his father's assistant. But looking at the caller ID on his desk phone, Tyler guessed his father was not on his desk as they spoke.

"I did not have time for that," answered John Fraser flatly.

"You need to make time to look into this, Dad. Jake Stellar, the man you appointed as Head of Finance for our company, has been diverting company funds to his personal account for the last decade. Do you want to know how he pulled it off, Dad?"

There was no response from his father, but Tyler could tell he was still paying attention by the sound of his breathing.

"He made fake payslips using a fake employee's name, but the money ended up going into his own bank account. He had his team create a purchase order for inventory from a fake company and approved the payment. Then Benjamin Clark, who you called a low-level employee working in the printing stationery room, was the man who did his job diligently to check orders. One day, he stumbled upon a fake bill for stationery that he never received. The bill was dated a month ago and marked as received but with no receiver's name. He shared his discovery with one of the female staff in accounts payable, who then escalated it to her manager, then eventually went to Jake. So, what do you think Jake did to cover his ass, Dad?"

In a way, Tyler could tell he was pushing his father's buttons. There was no immediate response to his query, but John Fraser's deep inhale signalled his readiness to listen.

"Go on."

Even though his father could not see him, Tyler's lips curved into a victorious smirk. "He made some phony bills and had the staff send payments to Ben. It just so happened that Ben had an ABN for his plant-selling business at the local market, so the money ended up going there. Then he reported Ben to the HR team. You know the rest of the story, Dad."

A momentary silence descended. No hang-up line sound, only John Fraser's audible exhale broke the stillness as Tyler stared vacantly to the window, looking at the tip of the neighbour's tower building. Jake Stellar exemplified greed. Despite being John Fraser's old friend's son and holding a prominent position with a hefty salary, he misused his influence for personal gain. Tyler dug out the information from some managerial staff under Jake, who was probably aware of the misconduct but feared reprisal. The company did not provide assurance and appropriate means for whistleblowers, a glaring issue that must be addressed to safeguard the legacy of Fraser & Co.

"I did not see that coming, son." His father's voice pierced through. "I thought he was a reliable man."

Tyler took a deep breath. Taking a moment to ponder the situation, Tyler realised the issue was bigger than just Jake. "Even if it was not him, none of us would see it coming, Dad," he said softly. "There are many loopholes in our current system, something that we must work on. For the sake of your good relationship with your old friend, I only fired him and cut off all his access. I did not report him to the police. But I will clear Ben's name."

"Ben deserves to be in prison. He possessed an illegal weapon and he shot you," grunted John.

Though Tyler acknowledged his father's point, he knew he had to do something to help Ben. He chose to seal his lips as he did not wish to argue further.

"Good job, Tyler." John's tone grew stern as he switched topics. "I think there's another matter that you need to look at."

Tyler anticipated where the conversation was headed, but allowed his father to continue.

"Are you out of your mind for giving half of your assets to your soon to be your ex-wife?"

He chuckled, envisioning the bewilderment on his father's face. "Yes, I am giving half of my assets to Janine. Speaking of which, the paper will be ready by today. My soon-to-be ex-wife is coming to my office..." He looked at his Rolex. "...soon. Probably in ten minutes, along with my lawyer, to sign the paper."

"I want to make sure that you're thinking properly. Do you realise how much your asset is worth? That's the reason I never wanted to divorce your mother."

The mere mention of his mother in this situation made Tyler's heart ache. While his parents never officially divorced, they did not fulfil the roles of husband and wife. Instead, they were essentially two individuals leading separate lives and pursuing their own interests. Without a doubt, both of them were skilled at keeping themselves entertained, as evidenced by their twenty years of doing just that.

"Have you thought about yourself and your children's future?

Rolling his eyes, Tyler scoffed, "We will not be living in poverty, Dad. Janine has been a good wife and mother to the children." He truly meant every word, even though he no longer wanted to be with Janine. "She deserves it. She deserves her happiness and freedom, as do myself and the kids."

John Fraser huffed. "You can do like what your mother and I do."

"I know. But I don't want that. I want to be with someone that I love and care."

A sarcastic laughter erupted from the other end. "This divorce is making you look like a weak man. How could you believe in love?"

Smiling sadly though his father could not see it, Tyler was unable to hold his tongue. "I do believe in love, Dad. I know you don't. That was the reason you did not grant the two hundred thousand dollars that Ben requested when he held me as his hostage."

His father's scream made him cringe. "That is different! You..." But he suddenly fell silent.

With bated breath, Tyler opted for silence, anticipating his father's boiling anger.

"Mind your words, son." The warning in John Fraser's voice was unmistakable.

The mere threat only served to trigger Tyler's anger. "Or what, Dad?" he retorted. "Are you going to fire me?" He laughed between being bitter and sarcastic. "I just solved a case that could potentially make our business lose five hundred million dollars. You still need me if you want to find a way to prevent this from happening again in the future. Sam will have no idea how to do this. Who do you think you can trust, Dad? Another Jake Stellar?"

Tyler knew his words hit the right mark as his father went quiet. Another momentary silence fell and he did not wish to say the first word.

"I hope you won't bring the past regarding the hostage anymore, son." His father's voice finally piped in, sounded sombre, then soon afterwards, followed by the hang-up beep line.

Tyler reclined in his chair and let out a deep breath. He had no idea whether he had to be grateful that his father discontinued the line. His limbs instantly became loosened as the tension melted away. Staring at the high white ceiling in his office, their conversation was replayed in his head . He did not mean to hurt his father's feelings. Though John Fraser's existence was rare in his personal life and more dominant in his work life, he was still his father, after all. He had not forgotten how fortunate he was to have been raised enjoying the privilege of a Fraser.

Another chime from his desk phone startled him. Pressing the speaker button, he already knew who was on the other end.

"Janine is here, Tyler. As well as Mr. Smith, your lawyer." Megan's voice reverberated through the room.

Tyler held a smile at how his personal assistant addressing his soon-to-be ex-wife. No personal grudges between the ladies. In fact, they had been good friends, a true example of women empowering each other. His personal life was no secret to Megan, and she had always been a supportive listener. She even complimented him for handling the divorce agreement fairly.

"Bring her in. And you need to join in as well, Megan, as our witness," ordered Tyler.

"Of course."

Tyler stood up, buttoning up his blazer as his guests and personal assistant entered his office room. What caught his eyes in an instant was the glow on Janine's face. Her freedom would be sealed on this very day. She looked gracefully beautiful in her bright yellow summer flowery dress, matching well with her glowing skin complexion, emanating absolute joy from her within. Tyler was unsure why, but the positive feelings were infectious, as warmth feeling flooded his heart. However, he restrained from moving forward welcoming her, rooted tall on his spot, as his three persons took a seat in front of his desk. He welcomed the handshake from his lawyer.

"How are we?" He propped himself on the desk with his hands crossed, in a teacher-like stance ready to impart wisdom.

A chorus of responses followed, "Good, good."

"Hope your morning has been good so far, Tyler?" Janine smiled cheekily, her finely inked eyebrow arched. "I heard your father just called."

"It has been fantastic, Janine," Tyler replied calmly. "I just saved the company five hundred million dollars. What do you reckon he thinks about it? Not thrilled about the divorce, though." He winked. "You are his favourite daughter-in-law."

Janine's gleeful laughter resonated in the room. "I like your sense of humour. I'm going to miss it."

Tyler tilted his head. "Shall we get down to the business?"

Janine's eyes beamed. "Absolutely."

Hearing the word, Mr Smith sprang into action. Spreading the documents on Tyler's desk, he explained where the conditions had been specified clearly on the paper. The second condition, out of the three, stated Janine was strictly prohibited from any further access to Fraser's assets, including asking for any single cent from their children. If there was a breach, the consequences would be severe, including possible sanctions to her event management business that potentially destroyed her. Janine happily accepted the terms, seeing her freedom was just around the corner.

A few minutes passed with just the sound of paper rustling and pens scribbling in the room. Mr. Smith neatly gathered up all the papers, gave one to Janine, and prepared to head out for his next meeting. Megan trailed after him, sensing that her boss might want to have a chat, or maybe a goodbye kiss to his now officially ex-wife. With a mischievous grin, she vanished behind the door, leaving Tyler amused and shaking his head with a light chuckle.

"Shall we celebrate?" He grabbed the decanter and poured some red wine into the glass.

Janine stood up from her chair and walked over to him. "Of course. Don't you have a meeting soon?"

"I suppose Megan informed you. Yeah, the next meeting is in five minutes. We still have a bit of time."

What happened next was something Tyler never thought it would be. As he clinked glasses with Janine and locked eyes with her, a feeling of triumph washed over him. They were separated but they were content. Being unattached except for their roles as parents, brought a sense of liberation.

"So, when is your next trip to your lover?' he asked with a smirk, noticing a subtle blush on Janine's cheek.

"Next week," she replied after she safely swallowed her drink. "There's one major event coming up. Then after that, I have more time."

"Where is he?"

"France."

His favourite city. Formerly was their favourite city. It was the destination where they passed the majority of their honeymoon. Sounded ironic as it was, but Tyler understood well why Janine got hitched in that romantic city.

The chime on his desk phone was a reminder that it was almost time for his next appointment. Though Megan informed that his guests were happy to wait since they had arrived early, Janine understood that it was time for her to leave soon.

Standing before each other as fresh individuals, not bound by the confines of marriage, brought a chuckle to their lips. It was a peculiar sensation, but also undeniably liberating.

"So.." Janine broke the awkwardness as she took a deep breath. "I guess this is it?"

"I guess this is it." Tyler nodded in agreement. "Perhaps the next time I'll see you is on Christmas? You're more than welcome to join us for the festivities."

A glimpse of melancholy drew on Janine's face as her lips curved into a timid smile. "Thank you, Tyler." Then she twirled around and walked towards the door with her head held high. Just as she was about to reach for the door handle, her steps came to a halt. Tyler furrowed his brow as he watched her elegant figure from behind. Rather abruptly, Janine turned around to face him.

"Are you sure you're not forgetting something, Tyler?" she asked with one side of her eyebrow raised and a tentative smile on her lips.

The question caused Tyler's lips to part as the crease formed on his forehead. he was positive he had not overlooked anything. Unless there was something that Janine expected him to do. A farewell hug perhaps. But Janine was still rooted in her place, showing no sign that she wished to approach him. Tyler pondered if she anticipated him to make the first move instead.

AMELIORATION: A CHANGE OF HEART

Approaching his ex-wife with measured steps, analysing her every expression, he had a feeling that Janine was not seeking a hug. Pausing halfway, head tilted, he awaited her explanation.

Janine's round blue eyes gazed at him with apprehension. "You mentioned there were three conditions before the divorce."

It clicked in Tyler's mind, his mouth moving like a startled fish before a smile spread across his face. "You remember."

"I do. Only two conditions were agreed upon and the divorce papers were signed. You're not considering reversing the divorce, are you?"

Though Janine's corner lips twitched and her eyes twinkled with mischief, Tyler noticed how she clenched her side dress tightly to conceal her nervousness.

"No, Janine. I have no intention of referring to you as my wife again," Tyler quipped.

Janine let out a sigh of relief, a wide smile spreading across her face. "Good!"

"But it doesn't mean I cannot impose the third condition," Tyler continued with a severe look.

A sudden cloudiness shadowed Janine's face as he spoke. Tyler used to delight in the meekness of his opponent, and Janine used to be counted as one. But a guilt-ridden feeling slipped in instead as Janine's chest heaved up and down.

Tyler's smug smile only added to her turmoil as he placed a hand on her forearm and opened the door for her. Her pout deepened and she shot him a fierce look as he guided her out the door.

"Just be happy, Janine."

Janine blinked in surprise. Her bright red sultry lips parted as she struggled to respond.

"That's the third condition. Just be happy," he repeated, then he let the door close as Janine's puzzled face slowly faded behind the door leaf.

Chapter Twelve

The Present and The Past Merges.

"Have you met anyone new lately?"

Upon hearing the question, Amanda resisted the urge to roll her eyes. Though she manages not to do it, Shannon – her psychologist, can guess what her patient has in mind and repress her smile.

"Well, yes and no," Amanda replies.

As she lays on the loveseat, Amanda is looking out the window and Tyler Fraser's face is flashing through her mind. She has known Shannon for a decade, since the hostage incident. They did not have regular sessions, but Amanda started seeing Shannon again after her divorce. She had not yet shared with Shannon about the trauma and stress she experienced with Tyler before the hostage situation.

Shannon has provided numerous tools and guidance for her to move on from her divorce. However, most of the advice simply goes in one ear and out the other, with no action taken. But when Amanda mentioned her unexpected friendship with Elena, she could see the satisfaction on Shannon's face, indicating that her advice had finally sunk in.

Shannon's eyebrow raised slightly upon hearing Amanda's response, and a warm, motherly smile adorned her lips as her eyes sparkled with anticipation, waiting for Amanda to elaborate further.

"I ran into my former employer from a decade ago, who now happens to be my daughter's superior. He had once propositioned me to sleep with him in exchange for job security."

Amanda sighs deeply at the memory. Shannon appears baffled momentarily but quickly masks her emotions with a facade of indifference. With two decades of experience as a psychologist, she is clearly adept at listening to intense narratives without displaying any visible reaction.

"I'm concerned that he may treat my daughter the same way. I urged her to resign from the company, but she refused to heed my advice. She enjoys working with him and cannot fathom that he could be capable of such misconduct."

Quietude settles in as Shannon jots down notes in her book, waiting for Amanda's next words. However, Amanda is lost in her own thoughts, her gaze distant. Shannon clears her throat to regain her attention.

"Why does your daughter believe that? Is she romantically interested in him?"

"Perhaps," Amanda responds, her thoughts tinged with fear. "They don't appear to be romantically involved, but she clearly looks up to him. She sees him as a charismatic leader, adored by his subordinates. It's a stark contrast to my perception of him."

"He may have changed over time."

Amanda finally shifts her gaze from the window. Shannon has been sitting beside her, giving her full attention throughout the session. Shannon's remark on the possibility that Tyler is turning into a new leaf sounds ridiculous to her ear.

"Can someone like him really change?" she scoffs.

Tyler's request to go travelling with him in exchange for Isla's project in Brisbane makes Amanda's blood boil with anger. He has kept his promise on one side, as Isla has been moving to Brisbane for about a month. Though her daughter does not talk much with her anymore since their argument in Bali, at least she writes a message informing her trip in their group chat message with Hamish. Tyler's subtle threat lingers in her mind, urging her to make a decision. As much as Amanda dreads Isla being away from Melbourne, having her back while still working at Fraser & Co seems even riskier. She must act before Tyler runs out of patience.

"People change, Amanda," Shannon states with her wise smile. "You've changed, too."

Amanda huffs. "Are you saying that he's possibly not a bastard anymore?"

Shannon shrugs. "I don't know. But it's common for people to act impulsively when they're young. But as they get older, they realise their mistake and feel ashamed about it. Think about how you viewed yourself a decade ago. How does it compare to now?"

Amanda cannot help the twitch on her lips. Clearly, her psychologist is trying to make her open up about herself more.

"I can't remember," she sighs, leaning back and gazing out the window at the clear blue sky. "But I doubt I was content back then either."

A decade ago, aside from the episode involving Tyler and Ben's hostage, she was struggling to rejuvenate her love life with her husband. The near-death experience was the one that kept reminding her to be grateful, despite every day her heart was slowly bleeding with indifference from Sean.

But she understands Shannon is right. She changes.

"I know I am still holding onto my resentment from the divorce," she says quietly.

"That's completely understandable, Amanda," Shannon consoles her. "Besides seeing Elena, have you attempted to join a support group for divorced individuals?"

Amanda shakes her head. Shannon should know better that she is not keen on meeting new people.

"How about seeing your ex-husband and his new partner?"

"That's out of the question," mutters Amanda. "If I were to see them, I might...." She pauses, her heart sinking at the thought of seeing Sean and Tom together.

"What will you do?" Shannon prompts her.

Her shoulders slump. "I'll likely end up yelling at them," she mutters softly. But another thought crosses her mind - does she really have to do that? Should she let out all her anger on Sean and Tom?

The idea of Isla and Hamish finding out fills her with embarrassment - they would see her as immature.

"You didn't do that when your husband announced the divorce?"

Amanda weakly shakes her head.

The particular day when Sean announced the divorce replays before her eyes. She just returned from work, and only two of them were in the house, because Hamish and Isla just moved to their own place, renting an apartment with friends in the city. It was another new chapter in their life, kids had grown up and left the house. She planned to prepare a special candle night dinner. To her surprise, Sean had been waiting for her, sitting in the dining room, with head deeply bowed down. When he lifted his head, tears streaming on his cheek. He kept apologising, confessing about his true sexual orientation, and then asking for a divorce. That day her world turned upside down. What amazed her was that she still stood tall before him, though she was totally shocked and numb. She was left wordless, and Sean took the opportunity to leave her behind.

Now she understands that her state of shock at that time lasted for quite a while. Even when the divorce paper was finally signed three months later, she could not feel anything. Her mind was in conflict, to gracefully accept the changes, to accept for what Sean was, especially even when their children supported him, but her heart said otherwise. The moment she witnessed Sean stepping out from their lawyer room, welcomed warmly by Tom's joyful smile, her anger bubbled to the surface. She felt like she had been ridiculed, and treated unfairly. But she did not have a chance, or given the opportunity to express her disappointment.

"Why?"

"I did not have a chance."

"Are you afraid of something?"

"Probably." Amanda takes a deep breath as her chest becomes tight. "I guess it's too late now. I just want to keep the peace with Sean for the sake of the children. I don't want them to see us fighting or screaming at each other." Looking back, that was what she had been doing. Swallowing her own disappointments countless times due to Sean's indifference throughout her marriage, she kept it to herself for the sake of the children.

"Do you think that action will bring you peace?"

Amanda weakly shakes her head again. "I'm not sure. Possibly."

Probably yes. Hamish and Isla are mature adults. Yet, they might cast a critical glance her way if she directs her frustration towards their father. Will she be able to live with that for the rest of her life?

"You have to let it go, Amanda." Shannon's tone is resolute.

Amanda shifts her head abruptly and locks eyes with her therapist. "Are you suggesting I should pay a visit to Sean and express my anger at him?"

"No. I want you to talk with him, expressing your anger and disappointment at him, not necessarily by screaming at him. Both of you are mature adults. You can speak calmly while expressing your thoughts. If you openly tell him that this will help you to move on from the divorce, I have a feeling Sean will do his best to help you."

Amanda quietly takes a sigh, admitting that Shannon is probably right. Knowing Sean's character, and recalling the past how he and Tom have been trying to include her in family gatherings with Hamish and Isla, Sean probably will not mind going through the process.

"Alright. I may try that," she says quietly, unsure of when she will muster up the courage to broach the subject with Sean.

As if Shannon can read her mind, she continues her advice. "The key is to let it go, Amanda. Consider this carefully. Clinging to resentments will not alter the past. Your marriage will not transform into the fairytale you desire. It only hinders your progress, preventing you from embracing new opportunities for potential happiness. Let go and set yourself free."

Amanda weakly nods as she looks out the window towards the bustling street below. The counselling room is on the second floor, giving her a perfect view of the passersby and the vibrant cafes and shops across the street. The session has been eye-opening, but her growling stomach reminds her that lunch is needed soon. Seeing one of her favourite cafes from the window only intensifies her hunger.

She is about to look at the time on her mobile phone, fully aware that the session is approaching to end anyway. But what pops up on her mobile screen makes her breath stall.

It is a message from Sean. He needs to talk to her.

. . . .

CRUISING THROUGH THE lush fields of Bright, adorned with a stunning carpet of golden wildflowers, has been Tyler's ultimate desire for the past month. This vacation is the one he has eagerly anticipated - a respite from his hectic work schedule, a chance to unwind his mind from work-related stresses. And perhaps, if he is lucky, a break from the endless conversations with his father.

It is not that he does not like to speak with the old Mr Fraser, but he cannot deny his lingering resentment from the hostage saga a decade ago. After the major transformation that he has successfully done to Fraser & Co, which improves the company culture and productivity, his father seems never to want to leave him alone. The call is every day and all is only about work.

Tyler knows his father still cannot change, and he does not blame him for that. He embraces him as he is. Despite their discussions typically revolving around work-related matters, Tyler understands that his father's intentions are simply to stay informed, not to exert control over him. But for this holiday, he has strictly instructed Megan that he does not want to be disturbed unless for something urgent or emergency. Nevertheless, Megan will not be able to stop the call from the old Mr Fraser.

This holiday is going to be short. If he can go for a full week without thinking about work, it will be considered a huge success. Even though he will have a break from work for seven days, there is one thing constantly on his mind.

Amanda.

She has not contacted him. He is debating whether he should be the one to make the first move, reminding her about their so-called little agreement. Slightly grimacing, he knows there was no agreement, but rather a veiled threat he had made. Regardless Amanda is coming with him or not, he will still send Isla for the digital development project in Brisbane. Isla has been eyeing to be part of that particular project. He has no intention of pulling her out, even if Amanda decides not to join him.

Taking a deep sigh, he has to think of other ways to get into Amanda. With no coercion or threat this time. He should genuinely approach her, asking her out for a drink or probably dinner. Laughing at himself, he finds the notion is rather absurd. Pursuing a woman is uncharted territory for him. Because he does not need to. All those women always seek him out. Things with Amanda will be harder and trickier, especially with their dark past.

Sighting the petite red brick gate and pulling into the driveway of his quaint cottage, he eagerly anticipates collapsing on the couch after his nearly four-hour drive. This brief getaway may just give him the clarity he needs to devise a plan on how to win over Amanda. Grabbing his lone suitcase, he steps inside the house. Instantly enveloped in the cozy atmosphere, he finally feels at ease.

Two years post-divorce, he purchased this quaint three-bedroom holiday cottage with the savings he had accumulated. Taking charge of the interior design himself, he collaborated with a professional designer whom he briefly dated during the project. Recognising the temporary nature of their relationship, he respected her work and appreciated her ability to grasp his vision for the house.

The building's structure is what captured his heart— from the cathedral ceiling and wall-to-wall windows with a breathtaking view of the hills, to the painted white brick chimney and gas fireplace. The open-plan kitchen with an island bench, art walls, knick-knacks, cream-coloured furniture, and cozy couches all contribute to the charming provincial theme that Tyler adores. This little cottage is exactly what he and his children need for a peaceful Christmas getaway, away from the hustle and bustle of city life. It is a quality moment that Tyler will always cherish.

Flopping onto the couch, the throw and cushions emit a pleasant cedarwood scent, thanks to the meticulous cleaning lady he hired. He must remember to personally show his gratitude once he is in town.

Just as he considers closing his eyes for a brief rest, his phone's ringtone interrupts with a groan-inducing sound. Reluctantly, he answers the call from the last person he wants to talk to.

"I'm on vacation, Dad!" Tyler immediately cuts off the caller before they can even say hello. "If you want to discuss work, I'll be back next week."

"Uh..oh.." John Fraser stutters. "Of course, son. It can wait till next week."

Hearing his father's hesitant voice, Tyler cannot help but frown. A momentary silence falls and he waits in case his father will hang up. But John Fraser's deep vibrato voice pipes in.

"So, where are you now? Have you arrived at your cottage yet?"

Tyler is taken aback by his father's sudden interest in his vacation. All this while every call from old Mr Fraser was only about work. Even at their Christmas gatherings, his father still managed to sprinkle in work-related talk, albeit in a more casual manner.

"Yes." Tyler sighs, reclining on the couch and shielding his eyes with his hand. "It's a long journey, but it was good driving. This town is truly stunning."

"Are you....with someone?"

Tyler can sense the hesitancy mixed with curiosity with the question. Something is tickling him and makes him ponder on his father's interest in his personal life. He never bothers himself with what his father does. Likewise, his father does the same. Probably it is their way to respect each other's space.

"No. I'm alone. Why?"

"Ah....nothing."

Another awkward silence follows, leaving Tyler to wonder if his father needs his help.

"Are you alright, Dad?"

"Yeah, I'm good."

Tyler attempts to remember his father's current schedule, recalling that no trips abroad are planned. This suggests his father may be in Melbourne.

"So, why are you calling me? Do you need anything from me?" Tyler hates that the questions spill out from his lips. Any parent will not like to be asked that. It is a sign that the children feel bothered with the parent's call as if it's just a nuisance. Aaron and Kylie sometimes do it to him too, and he despises it, while his true reason is only to find out how they are doing. It is probably a lifetime curse as a parent. And now he feels like a teenager, for speaking like that to his father.

However, to his recollection, his father's daily communication with him is not motivated by a genuine interest in his well-being. The discussions revolve around work-related updates, with little regard for his personal life. Determined to set boundaries, he firmly asserts that he does not want to discuss work for the next seven days.

"Well..."

Tyler grits his teeth despite his father cannot see him anyway. "You want to talk about work," he supplies his father's next words.

"Well, yeah. Because that's the only way I know you're alright."

Tyler is taken aback, and almost cannot believe his own hearing. "What do you mean?"

"I call you daily for work updates so I can have peace of mind knowing that you're safe."

If Tyler is not left gobsmacked, it is safe to say it is an understatement. Utterly speechless, he struggles to decipher his father's words. Another awkward silence descends as his lips part and the crease on his brow deepens.

The heavy sigh from John Fraser resonates through the phone. "Well, son. You were under hostage of a gunman before. You had no idea how it affected me when the first time I heard about the news. I know that I did not handle it well. But I was totally relieved that you were safe. I am not...." Another sigh, and then John Fraser's voice begins to tremble. "I am not good at words. I am sorry if it's annoying you that every time I call, it's always about work. But I do want to talk to you."

Though he cannot see his father's face, and now it makes him realise that they almost never do video calls, Tyler begins to comprehend his father's true intention. The conflicts stemming from Ben's hostage situation have brought him to tears at times, but he chooses to forgive and embrace his father's aloof demeanour. It dawns on him that John Fraser may not appear as a warm, affectionate father, but deep down, he still harbours paternal love and concern for his children.

"Thanks, Dad." Tyler finally manages to speak. Pinching the bridge of his nose, his father's words almost bring tears to his eyes. Swallowing hard, he prays that his voice will not tremble with emotion the next time he speaks. "Are you in Melbourne now?"

"Yes, I am. In my office."

"No meeting?"

"No."

Yet another uncomfortable silence descends. Tyler yearns for more natural conversations that do not revolve around work. The deeply ingrained habit seems impossible to shake. Perhaps he is also to blame for not showing any interest in his father's personal life. He believes in respecting each other's privacy. Honestly, he does not want to know with which woman or friend his father is mingling with.

"Any exciting plan this week?" Tyler must compliment himself for prompting the question that he usually posts to his children. It is a simple trick to dig out his children's personal life.

"Well, nothing much. There's a business conference on Friday." His father's reply sounds flat, but then he trails, "I wonder..."

Tyler's curiosity is piqued. "Yes?"

"Can I pay you a visit tomorrow?"

Like another bomb just being dropped in his world, Tyler's jaw drops, as if any flying insect could fly right through it. He quietly feels grateful his father cannot see his shock, but the awkward silence speaks volumes of his reaction.

"If you don't mind, of course, son." John Fraser's voice interjects hastily. "I know you're on vacation, but I promise I won't talk about work. I never have a look at the place since you bought it."

Tyler's heart is beating fast, feeling like he is under the spotlight on stage. This conversation turns out into something that is totally unexpected. He never imagined his father would seek out this bonding opportunity, let alone take the initiative. Although his plans for the holiday may need to be adjusted, Tyler cannot help but feel hopeful that this change will only lead to something better. Quietly taking a breath, he clears his throat.

"Of course, Dad. Feel free to come," he says quietly. He can picture the happy smile on his father's face, mirroring his own.

"Thanks, son." John Fraser's voice turns brighter. "I will let you know what time I will be there. But whatever your plan tomorrow, please go ahead, don't wait for me."

"There is a key deposit box, Dad. I can leave a spare key, and let you know the code."

"Sounds terrific to me, " a satisfied sigh exhaled through the phone. "I'll see you tomorrow."

"See you tomorrow, Dad," Tyler replies. Once the phone is hung up, his lips curve with a smile. For a moment, his eyes are still lingering on the mobile phone screen, in disbelief at what just happened, a warm glow in his heart. His holiday has just begun, and from the look of it, it is shaping up to be amazing.

Deciding to prolong his relaxation, he set his phone on the coffee table before easing onto the couch. However, his peace is short-lived. Just as he begins to drift off, the loud ringtone startles him awake. He grabs it with a loud groan but is perplexed to see the caller. Slightly hesitant, he slides the green button.

"How are you going, Tyler matey?"

Chuckling while rubbing his sleepy eyes, Tyler replies, "What's up, mate?"

The caller is Matthew, his only friend as well as his neighbour in this town. Matthew came up to him to introduce himself when he bought the property. Unlike him who is only a tourist to the town, Matthew has been a true local of Bright. Every time Tyler pays a visit, Matthew is the first one who welcomes him. Matthew helps to keep watch of the property when it is empty, or being rented out to other holiday visitors. He also has been the one that helps to organise the cleaner and any handyman to help maintain the property.

"I know from Grace that you will be arriving today," says Matthew. Grace is the local whom Matthew engages to clean the property before Tyler's arrival. "I am sorry to disturb your holiday. Have you seen the emergency SMS?"

Tyler furrows his brow and puts Matthew on speakerphone, quickly swiping his phone screen to check for messages. He notices a new message from the local SES, stating that volunteers are needed to search for a missing person.

"Oh no..." Tyler groans. After eight years of holidaying in Bright annually, he can only recall one instance of a missing person report. The Alpine area, just an hour away from Bright, is known for attracting avid hikers and campers. It was Matthew who convinced him to volunteer his phone number for emergencies. Tyler does not view himself as a seasoned hiker, but he always goes on hikes during his visits, all thanks to his friendship with Matthew.

"Yeah, I know. Bad timing," sighs Matthew. "But I'll be heading there soon. Any chance you could join me? Having an extra volunteer could greatly speed up the search for the missing person."

"Do you have any idea who we're looking for?"

"A pair of young lovebirds. I think they're just off on their own little adventure. They tend to wander off from the group."

Tyler cannot help a small laugh hearing Matthew's joke.

"I heard the girl is a quite experienced hiker," Matthew continues. "The boy is first timer. Hiking at Mount Feathertop sounds a bit too aggressive for a first-timer, I would say. The rest of the group has returned since this morning without them. I suspect one of them is injured. So, they have been missing for almost eight hours."

Tyler has a peep at the window while listening. "The weather looks pretty good." The sun shines quite fiercely for Spring weather in his opinion. "What's the forecast for the next few days?"

"Rain is developing tomorrow afternoon," replies Matthew with a sombre tone.

Tyler takes a sigh understanding what it means. Once the weather changes, it will be much harder to locate the missing people. Time is of the essence. On the positive side, daylight savings time is in effect, giving them more brighter sky before dark. Glancing at the time on his mobile, they still have approximately six hours before the moon settles in.

"Alright. Can I join your car?"

"Rightio. I'll be there in a sec."

"Cheers, mate."

Letting out another deep breath after ending the call, Tyler acknowledges that this holiday is bound to be unforgettable.

Chapter Thirteen

A manda is in disbelief that she has been driving for nearly five hours. The sight of cherry blossoms cast in the sunset, along with a couple of shops gives her hope that she is almost reaching the centre of the town.

Perhaps this is what people refer to as a mother's curse. When her mind is plagued with worry for her children, she can momentarily forget the pain she endures for their sake.

Upon receiving a text message from Sean, she jumped out of her session with Shannon. Sean called her not about her or their relationship, but rather to deliver devastating news that their son, Hamish was reported missing during a hiking trip. This is the most terrible news Amanda could imagine, even more heart-wrenching than her divorce.

She immediately drove to the place where Hamish was last seen. She keeps whispering to herself as if her voice will be carried by the wind to Hamish's ear, 'Hamish, please be okay." That has been her litany throughout her journey. She even vows to attend his birthday despite that she has to endure the pinching pain of seeing her ex-husband and his new partner.

Sean has offered her to go in one car together with Tom, and she is glad that she did not take the offer. It is better for her to be on her own. Being in one vehicle with them requires an extra effort that she did not need at this critical time. She took a rest in a town after the first two and half hours of driving. Quietly she hoped she would not bump into Sean and Tom in the same town. While she acknowledges the inevitable encounter, driving provides her with the opportunity to mentally brace herself.

Slowing her car down as she pulls into a nearby parking lot, she swiftly scans her messages for any new updates on Hamish from

Sean. A call from Sean fills her with anticipation, an immediate response to her inquiries.

"Where are you now?" Sean's voice is full of anxiety. He beats her to the question by just a split second.

"According to my navigation, I'm in Bright," she replies. "And you?"

Sean exhales deeply. "Awesome. I'm also in Bright. At the hospital. They already found Hamish."

Amanda feels a wave of relief as the news washes over her soul like refreshing water. She exhales deeply, laughing and tears streaming down her cheeks. Even though Sean cannot see her, he can surely hear her emotions.

"Is he.." Her voice is cracked with emotion, mixed with her sobs. "Is he alright?"

"He's fine. It's just a minor injury on his leg from not wearing proper shoes. Silly mistake. He's a bit dehydrated, but overall he's in good fit."

Amanda shuts her eyes as another roll of tears falls. "Thank God."

"Amanda, everything is fine," Sean's voice is soothing. Amanda cannot help but feel a pang of longing for this tender side of her ex-husband's voice. Reflecting on the past, she struggles to remember the last time Sean spoke to her with such affection. How could she have missed the signs of his changing behaviour? Was she truly that blind?

Shaking her thoughts from being sentimental about the past, she quickly opens the navigation apps on her mobile phone and starts typing. "What is the name of the hospital? Alpine Health? Is that the one?"

"Yes, that's the one."

"I'll be there shortly."

"Sure, see you soon."

Amanda is not replying to the last sentence, as apprehension suddenly takes over at the thought of seeing Sean and Tom soon. Hanging up the phone, she takes a deep breath and inwardly steeling her mind that she will be able to go through this. She reminds herself to stay focused on Hamish and not let the presence of Tom and Sean affect her.

In less than five minutes, she reaches the hospital and quickly approaches the receptionist, mentioning Hamish's name. A young nurse named Sally personally escorts her to Hamish's room, providing updates on his condition as they walk down the corridor.

"He's doing well," Sally assures her. "The rescue team who has found him are also here to see how he's doing."

"That's awesome," Amanda breathes. She is eager to personally thank her son's saviour.

As Sally's footsteps gradually slow down, Amanda detects that the first double door ahead is likely Hamish's room. Sally confidently pushes the door open wide, allowing her to catch a glimpse of the individuals inside before entering. Instantly, her eyes lock onto the familiar figures of Sean and Tom, positioned by Hamish's bedside with their backs facing her.

Amanda always assumes that seeing Sean and Tom will make her heart beat faster, as apprehension will take over, creating uneasiness about how she should behave in front of them. There are definitely sparks of anger that she will try to tame. Having outbursts at them in front of her children will be the last thing she has in mind. However, what she feels as she steps into the room is totally beyond her expectations.

She is breathless. Because of utter shock.

Her mouth parts as her lips become dry.

The sight of one of the two men directly standing facing the door causes all the colour to drain from her face. Her body stiffens, and her heart feels as though it stops beating. The room air freezes, with no sound or movement for a few moments.

The man returns her stare, mirroring her shocked reaction. Uncertain of how long they openly stare at each other, noticing the man is wearing the orange SES uniform, Amanda wishes this is just her hallucination.

Yet, even after blinking her eyes a few times, the scene remains unchanged. The confused question from Sean as his eyes bounce between her and the man is a light slap of reality that what she has before her is undeniably real.

"Do you two know each other?"

The question serves as another stark reminder that she must come to terms with this unpleasant reality.

Tyler Fraser is one of the men responsible for saving Hamish.

• • • •

HE HAS BEEN DREAMING about her, holding her hand, strolling together through the beautiful colourful spring in one of the city parks in Bright. Though her scowl accompanies their imaginary walk, he is content simply knowing she is at least beside him. He pledges to make their time together in this enchanting town unforgettable for her.

Of course, when he, in the end, drove by himself to Bright this morning, Tyler knew it was only a dream. He realised that he could not force his wants on her. She is the ultimate reminder that despite what he owns in this world, is not tempting her enough to be with him. On the other hand, the more he shows off himself as a proud wealthy man, the more she despises him.

Amanda is the one humbling him.

In a way, his dream to be with her in this town comes true. Now finding her standing before him with an utter bewilderment, Tyler feels an indescribable sensation in his heart. The moment her oval round face emerges from the opening door, with her long hair piled into a bun, his heart trembles with the flash of memories of seeing an angel when he was fighting for his life. However, seeing the crease that slowly forms between her brows as she registers his presence, he totally understands that she is clearly far from thrilled to see him.

"Do you two know each other?"

The voice from Sean, whom he was introduced as the father of the young missing man, breaks their trances. The curious glance from Matthew prompts him to lower his eyes, as a sudden uneasiness creeps in. This is different from their last meeting in Bali. While he had some inkling due to Isla and Amanda's relationship, he is completely in the dark about how this missing young man is related to Amanda.

The question goes unanswered. He discreetly checks if Amanda will respond. However, her lips are tightly pressed together as she boldly holds his gaze. Something that he has to admire her from openly daring him. Clearing his throat to regain composure and assert control in the midst of conflict, he lifts his head.

"We do." His voice pierces through the room. "Hi, Amanda. I suppose you're the mother of this young man. So I guess..." He smiles at Hamish who is lying on the hospital bed, watching him with open mouth. "You're Isla's brother."

"You know Isla?" The surprise tone of Sean's voice is evident.

Tyler nods his head in affirmation. "Isla works at my company. Fraser & Co."

"Wow!" exclaims Hamish as his lips break into a laugh. "Are you Tyler Fraser? Isla told me that you and my mum met in Bali."

Tyler nods once more, a timid smile playing on his lips. He quietly steals a glance at Amanda, who relaxes slightly as she crosses her arms on her chest as if challenging him to say more words.

"Right." Sean's lips break into a grin. "What a small world. Who would have thought a CEO like you would be volunteering here? Isla speaks highly of you. She truly enjoys working with you. Thank you for providing her with growth opportunities in her career. And now you've also saved her brother. She called me earlier, considering flying from Brisbane to be here. Perhaps we should call her together and reveal that her boss was the one who rescued her brother!"

A light murmur of laughter fills the air, which somehow melts the tension in the room. Tyler is quietly relieved by the change in the atmosphere.

"It's just a coincidence. I'm actually on vacation here." He inevitably glances at Amanda as the word 'vacation' is mentioned. She is still rooted in her place, staring at him impassively. "Matthew, my friend here...," he adds, giving Matthew a friendly slap on the shoulder. "..who has been the regular volunteer. He just dragged me along this morning when we received the news about Hamish. Tell them how we found Hamish, Matt."

Intentionally steering the conversation towards Matthew, he hopes his friend will help to dispel the remaining awkwardness.

Matthew shrugs and sheepishly smiles. "We did not find them. This young man and his girlfriend found us instead. Tyler and I had only been searching for about two hours when suddenly Angela shouted for help."

"Angela is my friend, Mum." Hamish supplies the information.

Amanda blinks and smiles timidly at her son. As if just being reminded why she is in the room, she walks over and gives him a tight hug while kissing his head.

"I'm alright, Mum," chuckles Hamish. "I was silly for not wearing proper shoes and ended up getting lost while walking too far behind the group. Thankfully, Angela has been by my side the whole time. She knows the area well and stays calm and confident that we will be found. Despite taking many breaks along the way, we persisted in walking forward."

"Yeah, all good," Matthew adds in. "Not needing a chopper to track them down is a good sign. Thankfully, it's still daylight saving time. And you found us at the right time before sunset." He winked at Hamish. "We fed them with plenty of snacks and water, then we decided to bring them here for a thorough check-up."

While still holding her son in her arms, Amanda murmurs a thank you to Matthew. Tyler feels his heart leap as she expresses her gratitude to him as well, although her smile does not quite reach his eyes.

"Well, I guess it's time for us to give you some privacy. I bet you have a lot to catch up with your son."

Tyler quietly feels grateful for Matthew's initiative to leave before further awkwardness.

"Thank you once again for rescuing Hamish." Sean moves forward to shake Matthew's hands and his. When their hands meet, Tyler can feel the strong, intense grip and the heat of Sean's gaze on him.

"Don't mention it," Matthew responds. "We are glad he's found." He nods at Amanda who offers another grateful smile. As Tyler trails behind his friend towards the exit, he instinctively seeks out her gaze. Her eyes are indeed on him, so sharp as if a knife piercing through his soul. But Tyler lifts up his chin, refusing to be intimidated.

"Good night all." He darts another intense gaze at the woman who has been haunting his mind. "Good night, Amanda." Then he strides towards the exit door and inevitably catches the curious glances from Tom and Sean on the way out.

The crips night air greets him as they step out from the hospital and stroll towards the car park, providing fresh air to his lungs. Quietly taking an exhale, the tension in his limbs starts to loosen up. Matthew gives him an arched eyebrow and a smirk while opening his ute door, signalling a forthcoming conversation on their ride back. However, their steps are abruptly halted by a stern voice.

Tyler's head snaps around recognising the voice. In the hospital driveway, illuminated by the street lights, the silhouette of Amanda's slender figure strides confidently towards him. Every step resonates with the click of her high heels. Swallowing his nervousness on anticipating what she might say to him, he clears his throat until she lands exactly an arm's length before him, looking at him squarely in the eyes.

"Can we have a talk, Mr Fraser?"

The way she is still addressing him formally gives him a strong feeling that whatever she is going to talk about will not be pleasant. He cannot entirely blame her, because so far there is no reason that they will have a nice conversation. Catching Matthew's eyes, his friend gives him an understanding but cheeky smile.

"I'll wait for you in the car,"

Tyler responds with a timid smile and a quiet sigh in return.

Aware of potential eavesdropping, Amanda moves a couple of metres away from Matthew's car and stops right under the street light pole. It is probably a good spot as Tyler does not think talking in the dark will be a good idea either.

Standing tall before him despite she is just about his chin height, she lifts her chin to look at him in the eyes while crossing her arms on her chest. Dressed in a long sleeve high-neck floral spring dress, Tyler shudders with the ripple in his chest admiring how graceful she is.

"What do you want, Mr Fraser?"

Her sharp voice slaps him awake from his dream of embracing her in his arms after admiring her beauty.

"Why are you hovering in my children's life?"

The harsh question should be expected, and yet Tyler feels it is a brutal accusation.

"I am NOT hovering in your children's life," he mutters.

"Are you not?" Amanda shoots him an arch sarcastic eyebrow as she tilts her head. "Then why, out of all the places in Australia, did you choose to be here?"

Witnessing the fiery range in her eyes, plus her severe words, puts his patience to the test. "As I mentioned before, I am currently on vacation," he snaps in frustration. "Do you not remember that I mentioned my vacation plans about two months ago in Bali? And if you recall, we had an agreement. I have kept my promise to keep Isla away from me like you wish." Inwardly, he berates himself for bringing up the despiseful thing he has done to her.

"I never agreed to that," she defends herself.

It is true and Tyler has to bite his own words. He restrains himself from speaking further which deepens her hatred towards him. If he even hints at bringing Isla back to Melbourne to annoy her, he is a hundred percent sure she will strangle him now.

Taking a deep exhale, exhaustion suddenly washes over him. It has been a long draining day. All he wants now is to retreat. Raising his hands in surrender, he shakes his head in frustration.

"Whatever you think, Amanda, I don't care! Today's meeting with Hamish is purely coincidental. If you doubt it, I'm absolutely fine with it!"

She looks slightly taken aback, but he can read that her suspicion stays.

"So what are your intentions with Isla?"

"Nothing!" His arms flap in frustration. "Like I told you, I appreciate her as our valuable employee. She will have a bright future in Fraser & Co."

"But you're threatening me! Just like you did!"

Her voice is pitched an octave higher, her body trembles as she breathes hard through her nose. The vein in her graceful neck swells as her face flushes with anger. But it is her wide furious eyes at him that knocks him back to all the past mistakes he has made. Tyler now realises, that the more he desires her, the more she misunderstands him. Instead of earning her trust, on the other hand, her suspicion towards him only grows. All is partly due to his pride, as he insists on imposing his desire, without considering what she truly wants.

A moment of silence falls upon them, drowned out by the chirping of grasshoppers. Completely beaten, Tyler closes his eyes briefly, silently praying that his next words will finally resonate. Exhausted physically and spiritually, he longs for the opportunity to reveal his transformed self to her. But the more he attempts, the more she only sees the remnants of his past self.

"I am sorry, Amanda." His voice sounds feeble to his own ear.

That is probably the only word that does not effortlessly escape his lips. He is a man accustomed to being revered and respected as a leader, assuming faultless all due to his power and status. But now, facing the woman he has been trying to convince of his change, a realisation suddenly dawns on him that he still owes her *this* compelling word from a decade ago. How can he prove himself if he is too proud to admit his past mistakes to her?

"I did not mean that. I just..." he trails off.

Beneath the harsh street light, she looks rather stunned witnessing his sudden display of timidity. Her luminous grey eyes fixate on him with bewilderment.

Tyler squeezes his eyes shut in agony. A pang of pain grips his heart as he observes her reaction. Pinching his nose bridge, a habit he does in moments of distress, desperately searching for the right words to say.

Bracing himself, he snaps open his eyes. "All I ask for is a chance."

Her brow furrows deeper at his words. Narrowing her eyes, her voice sounds raspy. "What exactly do you mean?"

"I ...." Tyler swallows hard. Acknowledging his intense feelings for her would only complicate things further. "I owe you a life. Despite my poor treatment of you in the past, I cannot forget your kindness when we were under Ben's hostage. I just hope..." He knows he cannot say that he wants her to be his. "I hope you can find it in your heart to forgive me and maybe we can start over as friends." At the last word, he lowers his eyes, not entirely meaning it. He hates lying though it is for the best.

As he anticipates, silence envelopes them once more. Tyler can feel his heart beating fast, waiting in apprehension on the verdict of his vague confession. Fixing his eyes on the woman before him, Amanda looks dazed as her eyes fall on the ground, trying to decipher his words. He longs to grasp her by the forearms, expressing his desire for her acceptance. But he has made many mistakes and he cannot keep risking her trust by being impulsive.

After it seems an eternity, she raises her eyes. As if she finally found her resolution, she takes a deep exhale and returns his gaze with determination.

"I am grateful for your help in saving Hamish today." Her gentle voice breaks the quietitude of the night.

To Tyler's ear, her tone sounds sombre. He swallows hard, preparing himself to hear for the worst. Time stands still, as his eyes anxiously look at how her lips move a couple of times but no words are uttered. The flame in her eyes has dissipated, replaced by the kind gentle eyes she had when she held his hand in his near-death experience.

He understands the meaning of that look.

It was a compassion. And this time is no different.

As much as he hates being pitied, Tyler has to accept that the best that he can get from her for now.

"Let's consider us even, Mr Fraser," she says softly. "Good night."

Before he can utter a response, she twirls and strides back to the hospital. The soft echo of her footsteps against the concrete street is the only sound Tyler can hear as the sight of her figure slowly disappears in the dark.

AMELIORATION: A CHANGE OF HEART

It is a visualisation that brings back memories of a recurring nightmare.

He was bleeding to death, his vision slowly became dark as her image slowly vanished.

Chapter Fourteen

Staring absentmindedly out of the splashback kitchen windows, Amanda's gaze falls upon the green vine adorned with blooming English Ivy flowers. Appreciating the meticulous placement of the crawling plant, a bitter smile gradually forms on her lips. She is certain whose brilliant idea it must have been.

Her ex-husband is an avid gardener. It has been his favourite hobby and Amanda has to admit his choice of creating a beautiful lush garden is always fascinating, much better than her. She fondly recalls how in the past she always smiled watching him pushing the wheelbarrow, diligently moving soil and planting seeds for his creation, finding solace in the therapeutic activity. Despite feeling neglected at times, Amanda always let him. But now standing in the kitchen in his house that he shares with his new partner, she ponders if she should have made more effort in the past to potentially save their marriage.

Taking a deep sigh, she is quietly grateful for approaching footsteps which pulls her mind back to the present. Elena enters the kitchen with a solemn smile drawn on her lips.

"I can see Hamish is absolutely thrilled to see you here."

Amanda responds to the comment with a wistful smile.

Yes, she is finally in Sean and Tom's house for her son's birthday. She promised herself she would make it happen after Hamish went missing while hiking on Mount Feathertop. Each step towards the modern house Sean and Tom built feels heavy as if she's carrying a rock tied to her feet, but she made it here at last.

It is only her first thirty minutes in the house, and she has been looking at the clock, eager to leave soon. In reality, she still has to endure for at least another four hours before the birthday song is sung for the birthday boy.

AMELIORATION: A CHANGE OF HEART

The only thing keeping her at ease so far is Elena's presence. As if she could sense her discomfort, Elena whisked her to the kitchen to help prepare the salad and skewers for the BBQ. This distraction saves her from having to engage in conversation with Sean, Tom, and the rest of Tom and Elena's children.

As much as she feels uncomfortable, she is amazed at how Elena can navigate the house as if it's her own. Elena knows where to find all the kitchen utensils without any trouble. While she finds it strange, she admires how Elena and Tom still form a good friendship despite their divorce. This makes her question whether she can do the same with Sean. The thought of it seems still far from possible.

"I wonder if Isla will be arriving soon. Will Sean be picking her up from the airport?" Elena's question seems to help her dispel her uneasiness.

"Yeah, I believe so," Amanda replies softly while slicing the cucumber for the salad.

"Have you two been talking?"

Amanda shakes her head weakly, understanding Elena's question about her relationship with her daughter. "Not really. Just a few messages in our family group chats." She lets out a quiet sigh. Despite their divorce, she and Sean have agreed to maintain their family group chats to keep each other updated on their children's lives. It was through these chats she learned about Isla's work project in Brisbane.

"I'm sure she is also thrilled that you're here." Elena squeezes her forearm, assuring her.

But Amanda does not share the same optimism. "I hope so," she mumbles quietly.

The next half an hour flies as she has successfully made herself occupied with all the food preparation. When her mobile phone rings, her mother's number appears on the mobile phone screen.

Sliding the green answering button, the motherly face of Mrs Johnston brings comfort to her heart.

"How are we? Where is the birthday boy? Oh, I shouldn't call him a boy anymore, should I?" Mrs Johnston laughs. "How old is he now?"

Half chuckling, Amanda's eyes roam locating where Hamish is. "He's twenty years old, mum."

Her sight finally captures the skinny tall figure of her son in the outdoor alfresco, helping Tom with the BBQ. The sky is starting to cloud over with rain on the horizon according to the weather forecast. It is just another unpredictable Melbourne weather at the beginning of summer. Despite this, Sean and Tom insist on going ahead with the BBQ plan. For the backup plan, they pre-cook all the meat before the guests arrive. If the rain comes, they can have the meal ready indoors.

"He's grown into a man now. You must be proud of yourself, Amanda, for raising him so well. So, tell me what happened when he got lost in hiking?"

Amanda laughs as she makes her way into the alfresco and approaches her son. "Let Hamish tell you himself, Mum."

Upon hearing her voice, Hamish turns around. Amanda mouths the word 'grandma' and he laughs while taking the mobile phone. The grandma and grandson have a delightful video chat for the next five minutes, until the drizzling starts. Half panic, all the BBQ crews including Hamish rush into the house with all the marinated meat and cooking equipment.

Amanda retrieves her mobile phone and swiftly retreats inside the dry comfort of the house. While the rest of the people are pooling around the living area and kitchen, she seeks solace in the small lounge near the entrance door of the house.

"How are you, my dear?"

Probably her mother can see from the screen that she is intentionally isolating herself from the rest.

"I'm alright, mum."

"Sean and Tom have such a lovely house," Mrs Johnston comments.

Amanda is unsure whether the topic of this new modern double-storey contemporary house that Sean built together with Tom is a good idea. She also once dreamed of building a new house together with Sean in the past, but obviously, it was only her dream alone, not Sean's. On the contrary, after the divorce, she now resides in a small three-bedroom house built in the 80s that is probably still too spacious for her alone. However, she chooses the place as if expecting one day Isla and Hamish will use the extra rooms.

"Yeah." She smiles timidly.

"How are you feeling?"

Amanda understands that her mother can sense her trepidation being in her ex-husband's house. She lifts her shoulder nonchalantly. "I'm okay, I guess. I've been helping in the kitchen."

"I saw Tom earlier. Where's Sean?"

"He's picking up Isla from the airport."

"Right." Mrs Johnston nods vaguely but slowly a comforting smile curved on her lips. "I want you to know that I'm very proud of you. I know you're not comfortable being there, but you're doing it for the sake of Hamish. He must be very proud of you."

Amanda is uncertain of what to say, merely nodding in agreement as everyone echoes the same sentiments. They are definitely surprised and want to appreciate her effort to be in this house, despite she hates it, the encouragement fails to uplift her spirits. On the other hand, she feels everyone is looking at her warily as if she will either break down or explode at one point. This situation brings back memories of her conversation with Shannon, where she admitted her potential anger towards Sean and Tom. To her own surprise, she has been calm since she steps into the house. She exchanges short greetings with Sean and Tom without much expression. She just feels.....*numb*.

"Alright, I'll let you go. Your Dad and I are heading to an early Christmas party in Uncle Sam's house."

Amanda cannot help but laugh, noting that it is only the last week of November. "Christmas party already?"

Mrs Johnston joins her daughter in laughter. "Yeah, Uncle Sam will be travelling by cruise during Christmas, and he tries to match everyone's schedule. You know, this happens."

Amanda nods in understanding. "Alright, Mum. We'll talk again soon."

"Absolutely. Talk to you soon."

Once the call is hung up, as if it is a habit, Amanda instinctively takes a deep breath. She never fails to appreciate her chats with her mother, and this time is no different. But as her eyes catch the provincial theme interior in the lounge, the reality of her prolonged stay in this place sinks in. Trying to shake her negative thinking, she jumps out from the couch, thinking to get herself useful in the kitchen again.

As she rises and straightens her skirt, the door swings open. Her breath catches when Isla enters with her father. Yet, Amanda cannot help but feel proud of how poised Isla is when their eyes meet. Her daughter approaches, and they share a hug which immediately dissolves the tension in Amanda's limbs. She only needs this and she will be content.

"How are you, my dear?" Amanda does not want to miss the opportunity to be able to see her daughter closely. Her hands are still on Isla's forearms as she squeezes them gently. "Do you have a lot of fun in Brisbane?"

"Very much, "Isla replies. She has a good look at her mother before continuing, "I'm glad to see you here, Mum."

Again. Another word that is meant to appreciate her presence here. But Amanda inwardly takes a sigh and silently wishes to dispel the awkwardness. She longs to scream, urging everyone to stop treating her differently, and just accept that her presence is natural like Elena.

"Of course. It's Hamish's birthday. I will not miss it," Amanda muses, quietly complimenting herself for being able to form a wise answer. "Especially after he's almost missing in his hiking. Thankfully he has been found safe and sound."

"That's right, Mum." Isla laughs softly. "I don't want to miss this special moment. I miss him a lot."

Just then, Hamish pops in and the lounge is filled with warm laughter as the brother and sister share a big cuddle. Amanda feels tears welling up in her eyes, witnessing the harmonious relationship between her children. Glancing at where Sean stands, they exchange a proud smile for their children.

Unfortunately, the heartwarming family moment that briefly eases Amanda's discomfort momentarily, must come to an end. The doorbell rings, an indication of the arrival of their guests. Sean answers the door and Amanda feels her breath is stolen once again, as one person, the last person she least wants to see at this moment, steps in with the group.

Tyler Fraser.

To be in this place is hard enough for her, but it seems the world does not smile favourably at her at this point. Tyler and Matthew arrive together, and Amanda understands the reason for their presence. She must take pride in Hamish's gratitude, inviting the two men to his special day.

As if there is magnetism between them, as she stares at the man who has been troubling her mind recently, Tyler's luminous brown eyes finally meet hers. Their gazes lock and the room seems to stand still, with only the two of them existing at that moment. Their unspoken communication fills the air with a silence that speaks volumes.

A soft whisper, like a gentle breeze, sweeps through her heart.

He apologised.

Ever since their last encounter three weeks ago, his apology words kept resonating in her head, clashing with Shannon's voice. *People change. You have changed.* Amanda could not ignore the sincerity in his words when he apologised and begged for friendship. If it was just an act, he was surely a phenomenal actor. The apology may not make any sense to her. And yet, she is convinced that he is being sincere. Her conviction somehow surprised her as well.

The chattering between Hamish and his friends finally breaks their trances. Slowly motioning everyone to the living area, Amanda purses her lips and decides to be the last in line. Her heart ripples as she witnesses Tyler and Isla exchange light pecks on the cheek. She has to admit that their chemistry looks like an affectionate father-to-daughter slash friend. Although Isla's face lights up the moment they speak, their body gestures show a respectful distance.

Contemplating another escape to the kitchen, Amanda stealthily moves behind the island bench, where Elena is removing quiches from the oven. Her friend gives her a knowing look, gauging how she is handling the situation. But Elena should be aware that there is little that can be done. She must simply endure this.

"Does Hamish know about your past with Tyler?" asks Elena quietly, her voice barely above the whisper.

Amanda weakly shakes her head. "I have no idea. Probably Isla told him."

"Right."

Elena's question does make her think. If her children were privy to the unpleasant past she shared with Tyler, would not they consider her feelings before inviting that man to this place? The answer to the question makes her conclude that Hamish has no idea at all. Her son is probably only seeing Tyler as his saviour, and Isla's relationship with Tyler makes him feel is natural to invite Tyler.

Shaking her negative thoughts, she helps Elena arrange more quiches on the baking tray before they are chucked into the oven.

"I guess his presence here does not make you feel better," remarks Elena. Her eyes glance at where Tyler is, in a circle talking with Hamish, Sean, Tom, Isla and Matthew. "But I can assure you that there's nothing romantic between him and Isla."

Amanda understands that her friend just wants to console her. She blurts, "He apologised."

Elena's eyes widen as she scoots closer to her. "Do you mean Tyler? He apologised to you?"

Amanda weakly nods. "For our past."

The sentence only sends another shock to Elena as her jaw drops. However, realising that they are in the middle of the party, it is not the right time to talk about it.

"You have to fill me in soon, love," Elena whispers with a curious twinkle in her eyes. "Tonight, after the party. Damn! Why didn't you tell me sooner?"

Amanda arches her eyebrow with a twitch on her lips. It is not she does not want to share the story with her friend. While she is occupied with Hamish's recovery from hiking, Tyler's apology, and another session she has with Shannon, Elena has been busy with her new love. They just returned from a short holiday together in Cairns.

"I don't want to spoil your fun time," she teases. "Is he joining us tonight?" She is referring to Chris.

A shade of blush appears on Elena's cheeks. "Yes, he will be here tonight." She grabs her mobile phone from her kitchen apron pocket. "Oh, I should let him know that Tyler is here. Just to give him a heads up."

Amanda chuckles lightly, amused to see her friend is falling in love like a teenager. It dawns on her like a revelation. Probably that is the reason why Elena can move on from her divorce and forgive Tom easily. She has found someone new. It makes Amanda ponder whether she can finally move on like Elena. Yet, the idea of seeing someone new seems to require a significant amount of effort.

One hour passes before the rain pours down heavily from the sky. All seek shelter inside the house to stay dry. The chatter inside intensifies as everyone occupies themselves. Amanda seizes the chance to blend into the background. But she cannot ignore the scorching on her skin, sensing a burning gaze from someone in the distance. Without much thought, her eyes scan the room until they land on the tall broad shoulder of Tyler Fraser, meeting his dark consuming eyes.

Those pair of eyes were the same as a decade ago. However, what is baffling her is how it feels so much different now. It no longer intimidates her but instead, sends a warm, indescribable feeling. She has seen him in a different light, all because of his humble apology.

But now he is asking for a friendship.

A bitter smile tugs at her lips at the mention of 'friendship'. The concept feels foreign to her, especially considering she still struggles to form a friendship with the father of her children, let alone with a man who once bullied her.

Suddenly feeling a creeping heat on her neck, she breaks off her eyes from him. The sight of Sean and Tom with their arms on each other takes over. The bright smiles on them are clearly the reflection of their happiness of being together. Amanda recalls how the bitterness began to pinch her heart the first time she witnessed them together as a couple. This time is not much different, though probably in a much lesser intensity. She ponders on the change, whether time may have healed her pain.

Sipping her wine until her glass is empty, she decides to find a solitary place. The comfortable couch in the lounge is the first place she has in mind. Slightly walking tipsily, she chuckles at herself by crawling the wall in the corridor, making her way into the lounges and collapsing at the loveseat. Taking a deep breath, the quietitude in the room makes her feel at peace.

The temptation to shut her eyes is overwhelming, and she fails to notice that someone is approaching. A soft clearing of the throat startles her awake.

"I hope I did not disturb your sleep. I'm just checking how you're doing."

Sean leans against the wall, with a crossed arm on his chest as he watches her. Unsure of how long he has been standing there, still with heavy eyes, Amanda stays unmoved from her loveseat, returning his gaze with a faint smile.

"I'm alright. Thanks for checking." She almost rolls her eyes, feeling like everyone is checking up on her because she is in her ex-husband's house with his new partner.

Sean straightens up and puts his both hands in his pockets. Observing his appearance briefly, Amanda notices that Sean's fashion tastes have not changed much. He looks comfortable in his polo shirt and khaki pants, her favourite outfit for him. Probably it was that made her fall for him in the first place.

"I want you to know that I am really glad you're here, Amanda." His voice sounds rather trembling. His Adam apple bobs nervously. "I know you are here for Hamish, but having you here means a lot to me. I hope..." He lowers his eyes and smiles sheepishly. "I hope we can be friends again."

The word 'friends' sounds like a sharp blade slicing through her heart ever so slightly. Amanda understands that there will be a time when they must work together as their children's parents. They used to be friends, and based on their compatibility and friendship, they decided to tie the knot. It sometimes makes her ponder if their relationship was ever truly fueled by romantic love. Despite their joy in planning for children together, their ability to be great parents does not guarantee everlasting love and companionship.

Amanda hates to lie. She averts her gaze, staring vacantly at raindrops splattering the glass window. The sky is crying, reminding her how she sobbed uncontrollably on the first night she was alone after the divorce paper was signed.

"I wish you can find your happiness as well, Amanda," Sean's gentle voice continues. She remains unmoved as if his voice is simply a passing breeze. It is so easy to tell others to find happiness. Her ex-husband has undoubtedly found his, possibly at the expense of her own. As much as she wants to be sarcastic, she cannot bring herself to express it to the father of her children.

As no response from her, a heavy silence envelopes them. Only the murmuring noises from the living room are heard from the distance. Sean remains rooted in his place, visibly uncomfortable at her lack of response. Amanda quietly hopes he will retreat away, as she has no energy to be courteous. She cannot deny the wounds of the divorce are still raw in her heart.

"Isla mentioned that you used to work with her big boss." Sean's quiet voice finally pierces in.

Amanda stiffens at the words, glancing at her ex-husband who quickly checks the corridor for eavesdroppers before turning back to her with a serious expression.

"Is Tyler...?" He gives her a hesitant look. "Was Tyler your ex-boss in Fraser & Co, the one who was shot during the hostage situation you went through?"

Amanda weakly nods. Apart from her parents, Sean is the one who also knows whom she was with during Ben's hostage drama. She wonders whether Sean remembers her complaints of stress working under Tyler's pressure.

Sean's lips are parting, a sign that his finding surprises him. "So, he's the horrible boss you worked with?"

Amanda nods again. "Yes, that's him."

"But Isla seems happy working with him."

Amanda lifts her shoulder nonchalantly. "I don't get it either. But he's the same person."

"Right." Sean nods his head with a loop of a smile on his lips. "He looks friendly and down to earth. "

Amanda arches her eyebrow and tilts her head, trying to decipher her ex husband's behavior. A sudden realization dawns on her as his last words trail off. He's not convinced.

"What exactly did Isla tell you?"

As if realising that he might have slipped up, Sean quickly shrugs. "Not much. She just mentioned that you already know him. But you never mentioned anything when Isla got her job. Well..." He chuckles rather amusingly. "I get it if you didn't want to bring it up. I know it's all in the past now. We were married back then, but I understand, Amanda."

Like a sudden thud hitting her chest, Amanda straightens herself up from the loveseat. Sean's words ignite an ire within her, signalling where this conversation is going. With nearly two decades of marriage with this man, she can interpret well the meaning behind the twinkle in his eyes. She is familiar with how his mind operates. They may have divergent thought processes, leading to different conclusions.

Differences in marriage are common. Amanda accepts that, and she always tries to accommodate it. However at this time, with lingering wounds from the divorce, her tolerance is wearing thin.

As the colour of her face drains, her chest heaves up and down as she tries her best to calm herself.

"What...?" Her speech falters in disbelief. "What are you saying?"

Though it seems he is taken aback by her reaction, Sean replies calmly. "I noticed the way you two looked at each other earlier. Surely that shows you have a past together."

Amanda can imagine her face must have crumpled as her chest tightened. "What kind of past do you think it was? What exactly did Isla tell you ?" She has confided one of her darkest pasts to her daughter, a memory she wishes she could erase. It makes her difficult to breathe, thinking how her daughter has taken her story as a twist.

"Isla only mentioned that you have a history with him," Sean replies. His tone sounds defensive. Amanda can sense that his answer is merely to protect Isla. "It's alright, Amanda. Like I said, it's already a past. I won't make a big deal out of it. I have moved on. You can too."

The words only intensified her exasperation. Amanda feels her vision spins as she grasps the edge of the loveseat for support. This is worse than her divorce. The divorce has made her feel dumb.

But this!

This is an ultimate betrayal.

"So, you and Isla believe I had an affair with Tyler when I was working with him?" To her own surprise, she finally drops the bomb. Every word tastes bitter on her tongue, sending a stab to her heart. Looking at her ex husband squarely in the eyes, she has confirmed what he has in mind.

Sean purses his lips but does not deny it. Taking a deep breath, he raises his hand, as if wishing to calm her down. "It's alright, Amanda. That's all in the past. I don't hold any grudges against you."

Amanda's eyes widen, totally shocked by what she hears. A soft gasp escapes her parted lips. Her breathing probably halts at that particular second before finally, she breaks into a small laugh. - a bitter dry laugh, as she shakes her head and tears prick in her eyes.

"Grudges, you said?" Her voice shrieks. "Hold grudges against me for being sexually assaulted?"

Sean's head snaps back, totally stunned. But Amanda ignores him as the heat of anger burns inside her. Darting him a venomous look, she continues, "Don't you remember when I told you I was unhappy working under him? How demanding he was? Do you think I was lying?"

The shock fills Sean's face, but he stays still and tight-lipped as Amanda forges ahead.

"He groped me and forced me to sleep with him, otherwise I would lose my job! This was when you were being laid off. I tried to tell you." Tears stream down her face as she recalls the moment how badly she wanted to tell him, but never found the right time as he preferred to be with his best mate's companion. "But you avoided me." Her voice cracks mixed with her sobs. "You chose to spend time with Tom, making an excuse that you needed to find a new job soon, and Tom had some help for you."

Then the hostage situation unfolded, they moved to Brisbane, and she had no choice but to keep the story to herself, because she desperately only wanted to move on.

A lump passes through Sean's throat. "You could have told me..."

"Did you even give me a chance?" She cut him off as another sardonic laughter slips from her sobs. "Did you ever truly care?"

The cold of loneliness haunted her every night she went to bed, creeping back to her. Even when they were on the same bed, Sean seemed distant away as his mind was never about her.

"All you ever thought about was yourself and Tom. I just wanted to move on from that horrible past. It was not only the hostage drama that gave me the trauma. That is why I never told anyone at the end. And now..." She gazed up at the ceiling with a bitter smile drawn on her lips. "When I finally open up..." Her forlorn eyes fall back to her ex-husband. "All of you think is I am a liar."

Completely shattered, Amanda feels all her limbs growing feeble as her strength drains away. Sinking back into the loveseat, the profound pain penetrates her soul, leaving her gasping for air. Her vision blurs, yet she remains aware of her surroundings. The chattering noises from the living room still reach her ear, but they cannot drown out the dreadful silence that hangs heavily between them.

Sean's trembling exhale pulls her back to the present. Slowly she raises her gaze to find her ex-husband standing before her, totally dumbfounded and rendered speechless. The crease in his forehead speaks volumes, he is just seeing a new transformation of her that he has never seen before. Chuckling bitterly, Amanda never denies Shannon's observation that she has changed. Her past trauma and her endurance over an unhappy marriage have moulded her into a bitter lonely person.

"I am sorry, Amanda." Sean's sombre voice pierces in. He carefully approaches her and crouches at the edge of the loveseat, gently touching her forearm. "I did not mean to neglect you. I know I have been unfair to you throughout our marriage." Tears well up in his eyes as his voice quivers. "I realise I will never be good enough for you. You always stay strong. For us. For the children. To the point that I feel you don't need me."

A wistful smile graces her lips. Amanda cannot deny that she only wants to stay strong for her family, especially for the children. She had been keeping herself afloat in the cold marriage, trying to stay positive for the sake of commitment, that she should never simply give up. Every effort she would put to bring back their romance and intimacy, to keep their marriage alive. Clearly, in the end, all her efforts went fruitless. Sean's heart ultimately belonged to someone else.

"So, is this all my fault?" Her voice is raspy, and she cannot help the sarcasm in her tone. Burying her face in her hand, tears flowed like the blood from her wounded heart.

Sean vehemently shakes his head. "No, that's not what I meant. Oh, Amanda!. I am not the right one for you. I'm sorry."

If Sean had said those words five or even ten years ago, perhaps she would have moved on by now. But cruelly, reality has hit her with full force. Two years is not sufficient to heal the betrayal pain of being kept in the dark for a decade. She has been having a hard time accepting the reality, to the point her children might think she has been delusional. And now, the subtle insinuation that she is a liar is like a sharp knife plunged deep into her chest. The pain is so intense that clouds her thoughts.

She has enough. She is exhausted.

As if a switch flipped in her mind, Amanda springs from her seat. Sean seems taken aback and quickly stands up, giving her a concerned look. Ignoring his question, she grabs her purse, her mind is only set to get herself out from this space. Despite her unsteady walk, she is fully conscious and heading in the right direction.

Towards the front door of the house.

Until a voice halts her.

"Mum! Are you leaving?"

Pausing in her tracks, Amanda looks back to find Isla standing next to Sean with puzzlement on her face. The clueless shock on her daughter's face only deepens her sorrow. Isla is likely oblivious to the hurt she has caused. Regardless, Amanda feels cornered, as it seems the father and daughter, and possibly her son, are all against her. The cold loneliness seeps into her soul.

Exhausted and unable to retaliate, Amanda spins back around and resumes her stride, ignoring Isla's frantic plea echoing in the background.

"Mum! We haven't sung for Hamish yet!"

Despite the lingering sense of motherly duty and responsibility in her heart, Amanda does not heed the words anymore. She came for the sake of Hamish. She always wanted to be a great mother whom her children could look up to. But all her efforts to be a perfect mother have gone in vain. None of them believes her. She has failed. She just had enough.

Stepping out of the house, greeted by the relentless downpour, she strides towards her parked car without glancing back. Ignoring the instant soaking of her body, various voices calling her name fade into the background as she enters her car. The dreadful silence envelops her, leaving her feeling completely numb. She starts the engine and drives through the heavy rain which depicts clearly her heart.

Chapter Fifteen

The loud rumbling of the rain thunder causes everyone in the room to flinch. Even the electricity in the room flickers for a moment. The sky outside is unnaturally dark despite it is not sunset time yet. Capturing his own reflection from the glass alfresco window, Tyler quietly feels grateful he is not outside there, battling with the fierce nature.

Despite the lively chatter surrounding him, Tyler isolates himself in the corner, eyes roaming around, searching for the lean figure of the woman who holds his heart. However, there is no sight of Amanda in the room. He squints, scanning for another round more carefully, but his effort is to no avail. He is pretty sure Amanda is not in the room.

The temptation to help himself explore the house is huge, but he must remain discreet. Somehow, the moment he makes a move, someone inevitably catches him in the eyes and pulls him for a chat. Not only Isla but also Hamish, Chris, Tom and sometimes Matthew. He is introduced to some of Hamish's friends, a group of young blokes who are amazed at his heroic act of saving Hamish. But his thoughts are consumed by Amanda.

He needs to see her. He is desperate to speak to her again. She merely mentioned they were on equal terms, nothing about forgiveness or friendship.

Probably he is asking too much. Probably he's rushing it.

Taking a deep exhale, all he desires is to catch a glimpse of her. He craves another opportunity to conversate with her, with the hope of unveiling his transformed self to her.

His nervousness is palpable, drawing an inquisitive look from Matthew, who has been chatting with a group of intrigued youngsters about his hiking adventures. Concealing a smirk behind a sip of his beer, Matthew strides toward him.

"Getting bored, mate? It looks like you're ready to get out of here soon."

Tyler does not respond, flashing a timid smile. Matthew seems reading his mind well.

After his last conversation with Amanda in Bright Hospital car park, he hopped into Matthew's ute, utterly devastated. Matthew shot him a wary look but did not press him with questions throughout the journey home. Tyler quietly appreciated his friend's respect for his privacy. However, in the end, he was the one who told him everything.

Matthew had been a great listener, offering no comment or opinion, just quietly listening with no judgement.

"Are you looking for her?" Matthew quietly asks, moving closer to him so no one else can hear them.

Tyler's weak nod is his only answer.

Another loud grumble of thunders shakes the room, accompanied by flashes of lightning. Gasps echo then followed by relieved giggles. At that point, Tyler catches Isla and her father emerging from the corridor, worry written on their faces. Tom approaches them, and they whisper among themselves. Hamish joins the group, deepening his frown as Isla and Sean engage him in discussion. His father gently taps his shoulder he nods weakly. Narrowing his eyes as if he is trying to do lips reading, Tyler can sense something is not right, and it must be something to do with Amanda. Tom claps his hands to gather everyone's attention for the birthday song, confirming his suspicion that Amanda has left the house.

Glancing back to the alfresco glass door, the sky becomes pretty dark as if it were midnight, despite time only showing eight o'clock in daylight savings time. His heart suddenly beats faster, as a negative thought haunts him. It is not safe to be on the road in this kind of weather. Why does Amanda have to leave the house at this time?

However, everyone's attention is drawn to the birthday boy, who is standing sheepishly in the middle of the room. The lights have been turned off, and the candle lights cast a soft glow on Hamish's face as Elena presents him with a large rectangular cake. It dawns on Tyler that Elena is completely unaware of Amanda's absence, absorbed in the celebratory mood. Tyler cannot blame any of them, and yet he feels for Amanda. Why isn't anyone questioning her whereabouts?

Should Matthew not suddenly grabbed his arms, Tyler would not have realised he was about to leave the room.

"We should at least say farewell to the host," Matthew suggests. Tyler nods in agreement, trying to calm himself from his sudden anxiety. After the song ends and the cake is served, he follows Matthew to bid goodbye to Sean and Tom as well as Hamish.

"Please send my regards to your mother. May I know where she is? Is she in another room?"

Tyler inwardly applauds Matthew's insightful question. His friend definitely can read his mind well, and try to help him to dig out information.

"Mum is not feeling well, so she decided to go home," Hamish replies with a shade of disappointment on his face.

"I hope her place is not too far. The weather outside is horrible." Matthew smiles at his own comment. "Having said that, I must also take my leave. Thankfully, my brother's house is only five kilometres away from here. Thank you for having me in your party, Hamish."

"Thank you for coming," Hamish replies.

Tyler is following Matthew's lead as everyone is shaking hands. But the moment he shakes Sean's hands, he can sense Amanda's ex-husband does not look him in the eye. His handshake is brief and cold, in contrast with their earlier interaction when he just arrived. Tyler has a gut feeling something might have happened. It crosses his mind that Sean may have uncovered his true past with Amanda.

As they walk towards the door, Isla turns up to bid him goodbye as well. Planting a light peck on her cheek, Tyler can sense her turmoil from her dejected expression. It crushes him to see her that way.

"Is everything alright, Isla?" Tyler cannot restrain his fatherly gesture towards the young lady.

Isla weakly shakes her head, tears glistening in her eyes "All good, Tyler. I'll tell you the next time we catch up, alright?"

Tyler nods his head as he understands he cannot push her. Besides, Isla is safe in her father's house. It is not the time for him to interfere when he is not being asked to. Furthermore, at this stage, his mind is set to find Amanda, though he has no clue where to begin.

Once he and Matthew jump into his car after hopping through the rain, he quietly takes a relieved sigh.

"Thanks, mate," he murmurs softly. "I couldn't do this without you."

Matthew chuckles and shrugs. "I didn't really do anything, mate." As the car starts moving, he gives his friend a worried glance. "Where will you find her? Do you want me to come along? This weather is horrible."

As Matthew is speaking, another lightning bolt flashes, followed by thunder. Tyler has no choice but to agree with his friend, as the road ahead is becoming increasingly difficult to see. The journey to Matthew's brother's house is fortunately relatively quiet and only one suburb away. Despite the unanswered question lingering in the air, Matthew does not push the question, letting him focus on the road, allowing them to reach their destination in five minutes.

"Are you sure you don't want to come in first? Maybe wait for a bit for the weather to improve."

Tyler swallows, thinking hard. His friend's offer is quite tempting. He still has no idea where to find Amanda and driving in this weather is not a good start. At least he has managed to escape the party.

"Come on, mate!" Matthew insists, not accepting a 'no' answer as he gives Tyler a firm slap, urging him to get out of the car. "Let's have a drink inside and we can come up with a plan."

Tyler is unsure how to respond. Reluctantly he steps out of his car, hopping through the rain again like a little rabbit, following Matthew to enter the house.

Matthew's brother's name is Sam. Sam lives with his wife and his two primary school kids, one boy and one girl. Seeing the children brings a sentimental feeling for Tyler, reminiscing about Aaron and Kylie when they were about the same age. The difference is Sam has a harmonious marriage with his wife, unlike him and Janine. Tyler has to be quietly grateful that despite the estranged marriage relationship he had with Janine, Aaron and Kylie can lead normal lives. Strangely enough, he has formed a friendship with his ex-wife post-divorce. Janine has been happily married to her own man, and they constantly stay in touch talking about their children's wellbeing. It's funny how the separation makes them a better person.

However, it turns out different for Amanda.

Watching the raindrops splashing hard on the window, his mind immediately flies to her. How she can survive driving in this horrible weather after the potential argument she had with her ex-husband, makes him wonder. Divorce instead makes Amanda bitter and lonely, shutting herself off from the world. Isla has shared stories of her mother avoiding almost everyone, including her own children. Tyler believes Amanda does not mean it, but she cannot help it.

He ponders what exactly the conversation she had with Sean earlier. Whatever it was, it must have ended badly, that pushed her to leave the place without even considering she was leaving her beloved son's birthday party. He takes a quiet sigh, and wonders where she could be.

His reverie is severed when a gentle hand slaps on his shoulder. Matthew hands him a bottle of beer, which he receives with a timid smile.

"The rain is predicted to stop soon," Matthew remarks as he joins him gazing at the window. "It is still heavy drizzling, but at least no sign of thunder or lightning anymore. Do you know where she lives?"

The question sparks an idea in Tyler's mind. He could easily find out her address with a quick call to HR. Isla must have listed her mother's address as an emergency contact. Asking Sean, Isla, or Elena directly would only arouse suspicion, even though his intentions are good.

"Thanks, mate." He flashes his gratitude smile to his friend, who continues to inspire him. "I need to make a phone call."

Within minutes, he is on the phone with his trusted person in HR, who quickly locates the information. When Amanda's address is supplied, Matthew gives him an arched eyebrow.

"That's quite a distance from here. Almost a forty-five minutes drive," remarks Matthew. But as if he realises that his words might aggravate Tyler's anxiety, he quickly adds, "The weather seems to be improving." They both look out the window and notice the drizzle slowing down. "Do you need me to come along?"

Tyler shakes his head. "No, mate. I'll be fine on my own." He is aware that Matthew needs to return to Bright early morning tomorrow. "Thank you for everything."

"I didn't do much, mate," Matthew replies as they share their buddy handshakes. "Let me know how things go."

"I will."

After he bids goodbye to Sam and his family as well, Tyler promptly jumps into his car. Even though the rain has stopped, the street remains wet. Carefully driving his car through the traffic and the freeway, he finally arrives at the specified address in an hour as expected.

Amanda's house is a typical Melbournian house likely built in the 1980s. Her front yard garden is adorned with lush gardens filled with carnation bushes and a towering liquid amber tree. The well-maintained garden reflects the owner's passionate love of gardening. Tyler smiles imagining Amanda tending to the garden, plucking out wheat. However, the imagination is far from reality at this point as the wet weather has left the garden completely soaked.

The sight of a small cream Toyota hatchback car on the driveway makes him quietly take a sigh of relief. He recognises the car as Amanda's. That means she has safely arrived at home.

For a moment, he is contemplating whether he should knock on the door. The house is in pitch dark, with no sign of any lights from inside the house. If her car is already in the driveway, wouldn't she be inside the house? Tyler wonders whether she has fallen asleep. However, it still does not feel right to sleep in total darkness. Not for him, but probably it is okay for her.

His apprehension mixed with his concern for her welfare pushes him to jump out of his car and decide to knock on her door. He is willing to risk being chased out because all that matters to him is ensuring her safety.

The first and second knocks are gentle. No answers or any single sound he can hear from inside. He tries again, this time harder, and takes out his phone's torch to search for a doorbell. Only silence greets him. By the fifth attempt, he realises he has to find a way to get into the house.

During his youth, Tyler led a reckless life. He recalls, though sounds silly as it was, that some of his group of friends challenged each other to break into someone's house for the thrill of it, not for material gain. Students from prestigious private schools were wealthy enough. He managed to break into someone's house before and escape at the right time before getting caught. Then his friends started to challenge him to go for a bigger double-storey house, or a house with dogs, a house with guards et cetera. Tyler got caught once and had to be picked up by his father from the police station. That incident marked the end of his breaking-and-entering escapades.

Now, approaching the age of fifty, he finds himself incredulous at the thought of repeating the experience. But this is for entirely different reasons. Navigating through the darkness with the torch from his mobile phone, he successfully leaps over the side fence, confident it will guide him to the laundry area. Thankfully, he remembered to bring his jacket, which he uses to protect his hands as he shatters the glass window of the laundry room. Within two minutes, he successfully opens the door and gains access to the house.

The dark silence greets him. With the aid of his mobile phone torch, he cautiously proceeds down the corridor and makes his way into the living area. Sighting no one, he decides to find the light switch. His hands eventually locate one, and with a simple click, the living area is illuminated.

The first thing that catches his eye is the extensive wall bookshelves framing an inactive chimney at the centre bottom. When his eyes slowly roam, his breath stalls to see a motionless body on the floor near the chimney. Upon closer inspection, he realises it is the unmistakable figure of Amanda.

He swiftly lands beside her at lightning speed. She is lying on her left side, drenched in the dress that she wore at Hamish's party earlier. Her eyes are closed, but what prompts Tyler to quietly whisper a short prayer is seeing her chest rise rising and falling.

She is still breathing.

As panic gets into him, he tries to remain calm. Delicately touching her arm to avoid startling her, he notices her trembling and pale, dry lips. The flush on her cheek suggests she may have a fever.

Touching her forehead, he recoils at the intense heat radiating from her skin.

"Amanda." He whispers her name, checking whether she is conscious. There is no response and it immediately prompts him to get help. With trembling hands, he picks up his phone, fumbling and dropping it to the ground. When he is about to press triple zero, Amanda unexpectedly stirs, causing him to jump in surprise.

Her eyes flutterly open, and squint for the moment against the bright light. Tyler swallows, holding onto every second if she screams upon seeing him. But what she does next leaves him blinking hard wondering if he is dreaming. She pushes herself into a sitting position with a small grunt escaping her lips.

"What happened?"

Her voice is hoarse and dry as she looks around, briefly pausing at him, the crease forms between her brows, but she seems to struggle to register well his presence as her gaze drifts away. Then she pushes herself up, slightly wobbly, prompting Tyler to instinctively reach out and grab her arms for support.

"You are unwell, Amanda. You should change into dry clothes."

As they stand in close proximity, Tyler holds his breath. They are standing so close that he can feel the fan of her hot breath on his neck. Her eyes are on him, confusion is evident on her façade. After what feels like an eternity, she finally breaks herself away and walks tipsily towards one of the bedrooms.

Tyler walks closely behind her, getting himself ready if he needs to catch her if she falls. Despite her feverish state and possible sleepwalking, she miraculously manages to pick out dress pyjamas from her wardrobe. Restraining himself from entering the room, Tyler observes her from the doorway. But clearly, she is unaware of his presence as she strips herself of her wet dress.

At one point she is struggling to open her bra. It makes Tyler feel like a teenage boy. He has seen naked women before, but somehow with Amanda, he does not want to cross the threshold of being disrespectful. However, as her fingers fumble, he steps into the room and helps her to unhook the bra. He vaguely hears what she mumbles as thank you as she continues to undress herself.

He decides to be at the doorway again. However, within a minute he hears another mumble as Amanda is struggling to fit her head through the neckline of her dress, forgetting to unbutton the top part of the dress.

Between feeling amused and exasperated, he chuckles at himself. As much as he wants to help her as surely she needs assistance, touching her bare skin makes him feel like a boy in puberty. He has longed to hold her in his arms, squirming under his touch. Luckily his common sense overrules. Taking the dress from her trembling hands, he focuses on unbuttoning the neckline, all the while conscious that she is sitting on the edge of the bed without any layer of clothes. Refusing to let his mind wander, he swiftly pops in the dress through her head as if dressing up a child.

Another mumble of 'thank you' slips from her lips before she pushes herself into the bed, clutching the pillow tightly. Though he is worried about her health, it seems all she needs now is rest. Her eyes remain half open, staring vacantly at him while he slowly moves toward the door, keeping a watchful eye on her.

Then what he has feared is finally about to come. The crease between her brows deepens. Lifting her head from the pillow, the alertness on her face indicates she begins to register his presence. Tyler swallows as he recognises the fire in her eyes.

"You!" Her voice is weak, like a hiss, but resonates clearly in the calmness of the house. "What are you doing here?"

He raises his hand, wishing to calm her. But before he utters a word, she continues.

"All because of you! Ever since what you did to me, my life has been falling apart. Sean left me." She begins to sob. " And now my children too! You've destroyed my life!"

Her voice pitch rises with each word she utters. Although he anticipates her reaction, her outburst makes him realise she might be delirious. He remains on guard, silently relieved that she remains on the bed, showing no sign of jumping at him. Her face is wet with tears as sorrow consumes her.

"No one believes me anymore. They see me as a lunatic," she chuckled between sobs, a broken sound escaping her throat. "They see you as a saint. They refuse to believe that you bullied me. You must find this amusing, don't you?"

His feeble attempt at a head shake and pained expression is his only response. Laughing at her expense never cross his mind. Though he has to admit that he has been selfish for wanting her for himself, he only wants to make her happy. Witnessing her joyful smile will be his ultimate prize.

The room is suddenly filled with her laughter. A laughter tinged with despair, that slices his heart. As the laughter gradually subsides, she buries her face in her pillow, tears streaming down her cheeks.

Tyler remains silent, not daring to make a sound or a single move. His chest is tight witnessing the anguish of the woman whose heart he wishes to win. Despite all the wealth and power that he possesses, once again, he still fails to make her happy. On the other hand, he only gives her another misery.

For it seems like an eternity, the room is only filled with her wailing. Tyler is unsure for how long he is rooted in his place, but he is determined to stay, making sure she is alright. As if the tiredness finally gets into her, eventually, the weeping fades into stillness, leaving a heavy silence in its wake.

Chapter Sixteen

Amanda cannot recall the last time she felt this weak. Though the curtain in her room blocks out the sunshine, it does not deter the heat from pinching her eyes open. However, all she feels is fatigue. Unable to let go of the comfy pillow in her arms, she closes her eyes again, wishing to let herself lull into another good sleep.

But her mind is only half asleep. Her brain starts to ponder what day it is. She remembers Hamish's birthday party yesterday and the shattering conversation with Sean. She ran into the rain and drove through the storm to finally get herself into her dark and isolated small house. The loneliness consumed her, leaving her numb. The chill from her wet soaking dress made her shiver, but she did not give a damn care about it. What happened next is a blur. It surprises her to find herself in bed, dressed in sleeping attire.

A tantalizing aroma awakens her senses, prompting her to rise from the bed. The wafting scent, possibly from a neighbouring home, induces hunger and curiosity within her. Yet, the intense bacon fragrance leaves no doubt that it emanates from her own kitchen. But she lives alone, the notion of an intruder in her home sparks a moment of alarm. Someone else is in the house and using her kitchen? She chuckles at the absurdity of the idea. If someone were to break in, why would they be cooking such appetizing food?

Nevertheless, she is on her guard. Grabbing her mobile phone from her bedside table, and Hamish's old cricket bat that she always hid under the bed, she opens her bedroom door and cautiously from her bedroom through the corridor towards the kitchen and living area. A soft melodious humming from the kitchen confirms that she is not alone. Oddly enough, this sound provides a sense of reassurance, indicating the individual is not a threat. The first person who pops up in her mind is Hamish, though she has no idea that her son is into singing.

Placing her cricket bat on the corridor floor, she decides to put an end to her speculation. The moment she finally gets a clear view of her kitchen, her heart seems to cease for a beat. The person who is behind the island kitchen bench, plating up the food from the frying pan, is the last person she will ever think of. Blinking her eyes a couple of times, Amanda is sure she is not dreaming that the person is Tyler Fraser, acting like a chef in her kitchen.

Her lips are parting in shock, but she is totally wordless. Initially unaware of her presence, Tyler finally looks up and mirrors her astonishment.

"Hello." His lips finally break into a nervous smile. "Good morning." He carefully placed the frying pan on the stove. "How are you? I hope you're feeling better."

Amanda is quietly taking a shuddering breath as if she has been holding it for an eternity. Hearing Tyler's voice is like a knock on her head that the man before her is real. The reason for his unexpected presence still stuns her.

"How did you...?" She glances around, then suddenly becomes conscious of her state of dressing. Despite wearing a granny-type cotton nightgown, the lack of undergarments leaves her feeling exposed. She quickly crosses her arms over her chest, attempting to conceal her vulnerability. But a new realization dawns on her. Could this explain why she awoke in her nightgown this morning? Could it be possible that she...?

As a soft gasp escapes from her lips, she darts the man before her with wide eyes. Her facial expression is easily readable as Tyler quickly raises his hand.

"No! We didn't..." An exasperation spread on his face. "I mean I did not...touch you." His Adam apple nervously bobs as he returns her stare with unwavering conviction. "I swear, I did not touch you. You changed your dress on your own. You probably did not realise that, because you were feverish last night."

The term 'feverish' triggers memories in Amanda of the intense heat she experienced last night while shivering. Despite feeling uncomfortably warm, she chose to disregard it and simply curled up on the rug in the living room. Was her fever so severe that she was unaware of her actions afterwards? Her mother had mentioned in the past that she tended to sleepwalk when ill. Tyler's explanation seems plausible.

But he once tried to force himself onto her. Though he had apologised.

Still, it does not explain how he could end up in her house.

"Why are you here?" Her eyes scan around, wondering whether he may have arrived with someone holding a spare key to her house. She had given spare keys to Isla and Hamish, welcoming them at any time into the house. But she does not sense anyone else in the house except them. "How did you get in?"

Tyler lowers his eyes, a faint blush colouring his cheeks. "Through the laundry. I broke the window to open the door. I'll get someone to fix it soon."

Amanda narrows her eyes. "Why would you do that?"

"You did not answer when I knocked on the door. I knew something was not right, so I decided to break in."

"Why did you come looking for me?"

"You left suddenly from Hamish's party in the middle of the storm. So..." He lets out a sigh, closing his eyes for a brief while rubbing his temple. "I was worried about you. So I decided to come here, to make sure you're alright."

His response leaves her breathless. With lowered eyes and a hint of uncertainty, he watches her reaction. Out of everyone who witnessed her leaving the party devastated, Amanda never expected Tyler to be the one rushing to ensure her well-being. It was indeed a crazy storm last night, but Sean or Isla did not try to stop her.

AMELIORATION: A CHANGE OF HEART

Though there is a slight feeling of dejection and being forgotten, Amanda refuses to let negative thinking overtake her mind. Glancing at her mobile phone screen, new messages flood in. Probably one of them is from Isla or Hamish. She will check that later. At this stage, her mind is spinning with the presence of *this* estranged man - Tyler Fraser- in her house.

Amanda has mixed feelings about how she should respond. There is a tingling warmth in her heart knowing his concern for her. However, she has not forgotten that, apart from their horrible past, the return of his presence into her life recently is causing the ugly conversation she had with Sean last night. She is utterly shattered that no one believes her because Tyler is not the same person as before. And yet, she cannot entirely blame him.

But a flash of memory strikes her mind. She dreamt of venting her anger at him. Doubts slip in that it is actually real.

"Did I...?" Raking her hair with her fingers, a wave of embarrassment suddenly hit her. "What exactly happened last night?"

"Well..." Tyler breathes deeply. "I found you lying on the floor in the living room." He nods his head to the area by the fireplace. "You woke up when I called your name, then went to change into dry clothes in your bedroom. I waited for you to finish. "

His throat bobs as he speaks. Amanda narrows her eyes, assessing his honesty. He glances at her briefly as if realising that she is not buying his story entirely.

"I helped you a bit while changing. You were slightly struggling," he admits.

Amanda takes a deep inhale but restrains herself to react. Another swirl of warm feelings gets into her that she even cannot understand. He is being honest, and she should appreciate it. Though it means he might see her in a state of undress, her gut feelings tell her that he did not try to take advantage of her.

He adds, "Then you fell asleep." But his eyes drop to the floor, signalling that he is hiding something.

"That's all?" she arches her eyebrow.

He purses his lips for a moment, before returning her gaze with determination. "Yes, that's all. I swear I never laid a hand on you. If you don't believe me, we can do a rape test."

Amanda inhales sharply. Having a rape test is not what she has in mind. Though she does not believe him entirely, deep in her heart she has a conviction that she has not been touched inappropriately.

An awkward silence descends upon them. His determination to prove himself innocent makes her feel uncomfortable instead. If he indeed did something to her last night, would he still have the decency to be here this morning?

Taking a quiet shuddering breath, her eyes drawn to two plates of food on the kitchen bench where Tyler has been leaning. There is a slice of bacon, with sourdough bread, scrambled eggs, mushroom and sausage on each plate. The sight of the food is enough to make her tummy rumble. Unsure whether he might heard it or not, a repressed smile is drawn on his lips.

"The breakfast is for you. Go ahead." Tyler pushes one of the plates to her side.

Amanda cannot deny that she cannot wait to tuck in. Rather hesitantly, she moves forward and sits on the stool bench. Her hands grasp the fork and knife prepared on the side, and once a small piece of the food goes into her mouth, irresistibly she moans as the punch of great flavours of each ingredient dances on her tongue.

With a satisfactory smile curves on his lips, Tyler watches as he takes his food as well into his mouth.

"Did you cook these?" she asks with a mouth full of food. She doesn't want to pause eating while her stomach continues to growl.

He nods with a sheepish smile. "I hope you enjoy it."

"This is absolutely delicious," she remarks. Another warm feeling strokes her chest, reminding her of the rare occasions when someone cooked for her. Sean never bothered to cook for her, though he was a decent cook. His cooking was usually for the kids, not for her pleasure. She never let it bother her before, but now, it brings a twinge of sadness to realise his lack of effort in pleasing her.

"Hamish looked slightly disappointed after you left the party last night," remarked Tyler after a brief period of silence as they enjoyed their breakfast together. The statement makes her munch slower, as the memory of the previous night flashes back and causes a pinch in her heart.

"He does not need me," she mutters quietly.

"Why do you feel that way?"

She shakes her head weakly, tears welling in her eyes. "No one believes me anyway." She lifts her eyes at him, who is stunned by her words. "They trust you more than they trust me!" Her frustration starts to bubble up, but as he is flinching at her words, she is reminded that it is not entirely his fault.

"No one believes what you did to me in the past. Instead, they assumed we had an affair." A self-deprecating chuckle comes from her throat as tears begin to roll on her cheek. "They think I am delusional, while you, in their eyes, are a great man. Meanwhile,..." she scoffs. " I am just a bitter unreasonable person."

Another silence envelopes them. Her eyes stay on him, searching for his response. But Tyler lowers his eyes with guilt ridden pinching expression on his face. Somehow Amanda believes that he did not intend for things to turn out this way.

With a sad smile, she darts him a painful look. "Why? Why did you have to change, Mr Fraser? What is exactly your scheme?" Her question is laced with sarcasm and anguish.

His head snaps up as the question hangs in the air, his eyes widening. Instantly regretting her words as they escape her lips, she acknowledges the unfairness towards him. What hurts her most is the lack of trust from her family. Regardless of Tyler's true intentions, none of her family should doubt her.

Shaking her head in despair as tears streaming down her cheek, she chuckles bitterly. "I'm sorry. I shouldn't have said that."

She admits the current Tyler Fraser is not the same as a decade ago. His apology appears sincere, his eyes no longer dark and cruel. Instead, they hold a tenderness and compassion that sends a whirl of breeze in her heart.

"I..." His head shakes weakly. "I do not have any scheme, Amanda." His voice is so soft, almost above a whisper. "I am a changed man, because..." He takes a shuddering breath. "Because of you. You are the one who changed me."

His deep gaze at her somehow paralyses her. For a couple of seconds, what Amanda can hear is her own heartbeat. His luminous brown eyes speak volumes, conveying a depth of emotion she never thought possible. Her little heart is admitting the true meaning of those looks, though her brain is trying to deny it.

A decade ago, that was not how Tyler Fraser looked at her. He would give her a dirty look, that sent shivers of disgust down her spine. But this time is different. It sends a swirl of warmth in her heart.

It is not merely a desire. It is an admiration. It is a meekness.

Taking a shuddering breath, she cannot tear her eyes away from him as he moves slowly towards her. He halts next to her, their bodies are just an inch away from touching. His right hand slowly up, pausing midways for a moment. She is amazed that she does not flinch as if she is mesmerised by his handsome face in close proximity or probably because her own pride preventing her from backing away. Emboldened, he places his right palm on her left cheek, his thumbs brushing against her lower lips.

AMELIORATION: A CHANGE OF HEART

Amanda does not even remember whether she is breathing. The warmth of his palm feels like a gentle caress to her very being. She cannot remember the last time someone touched her delicately. Yielding to the irresistible urge, she closes her eyes, leaning into his hand, savouring the touch.

It has been a while. It has been too long.

His head tilts down, bringing his masculine presence closer, overwhelming all her senses with the comforting solace she craves. His lips brush her forehead tenderly, moving ever slowly to her eyes and nose, like soothing balms to her heart wounds. Feeling his warm breath on her lips, she is inevitably parting her lips. And before she can fight her dizziness with coherent thoughts, his firm lips take hold of her soul, leaving her breathless.

His kiss starts soft and tentative, gradually deepening as she reciprocates. It lacks fierce passion, yet is filled with adoration, as he worships every inch of her lips. When finally they pull apart for air, Amanda feels like she is floating. His palm lingers on her cheek, and she is desperate for it to stay. Her heart dictates her hand to catch his palm and press a kiss to it.

The delirious hazy look in his eyes reflects her own. As their forehead grazes each other, his heavy breath brushes against her face. She can feel the inner struggle that he is facing just as she is grappling with her own. Yet, she is reluctant for this moment to pass.

"It's all because of you, Amanda," he whispers. "I want to be a better person for you."

His words, spoken with sincerity, not only shake her to the core but also dismantle the walls she had unknowingly built around her heart since her marriage faded. It feels like a lifetime since someone spoke to her with such passion. This moment is all about her and for her.

Nevertheless, she has been the sole source of her own strength till now and is uncertain about how she should respond. Gazing hazily at the lapel of his shirt, her hand unconsciously reaches onto it and gently pulls him towards her.

Unbeknownst to her, this gesture serves as a clear indication of her interest. His arms envelop her, their bodies colliding as he captures her lips with a fervour that ignites her own desire.

Chapter Seventeen

It takes every ounce of his strength to restrain himself from ravishing her. Yet, to finally have the woman he has yearned for over the past ten years in his arms, threatens to drive him to madness. As much as Tyler tries to remind himself against frightening her as he once did, he is like a wild uncontrollable beast feasting at its prey.

The only difference is he wants to savour every second, planting each kiss on every inch of her body, tasting her skin, inhaling the purity of her essence. Burying his face in the crook of her neck, his hands explore every part of her as if she might disappear at any moment, clinging to her desperately because every part of him craves for her.

Her soft moan only intensifies his desire. Removing her original sitting position with impatience, he effortlessly scoops her up and carries her into the bedroom. Her eyes are hooded with longing he eagerly wants to fulfil.

His hands urgently explore her bare skin and unsure whether it is his or her conduct, or it is a result of their work together, her nightgown slips off from her head swiftly. Her nudity is a sight to behold as every cell of his body is burning with desire. Carefully laying her on the bed, her wavey hair cascades around her head like a crown. Witnessing her is like seeing his dream come to life. She is an absolute goddess he is eager to worship.

With his shirt unbuttoned, his eyes rake on her from the crown of her hair to her feet. A shade of blush on her cheek only inflames his desire to make it right for her. Moving closer like a predator, he pauses when their eyes meet. Her hand on his bare chest is another green light that encourages him to press the accelerating pedal.

This is what he has been dreaming of for the past decade. Feeling her skin against his, the heat of her body beneath him. His lip captures hers, brushing against the soft skin of her lips, moving ever slowly to her cheek, and down to her neck. His hands somehow find their way to her soft beautiful breast, moulding them as he devours them into his mouth. Her soft whimper followed by her squirm only increases his pleasure.

He moves leisurely towards her stomach, his face eventually nestled in her inner thighs. His eyes search for her answer. She returns his stare with a yearning, like a silent order for him on what exactly he needs to do, to which he obediently complies. The air in the room stays still as his fingers and lips are diligently giving her pleasure. Her soft moan slowly fills the air, before it finally escalates into a breathless scream that he always longs to hear.

It is not the first time Tyler has heard a woman's orgasm, but hearing it from Amanda's throat is priceless. He will do it over and over again to hear it.

For a moment, he remains motionless on his knees between her legs, seemingly wanting to etch her delirium into his memory. As she finally descends from the peak of her pleasure, her hazy eyes become clear. She blinks and a perplexed expression creases her brow.

His lips draw a small smile, suddenly feeling shy for being caught red-handed watching her. He crawls onto her to savour her lips into his while his arm holds her tights. While he is in paradise enjoying the nectar of her soft lips, his bliss is interrupted when her hand slips into his pants. Reluctantly tearing his lips away from her, he grabs her hand and holds them above her head. She lets out a soft groan, sounding more like a protest, but he keeps pinning her hands.

His intense desire drives him to nibble on her lips, moving slowly down to her neck and chest. He is taken aback when her hands slip between his pants again. This time she works quickly.

"No," he mumbles. However, her teasing touch renders him speechless as she skillfully removes his pants. He has guarded himself from giving in to his pleasure, reminding himself that this is all about her, but her grinding against him pushes him to the brink of self-control.

Grabbing her both hands and pinning them above her head, he darts her with a dark intense look. How she returns it with a lifted chin only fuelling his passion. He captures her lips with ferocity, which she matches with equal vigour. She is challenging him, and he knows the only answer to that is to give in to her.

He is completely at her mercy.

He thrusts into her. Quick and hard. Her eyes widen in astonishment as a gentle gasp escapes her lips. For a second, they stare at each other, and stay still, as if their hearts speak to each other that this could be... *a life changing*.

Swallowing hard, Tyler is determined to make it unforgettable for her. He begins to move with deliberate slowness, relishing in the sensation of being connected to her with each gentle thrust. Her lips turn into a white slash as a soft whimper echoes in the room and their bodies move in perfect harmony.

He longed to be intertwined with her eternally. In every movement, he is rewarded with her melodious moaning. Their hands are clutched together, which reminds him of when she held his hands during the hostage -the hands that he was holding onto for his life. Pausing for a moment to catch his breath, his lips are hungry to taste hers. And when she reciprocates, he soars to paradise.

As he nears the pinnacle of release, he yearns to bring her along. Sliding his hand between them, he gently touches her core, revelling the euphonious of her breathless scream and the graceful arch of her body towards his.

His speedy strokes finally take him to his climax. Clutching tightly on her hands, their bodies quake in synchronisation until a peaceful serenity finally washes over them.

Rolling himself to the side to avoid crushing her with his weight, he stares at the ceiling for a moment, before glancing to the side.

Amanda is dazedly staring up, her chest rising and falling with each breath. Unable to resist her beauty, he rolls onto her, pulling her into his arm, feeling her heartbeat. Their breath slowly in sync before finally sleep lulled over them.

Chapter Eighteen

Upon waking from her peaceful slumber, the first sight to meet Amanda's eyes is the cream-colored ceiling of her room. It feels as though she has just emerged from a beautiful dream, her body is still humming with contentment. A gentle snore beside her and the weight of an arm draped over her serve as reminders of reality. Still enveloped in the warmth of Tyler's arms, with only a thin layer of quilt between them, she feels safe and comforted.

It has been years since she felt this way. Her marriage bed had been cold for almost a decade, and the divorce only deepened her loneliness. She never entertained the idea of someone else warming her bed despite encouragement from all her family. But what transpired this morning was like a spur of the moment. An impulse. Something that is out of character for her. And yet, it is oddly....*satisfying*.

Glancing to the side, she cannot help but admire the alkaline nose of Tyler as his steady breath fans on her cheek. The memory of his firm luscious lips on every inch of her skin sends another hum to her core. His gentle and patient caress peeled away every layer of her self-guarded wall. He had diligently taken her to climax, bursting every cell of her body into the maximum pleasure she had ever experienced in her life. Trying to restrain herself from comparing, but she could not recall that she ever had such a glorious moment before with her ex-husband.

But Tyler used to be a bully. He coerced her and forced her to be submissive to him. Though it was a decade ago, and he even had apologised, it was a past that she should not simply let go of.

Amanda acknowledges that she is not the type of person who can easily grant forgiveness. And yet, what has happened for the past hour, she finds herself welcoming the new version of Tyler.

How can something feel so right when it appears so wrong on the surface?

Quietly releasing the tightness in her chest through a shuddering exhale, she shut her eyes again, wishing to be overtaken into sleep. Perhaps the next time she opens her eyes, all these worries will disappear. But before she can fall into her deep sleep, a soft chime of her mobile phone that has been left behind in the kitchen startles her awake. Inevitably it creates quakes on the bed, and Tyler's head snaps up. With sleepy eyes, he rolls away from her and she takes the opportunity to jump out from the bed. Feeling the cold kitchen tile beneath her feet, she realises she is running without any single layer of clothes.

Nevertheless, seeing the name on her phone screen compels her to answer the call without hesitation.

"Mum?" Isla's hesitant voice echoes in her ear.

"How are…" Her voice is hoarse and she quickly clears her throat. "How are you, dear?"

"I'm well, mum. How are you? Are you at home?"

Amanda takes a deep exhale. "Yes." Crossing her fingers at her back, she hopes Tyler will not make any sound. Looking back to the bedroom, she swallows hard as she sees him leaning against the door. The sight of his well-toned body makes her cheek warm, and she is quietly grateful at least he is covering himself with a blanket. As their eyes meet, there is a mutual understanding that he should stay silent.

"You left Hamish's party too soon, Mum."

Isla's accusation is evident in her tone. As much as Amanda wants to retaliate to defend herself, she manages to hold back. She left because of the upsetting conversation with Sean, not with Isla. Though probably her daughter does not mean it, whatever story her daughter has told Sean has been misconstrued.

"I'm unwell," she replies flatly. "I'll call Hamish later."

"Alright." Isla's deep exhale echoes on the phone, seemingly unimpressed with her answer. "I'm heading back to Brissy tomorrow. Can you give me a lift to the airport? I know it's a working day. Unfortunately, Dad has a morning meeting. I could just take an Uber, but I thought maybe we could catch up..."

"Of course, I can take you," Amanda quickly interrupts. The offer of giving a lift to Isla to the airport is like a mother's duty call. Her daughter needs her help, and when she became a mother, Amanda vowed to be there for her children as much as possible.

"Great." Isla's response sounds flat. "My flight is at 3 pm. So, I'll wait for you in Dad's at 1 pm."

"How about I pick you up slightly earlier? We can grab lunch before heading to the airport."

"Sounds great. Alrighty. I'll see you tomorrow."

"See you tomorrow, love."

Once the phone is hung up, Amanda breathes a sigh of relief. The conversation seems going well, and most importantly, Isla has no idea that she is with Tyler in the house. The mere thought of Isla discovering her mother has slept with her big boss makes her insides quiver. However, before she can dwell on it too much, a gentle cuddle on her back makes her gasp softly.

Tyler wraps her from behind with a blanket and himself. At least the thin layer of the blanket separates their bare skin from touching. But his gentle kiss on her neck is sufficient to send butterflies to her stomach.

As much as she longs to savour the moment, the harsh reality sets in. Reluctantly she untangles herself from his embrace, taking a few steps away from him. With a heavy heart, she turns around, gathering her courage to see him in the eyes. As she has expected, a frown is formed between his brows. His eyes reflect a sense of resignation for the verdict that is about to come. It is the sight that only adds to her inner turmoil.

But she needs space to think about *this*. While she is sorting out her mind well, they cannot keep doing this as much as she yearns for his touch again.

"Thank you..." She nervously swallows. "For taking care of me last night and making sure I'm okay. And also.." She glances at the leftover breakfast on the kitchen table. "For cooking the breakfast. They are delicious."

Does she need to say thank you for the glorious moment they have shared? The memory sends a tingling warmth throughout her body. Her brain tries to dictate her heart, wishing he could not see the possibility of a blush on her face.

He stands motionless before her. His round brown eyes gaze at her intensely, occasionally bouncing at her lips and her figure. It is enough to send another humming throughout her body. She curses inwardly for acting like a teenager. Torn between speaking her mind and causing pain, she nervously bites her lip, contemplating to say the words, the hurtful words that probably no one wishes to hear after a great time spent.

However, he supplies the words for her.

"You want me to leave." His voice is devoid of emotion, filled with disappointment.

He lowers his head, taking a deep exhale in dismay while raking his chestnut hair. Amanda quietly swallows. As much as she had expected his reaction, but never anticipated the sinking feeling in her own heart.

"Do you regret what we just had?"

His question feels like a weight crushing her chest, her mind is whirling hard to form the right words to answer it.

She cannot meet his gaze, fearing he can see through her heart. A wave of shyness washes over her like an inexperienced 18-year-old girl after her first intimate encounter. "I simply need some space. I need to..." Her voice trails off, uncertainty clouding her thoughts.

"I hope you understand, Amanda." His gentle baritone voice rushes in. "What happened earlier means a lot to me. I..." He moves closer to her, he pauses with his hands suspended in the air just before almost touching her. She holds back the urge to flinch as his intense dark eyes lock with hers, emanating uncertainty. He seems to understand her doubts. His Adam apple bobs nervously as he continues, "I want you."

His voice is soft, almost above a whisper. But Amanda can sense the profoundness behind them. Her heart is swamped with warmth that she cannot comprehend.

How she can react this way to Tyler Fraser is ..*unthinkable*.

He desires her as much as now she desires him, a notion that seems preposterous.

But she cannot let her wall down easily. Having previously poured so much of herself into a relationship that went unappreciated, the idea of giving her heart to someone like Tyler Fraser, who ironically used to be her bully, does not make any sense to her.

"You already had what you wanted, Mr Fraser," she mutters quietly, immediately regretting her unkind words. His blanched expression is like a stab to her chest, but she steels herself by lifting her chin. "I think it's best if we move on from here."

His eyes widen at her incredulously. "What do you mean?"

"What I'm trying to say..." She swallows hard. "What happened between us..." She shakes her head weakly. "What we had should not happen again."

He narrows his eyes. "Why? Do you still doubt that I've changed? I..." For a moment he seems breathless. "For the past ten years, I've been dreaming of you."

Whether she should be flattered or not, Amanda is unsure. His words sound sincere, and something strikes her mind on the true reason for his change.

He is enamoured with her because of the kindness she showed during Ben's hostage crisis. He feels indebted to her for saving his life.

"You believe I've saved your life," she mutters flatly. "It was the circumstances that forced us together during that terrifying ordeal." Her face twists with pain as she recalls the past before letting out a dry chuckle "We should be thankful we were saved, as everything happens for a reason." A flicker of annoyance sparks in her heart. "It's unfortunate how things turned out. Ben only got what he deserved - he was frustrated and ended up in jail with nothing to show for it. And you did nothing to change it."

He seems taken aback by her last sentences. "Ben, you said? What do you mean I did nothing?" Then, as if a light bulb had just gone off in his head, he softly gasps. "So, you still don't believe me because of Ben?"

Amanda looks away, wishing he could not read the sudden uneasiness of his question. She should not bring in Ben's name. Regardless, Ben is not the main reason that she is still in doubt about what they had, and Tyler was not the sole cause of Ben's reckless action.

With a deep breath, she closes her eyes. The complexity of the situation weighs heavily on her, and all she longs for is some time to sort through her thoughts. It is impossible to do that with the recent events fresh in her mind and him still lingering nearby.

"Please go...," she whispers softly.

His defeated sigh fills in their quietitude. "Alright. I will go for now, as you wish. But please Amanda..."

She keeps her eyes closed, facing away from him, but she can sense his eyes are still on her, so intense like scorching her skin.

"Can we please one day talk about this again? About us," he adds on.

With her arms wrapped around herself, she purses her lips, restraining herself to promise him any answer.

Another resigned sigh floats through the air. Slowly he retreats to the room. Amanda gathers her courage to sneak a glance at him while he is wearing his clothes. Once he is prepared to leave, she averts her eyes quickly to avoid being caught peeping. His footsteps echo, before slowly dissipating as he closes the door.

Chapter Nineteen

Tyler feels like a zombie.

Like an empty shell, he strides into the lift that will take him to his office floor. His body moves mechanically while his mind drifts far away, replaying over and over again the glorious moment he shared with Amanda yesterday. However, her indifference afterwards left him shattered.

He thought what they had was special, and yet it was not enough to capture her heart.

He remembers her words yesterday about Ben. He has to do something to prove to her that he did not only stay idle after the hostage saga.

Repeatedly taking deep breaths despite the early hour, he makes his way to his office floor with a slight headache. Greeted by Megan's cheerful smile, he sadly musters up little enthusiasm in return. His loyal assistant furrows her brow, trailing behind him into the office

"Is everything alright?" Megan's voice is filled with worry as she closes his office door.

Sinking into his chair, Tyler lets out another deep breath while staring up at the ceiling.

Megan has been one of his good listeners. She is one of the people who knows about his past with Amanda. No judgement or comment passes from her. Her motherly gaze on him while she is listening to his story is sufficient to give him some consolation.

"Yes," he responds wearily. "I'm just exhausted." Then, he remembers asking Megan to arrange for a glazier to fix the window in Amanda's laundry room. "Have you found a glazier for Amanda?"

"Yes!" Megan promptly replies. "The man came yesterday. I texted Amanda and she confirmed when the job was completed."

Although Tyler has not disclosed anything about his activities yesterday, he trusts Megan is perceptive enough to deduce that he had been at Amanda's house.

"Good." He gives a nod before absentmindedly tapping his fingers on the table, suddenly feeling lost about what he needs to think first. Megan's next information like slapping him awake.

"Your brother tried calling. He couldn't reach you earlier. He's inviting you to a crucial meeting with investors in Yarra Valley. I've arranged for a private helicopter to fly you out from Melbourne at 1 pm."

Tyler's lips are parting, as if his brain is still digesting the news. While it is not the first time Sam has dragged him along to important meetings, Tyler is sometimes slightly annoyed by it. In the past when Aaron and Kylie were still young, he would try to avoid it. But now, he has no more excuses. Besides, probably being away from Melbourne could be a great idea, allowing him to escape from the thoughts of Amanda.

"Alright," he sighs. "I guess I have to go. Has any meeting been cancelled because of the trip?"

"No." Megan shakes her head affirmatively. "That's why I promptly booked the helicopter. But if you have time, Isla is wondering if she could speak with you this morning before heading back to Brisbane."

His head snaps up as the name of the young woman who is related to Amanda is mentioned. "Sure! Is she already here?"

Megan nods with a solemn smile. "She is. Would you like me to bring her in now?"

"Yes, of course."

Megan twirls around and disappears behind the door. Within a minute, his office door is open and the lean young figure of Isla in her cocktail dress emerges. Her presence immediately sends a warmth of fatherly fondness into Tyler's heart. Rising from his chair, he welcomes her with a light peck on her cheek.

"I will not take up too much of your time," says Isla as she is taking a seat on the couch in the small lounge area, while Tyler plunges a coffee capsule into the coffee machine. "I never properly thanked you for helping Hamish. I'm sorry I did not have the chance during Hamish's party. There was a little bit of drama..." She rolls her eyes. "...with mum."

"All good," Tyler responds lightly, feigning ignorance of the drama at Hamish's party. "Rescuing your brother was just a happy coincidence. Besides, I would say Matthew deserves most of the credit."

Isla smiles sheepishly. "It's a small world," she quietly remarks.

"Yeah, that's true." Then his curiosity is piqued. He wonders whether Sean told Isla the content of the conversation that makes Amanda upset. "So, what exactly happened with your mother on that day?"

Isla's shoulder slumps as she lets out a deep sigh. "As I've shared with you before, Mum refuses to be around my dad and his new partner since the divorce. She came to the party for the sake of Hamish. Well, I guess what happened afterwards is bound to happen. She simply stormed out from the party after she had the argument with my dad even before we could sing Happy Birthday to Hamish."

"What was the argument about?"

Isla purses her lips for a moment as if thinking how to formulate the right explanation. "Well..." Her round turquoise eyes look up at him with hesitation. "It's something to do with you."

Tyler maintains his impassiveness as he continues sipping his coffee.

"I believe it's just a misunderstanding. But she claims you were a horrible boss when she worked with you."

Isla swallows as she keeps looking at him with apprehension. Tyler can read she begins to feel uncomfortable.

"Then?" He prompts her, encouraging her to continue. "How did it lead to a confrontation with your father?"

"Well, It seems like Mum has been holding on to some bitterness since the divorce. So, she tends to view everything from a negative perspective. Of course, you are a great boss. So, when I told Dad, he jokingly suggested that she just tried to hide the fact that..." She chuckles rather amusingly. "That she fell for you instead while still married to him. Dad said he was okay with that. But she was so furious. That was why she left."

Upon hearing that, Tyler quietly inhales a trembling breath as a punch of guilt hits his chest. Now he can understand clearly the flame of anger in Amanda's eyes when she vented her frustration at him. Sean must have misinterpreted their past relationship. She must be devastated that no one in her family believes her, especially when it is pertaining to him, the man responsible for her painful past. He himself wishes he could reverse the time and rectify his mistakes.

"Mum was being childish. Hamish was so disappointed, but what could we do?" Isla keeps talking, oblivious to his pinched expression. "Fortunately, she made it home safely despite the crazy storm. Worried by her lack of response to our messages, I called the next morning. I was between annoyed and relieved that she finally answered my call."

Tyler is not responding. His heart becomes heavy thinking of the pain that Amanda is going through with this. He just wants to change to be a better person, but never he thinks that it will twist the past against her.

Without realizing the unsettling quiet that fills the room when Isla suddenly stops talking, her voice startles him back to reality.

"Tyler?"

He blinks. Regaining his senses, his lips slowly break into a timid smile.

"Sorry, Isla."

"No! That's okay! All good."

Isla must have thought that his mind was preoccupied with work, but in truth, his mind is consumed with thoughts of Amanda.

"So,..." He clears his throat. "Do you believe that your mother's claim about her past experience working with me being terrible...." A shiver runs down his spine as he braces himself to ask the dreaded question. Gathering his courage, he meets Isla's guarded gaze "... was untrue? You think your mother is lying?"

Tyler realises that his past must be brought to light one day. Some long-time employees at Fraser & Co, like Megan, remember how he and the company used to be very different. Unfortunately, Amanda was one of the people who had suffered under the tyranny of him and his family. Despite the painful truth being revealed, especially to someone he cares about like Isla, Tyler is determined to do so for Amanda's sake. This is the sole path to his redemption.

Isla's discomfort is evident as she admits, "Well, it's not I don't believe her. She's just changed so much after the divorce. I feel she doesn't like to see anyone else happy because she's not." Then with her pair of round innocent eyes, she gives him a suspicious look. "She did tell me that you coerced her before. But...."

Probably she starts to catch the glimmer of admission from his eyes. A soft gasps slips from her lips as her hand flies to her chest. "Please tell me you were not, Tyler. You can't be."

How tight his chest has become, Tyler has no idea as he can only lower his head, unable to see the painful look from the young woman, who all this time looks at him with respect as if he is not only his big boss, but also his friend. Taking a moment to gather his thoughts, he closes his eyes, tightens his fists, and summons the courage to reveal his innermost secrets.

"It was a decade ago, Isla. I wasn't exactly an angel. " His voice sounds hoarse to his own ear. "People change. I wish I could go back the time and fix it. But of course, I can't. Therefore I need to make it right this time."

Isla narrows her eyes at him as a shade of disgust begins to appear on her facial expression. "What did you do to her?"

Tyler is aware that this will be the most difficult part of all and he knows it will bother him later on. The pressure in his chest increases to the point where he is not even sure if he is still breathing. After closing his eyes briefly to gather his courage, he finally takes a deep breath and steel himself to meet Isla's gaze.

"I sexually assaulted her."

Chapter Twenty

Glancing nervously at the clock on the car dashboard, Amanda takes a few deep breaths in an attempt to calm her anxiety. She is behind schedule for taking Isla to the airport. Fortunately, their lunch appointment being cancelled is not due to her running late. It turns out that Isla suggested cancelling lunch because of her busy work schedule. The original plan to pick her up from Sean's house is also altered, as Isla now wants to meet at Fraser & Co's office.

Amanda is not a regular patron of Melbourne CBD. Her workplace is in the suburbs, where she usually commutes by car. Consequently, she has forgotten to consider the congested city traffic. It has been fifteen minutes since she entered the city area, and her car is barely moving through the traffic. According to her navigation, her destination is still two minutes away.

As soon as she catches sight of the Fraser & Co building and Isla standing outside the lobby, she breathes a sigh of relief. Stopping her car on the curb, she quickly jumps out from the car to help Isla with her luggage.

"I'm sorry I'm late, sweetheart. ".

No response from Isla. On the other hand, her daughter is rather avoiding to look directly into her eyes. She places her luggage into the boot and gets into the car without uttering a word.

Amanda takes a sigh, guessing Isla's silence is due to her tardiness. Refocusing on her role as the driver, Amanda swiftly takes her place behind the wheel and drives off. Exiting the Melbourne CBD has proved to be quite a challenge, but it is a little easier than expected. In just ten minutes, they are on the highway heading towards the airport.

The journey is filled with silence. Amanda is quietly grateful that she has been turning on the radio, hence the music sound and the radio DJ's chattering help to alleviate the dreadfulness of their quietude. She focuses on her driving, accelerating her speed where possible within the rule limit, and maneuvering between cars. She has to applaud herself for arriving at the airport on time as planned.

As they make their way from the parking area to the airport terminal, Amanda takes a deep breath and steals a glance at Isla, hoping her daughter's irritation has faded. But her heart sinks when she notices tears welling in Isla's eyes.

Just as Amanda is about to speak, the lift door opens, signalling their arrival at their floor. Without a word, Isla exits the lift, dragging her luggage behind her. Amanda follows silently, deciding to hold off on any conversation until Isla finishes the check-in process. Glancing at the time, Amanda realizes they still have at least thirty minutes before boarding begins. This means they might have a bit of time to talk before their flight.

Much to her surprise, Isla seems to think likewise. After receiving her boarding pass, Isla suggests that they find a seat in one of the nearby cafés. Amanda is quietly relieved that her daughter at least is not telling her to leave right away.

"Thank you for taking me here, Mum." Isla's soft voice pierces in once they are seated down with a cup of takeaway coffee for each of them.

"It's my pleasure, sweetheart. I apologise for being late."

Isla weakly shakes her head. "No, you're not. We made it here on time."

Amanda notices another glimmer of tears pricks in her eyes. If her daughter is not annoyed with her tardiness, she is pretty sure that Isla is still angry with her because she stormed out from Hamish's party. "Are you still mad at me for leaving Hamish's party?" she asks carefully.

Isla seems taken aback by her question, revealing a glimpse of sorrow in her eyes.

"No, Mum. I'm not upset that you simply left Hamish's party. " Isla's voice starts to tremble. "On the other hand, I am so sorry that you had to leave because of me."

Confusion spread on Amanda's face. "What do you mean? I left because I had a little disagreement with your dad. I'm sorry if I acted childish."

Isla begins to sob as she shakes her head fervently. "No, Mum! It's all my fault! I told Dad about you and Tyler. I was assuming that ..." She takes a tissue from her bag and wipes her sniffles." ... you were trying to deny your true feelings toward Tyler. I am so sorry."

Amanda purses her lips as a deep crease formed between her brows. Isla continues between her sobs, remorse evident in her round eyes. "I am sorry for doubting your story about the horrible past you had with Tyler."

A swirl of victorious feeling surges in Amanda's heart as her daughter's eyes finally open. However, a rush of apprehension immediately follows, her mind is running wild about what may have happened to her daughter.

"What happened, Isla?" She grabs Isla's forearms in panic. "Did Tyler...?" Her anger begins to simmer within her. Just yesterday, she started to believe that man has changed. The fact that she even had welcomed him on her bed sends an ache to her chest as she might have too early to make a conclusion. She has been fooled! With a horrifying look, she searches for an answer on her daughter's face.

Isla vigorously shakes her head "No, Mum! Don't worry. He did not do anything to me."

But Amanda feels not at ease yet as she tilts her head, narrowing her eyes suspiciously at her daughter. 'Isla..'

"I swear, Mum! Tyler never touched me! " Isla returns her look sternly. "I am telling you the truth!"

The firm answer makes Amanda's furrow deepens. She still cannot fathom why Isla is so upset if Tyler isn't the cause of her distress.

"Tyler confessed to me, Mum," Isla quietly adds.

Amanda feels like a thunderbolt strikes her whole body. Her lips part as her breath is restricted. Her eyes stare at her daughter in disbelief.

"He acknowledged that he was a changed man from ten years ago. He...," Isla's voice falters as she swallows her sobs. "He admitted to me what he did to you."

Amanda is utterly speechless. As she hesitantly lowers her hands from Isla's shoulder, her mind races. Tyler Fraser has surprised her again. No one believes her because the current Tyler they see is faultless. Yet, he has revealed his true self to Isla, which has worked in her favour.

Her anger and shock instantly dissipate, and sighing quietly, the memory of the unforgettable morning when their bodies intertwined sends a tingling warmth in her.

Could he have truly done this for her?

"And you believe him?" Amanda hates that the question slipped out of her mouth. She does not intend to be sarcastic, but there is a hint of bitterness in how easily people believe Tyler, but not her.

"I'm sorry, Mum." Isla squeezes her eyes shut as tears stain her cheeks. "You've changed so much since the divorce. You've distanced yourself from everyone. I never meant not to believe you. But when you told me the story and asked me to leave Fraser & Co, I thought...." She chuckles dryly. "I thought it was just your bitterness speaking. You weren't happy to see others happy. You are still not happy for Dad and Tom. I am at the peak of my career, and I thought..."

"I'm not happy for you...?" Amanda quietly supplies the words as her heart slowly shrinks. How could her daughter perceive her as a horrible and selfish mother? Tyler's words in Bali resonate back in her mind. *You shut her out.* She acknowledges that she is partly to blame.

Isla weakly nods. "I'm sorry, mum."

Amanda shakes her head. "That's alright, my dear." As a mother, she has to be the wiser one here. Despite the deep hurt in her heart, her motherly love will eventually wipe out all the pain. She opens her arm, welcoming Isla into her embrace. Her daughter has grown up, unafraid to admit her mistake and she should be proud of her.

"Tyler also shared with me about the hostage ordeal that you guys went through," says Isla once they have released their hug. Her sobs begin to subside as her voice steadies.

Amanda feels her breath hitches at the mention of the past. But Isla gazes at her with a solemn look.

"He will never forget how kind you were to him when he was shot. That's why he decided to change. You should have told me about that ordeal, Mum."

"You were still young at that time, sweetheart."

"I know. But now I'm a grown-up," argues Isla. "Knowing about it helps me understand you better. It was a tough time for you, and I remember how you stayed strong for all of us. Moving out from Melbourne to Brissy, then back to Melbourne. Then the divorce. You've been through so much, Mum."

The words send a tremble to Amanda's heart. She has been self-reliant, the one people turn to for help, not the one seeking help. She prefers to work behind the scenes with little expectations in return. Her entire life has been dedicated to her children, despite the marriage struggle she had. The recognition of her sacrifices brings tears to her eyes, though she quietly resents it, feeling as if she is being pitied.

"Mum..." Isla's hands reach out to hers. "Will you forgive me?"

Unable to control her tears, Amanda chuckles and sobs. "Of course, sweetheart." She embraces Isla tightly, feeling all her pain melt away in the warm embrace. "I'm sorry for shutting you out since the divorce. I didn't mean to, but..."

"I understand, Mum." Isla quickly interrupts her, soothing her back. "I understand. It's not your fault. I understand if you cannot forgive Dad and Tom, yet. You need more time. I promise I will not push you anymore."

And those are the words that instantly alleviate the weight that seemed to have settled on Amanda's chest. All this time she is always trying her best to maintain the peace with Sean for the sake of the children. Hamish's party was one of the struggles she had to endure. However, Isla's words bring her immense relief and will allow her to open up to her children.

The announcement signals that Isla's flight boarding gate is now open, prompting them to release their embrace. Wiping the remaining of her tears, Isla wheels away her luggage. Amanda follows her until they have to part before the security check-up.

Hugging each other for one last time, and a whispered promise that they will see each other soon for Christmas in three weeks, Amanda plants a kiss on her daughter's temple and whispers a heartfelt thank you. The beautiful happy smile on Isla's lips as she waves goodbye is the best moment that Amanda will cherish. After the conversation they had, today marks a new beginning for them. She looks forward to setting things right this time.

Once Isla's figure slowly fades from her sight, Amanda twirls around, heading back to the lift that will take her to the car park, with a content smile on her face. Suddenly everything surrounding her becomes clear. When she and Isla arrived at the airport earlier, her focus was solely on ensuring Isla caught her plane on time. This time she begins to appreciate the vibrant Christmas wreath and garland adorning the airport walls. A couple of photo booths with an inflated balloon of Santa and the reindeer, along with Christmas trees are scattered in the corners. Everyone that she passes through looks jovial, probably looking forward to their upcoming holiday trips. It makes her realise the power of seeing things in a positive light.

It is liberating.

Pressing the lift button, she waits patiently until the door is open. In addition to herself, there is an old man in the wheelchair and a younger man who she assumes is his son, standing within her peripheral view. Without any intention of eavesdropping, she finds herself listening to their conversation. Based on the young man's speech pattern, she notices he stutters. The more Amanda listens, she has a feeling that the young man probably has speaking and understanding difficulties. However, his father patiently explains with loving tender care and gentleness.

The ding sound of the lift door opening severs Amanda's thoughts of the couple. Holding the button to allow both men to enter the lift before her, she has a better view of the face of the old man as he is wheeled in by his son. A thud hit her chest as she recognises his familiar face. The old man looks at her with a smile on his lips, which instantly triggers memories from the past.

It was the same smile that used to welcome her every morning and served as her solace when she had to drag her feet to work in Fraser & Co. The smile belonged to one man who had brought a bitter-sweet memory a decade ago. His luminous round blue eyes used to look at her with empathy as if he was the only one who could understand the pressure she had at that time.

This time the same eyes look at her gently, as if he can understand her recent bliss. Unsure for how long their eyes lock, but none of them wish to break it away. It gave her a sense of reassurance that she indeed remembered him correctly.

"Ben?"

AMELIORATION: A CHANGE OF HEART

"Amanda?"

Chapter Twenty-One

The buildings with their diverse towers and heights appear as miniatures from Tyler's vantage point. The propellers' swirling noise is a constant white noise to his ears. Being on the private chopper to commute for business meetings used to be his favourite. The trip gives him temporary solitude while he can enjoy the scenery drive. It is no exception for this time. It is his solace after what the thing he had with Amanda, and the painful conversation he had with Isla this morning.

He has confessed everything to Isla. The shine on the young woman's eyes changes from respect and admiration to shock, and slowly into disdain the more he revealed what he did a decade ago. When he explained the catalyst for his change of heart, stemming from the hostage situation, her face was softened, filled with empathy, mirroring Amanda's forgiving gaze when he apologized.

Once his narration ended, a dreadful silence filled the space between them, intensifying the torment in his heart. Isla stared vacantly at the window, triggering a vivid recollection of Amanda's fearful expression when they were both held captive in his office during the hostage situation. The sight sent another punch to his stomach, as he comprehended another unforgivable act he had committed against the mother and daughter.

Without uttering any word, Isla finally stood up from her seat, walked to the door, and moved past him with the breeze trail of her flowery perfume. He clenched his jaw, shutting his eyes in pain, still holding onto a sliver of hope that she would speak.

For a couple of seconds, he waited for the sound of the door closing, but it never came. Wondering if Isla had left it ajar, he turned around to get his breath hitched, seeing the young woman still standing by the door.

Their eyes bore at each other for a moment, but he could sense that she was holding back something. He silently wished she would just unleash her emotions, even if it meant yelling at him or slapping him for what he had done. But he had to admire her calmness despite her age.

"Thank you."

Her voice came out almost like a whisper, but what caught him off guard was the words chosen. Did he deserve to be thanked?

"Thank you for being honest with me," she continued. "It means a lot to me and my relationship with my Mum." She appeared a bit nervous as she glanced down briefly before meeting his gaze with determination. "I need to prepare myself to get into the airport." Then she swiftly disappeared behind the door.

Tyler knows for sure that they need another talk.

If Isla decides to leave the company because of this, he will do everything to convince her to stay. However, he will ultimately respect her decision, even though it means losing a valuable employee and a friend. She is a vital part of helping him feel connected to Amanda. If she leaves, he may deserve it. He will lose both her and Amanda.

Taking a deep sigh, he throws his sight to the expansive greenery nature passing by. he longs to be holding Amanda's hands, soaking in the beautiful scenery below. However, all will stay as a dream only for now.

Shutting his eyes for a brief while pinching the bridge of his nose, he knows he has to do something to make everything right. He just has to know how.

The sudden shake on the chopper startled him, causing his eyes to snap open. He realises that the heli looks unstable, swaying from side to side. As he is sitting behind the pilot and the co-pilot, who appears in distress in controlling the heli, an apprehension instantly rushes into his blood.

"What is happening?"

The co-pilot turns his head at him, and Tyler can read panic spread on his face.

"Something is not right, Mr Fraser! Brace yourself, we may need to make an emergency landing!"

Tyler feels a thud hit his chest. He can sense that something bad is about to come. Gripping tightly to his seat, he holds his breath, as his heart whispers a silent prayer. This reminds him of a decade ago, when he was shot, when he thought he could die. Thousand of memories flood his mind. Faces of loved ones appear before him like scenes from an old movie.

His parents, brother, Aaron, Kylie, and even Janine.

Amanda and Isla.

This could potentially mark the end for him. His only hope now is to be granted another chance at life.

Chapter Twenty-Two

❚❚ What a wonderful coincidence that we're able to meet up today!"

Amanda represses her nervous smile as Ben's trembling voice reverberates in the café at the airport, with steaming cups of drinks in front of them. Ben's son, Charlie, is stirring his hot chocolate, licking the spoon, and smiling happily to himself. For an age probably in his late twenties, his round blue eyes twinkle like a little boy with tousled curly hair partially covering his forehead. Despite his larger, more muscular frame compared to his father, Amanda cannot help but notice how Charlie's behaviour resembles that of a ten-year-old child.

Amanda tries to recall if Ben has mentioned to her before about his intellectually and behaviour-challenging son. She remembers that Ben was a single father when they worked together and had mentioned that his wife had left him. Amanda did not ask why, but she suspected that Charlie could be the reason. Quietly she admires Ben's perseverance and dedication to his son.

"How have you been, Amanda?"

"I've been well, Ben."

Her answer is partly a lie. Over the last decade, her life has been consumed by marital issues and ultimately divorce. Recent interactions with Tyler and misunderstandings with her children highlight that she is not in a good place. These experiences force her to confront the fact that she consistently masks her pain.

"I'm glad to hear that." Ben nods his head with a solemn smile.

"What about you?" She hesitantly inquires with a slight grimace, dreading a negative response. She berates herself for asking, realising she should have anticipated the situation. However, upon seeing him and his son in the elevator, all she felt was a positive energy. She may be overanalysing the situation.

"Fantastic!" Ben's grin is wide. "So, what brings you to the airport today? Is it for vacation?"

"No. I just dropped off my daughter. She's flying to Brisbane." She notices he glances at her surroundings whether she's carrying any luggage. She does likewise, not sighting any sign of luggage around him. "And what about you? Are you on vacation?"

"No, no, no," Charlie chimes in with a sheepish smile. "Aunt Jenny visited us. She's flying back home now."

"My sister," Ben adds on. "She lives in Brisbane, too. She came to Melbourne and stayed with us for a week. We're just sending her off today."

"That's lovely." Amanda quietly remarks.

"She's the only remaining family I have," Ben smiles fondly. "I am considering moving to Brisbane, to be closer to her. I guess at this age, being close to family is the important thing." His looks are suddenly filled with regret when their eyes meet.

"I owe you an apology, Amanda."

Amanda blinks in surprise, not expecting these words. She had always assumed that she would be the one to apologise. Ever since the hostage ordeal, she had avoided reaching out to him out of fear and guilt. She understood his frustrations and the desperate reasons behind his actions. She wished she could help him, perhaps even avoid jail time. But she felt too overwhelmed by her own problems to do so.

"I apologised for what I did ten years ago," he continues. "It was wrong of me to do what I did. I deeply regret ever aiming a gun at you."

Amanda weakly shakes her head. "No. It's alright." She quietly takes a shuddering breath, feeling the weight of their conversation hit her. "I know you did not mean it. I ...." She bit her lips nervously. "I understand why you did it, Ben."

"It was foolish," he mutters with a regretful smile. His gaze goes distant as his eyes start being glassy with tears. "All because of money."

Amanda lowers her head, sensing his deep remorse. "It's all in the past now, Ben," she murmurs, struggling to find the right words to comfort him. "The most important thing is that you and Charlie are safe and sound."

"You're absolutely right. I am grateful for that." He nods and wipes his sniffles with the napkin, his friendly grin returning. "But it's not something that I'm proud of." He takes a deep sigh. "I resent Charlie's mother for abandoning us when she learned about his condition."" He glances at his son who seems unfazed by his words, still happily playing with his drinks and munching his carrot cake. "But I am not a perfect father, either."

Amanda is quietly listening as the words also sink into her heart. She is not a perfect mother, either. But her conversation with Isla earlier, makes her feel whole again. Probably what that is called the joy of parenthood.

"I consider myself lucky to have a second chance," Ben continues as he gives her a meaningful look. "I served my time and deserved it. We were given lesser charges because of Charlie's condition, and our prison time was shortened due to Mr. Fraser's plea, partly because of you."

Amanda's brow furrows at the mention of Tyler's name. But what makes her taken aback is how she played a role in it.

"How..?"

Ben smiles, understanding her confusion.

"I hate to bring up the horrible moment when four of us were in Mr Fraser's office room." He gives her a concerned look, but as she is not giving any negative response, he continues. "I knew at that time I would end up in prison and would not get any cents of money that I wanted. But you tried to calm me down and asked Mr Fraser to promise that he would give the promised money once all of us were out of that place. As you probably know, it did not exactly end that way."

Amanda swallows nervously. This is the part that always sends a pang of guilt to her heart. It was not her promise, but she meant it when she said she wanted to help. At that moment, she knew Tyler agreed to it because his life was at stake. When finally the police caught Ben off guard, and they were saved, she already had a feeling that the promise would not be kept. Her heart ached for Ben and his son.

Life is not always fair and square.

However, she felt powerless, unsure how to help him. That was the reason she did not have the courage to even see him in prison. This purely coincidental meeting makes her nervous, though she is conscious things are beyond her control and responsibility.

"I'm sorry, Ben," she mutters sadly.

Ben's eyes widen and his lips slowly break into a smile. "Why are you apologising?" He laughs. "What I'm trying to say is that because of you, Mr Fraser kept his promise and gave me the money after I was released from prison."

Amanda cannot believe what she is hearing. For a split second her breath seems suspended as she gasps with parting lips and an incredulous stare. "He did? Tyler?"

Ben nods affirmatively. "Yes, Tyler Fraser. He investigated the case and found the reason I was dismissed unfairly. It was because of my naivety. I stumbled upon a missing order of stationery that was actually part of a fraud scheme orchestrated by the Head of Finance at the time. I forget his name, and I couldn't care less now. "

Amanda is still processing the story in her head as her heart is pounding. Ben smiles rather amusingly at her. Swallowing hard, Amanda takes a quick breath. "Then?"

"Tyler fired him immediately. He did not sue him for the sake that man was the son of his father's good friend. Then Tyler visited me in prison, telling me his plan to speak with some lawyers to reduce my sentence. Thankfully, my good behaviour led to an early release three years ago." He flashes a grin. "Tyler was the first person Charlie and I met first when we stepped back into the world again."

Amanda remains in a state of shock, rendered speechless by the story unfolding before her. Her eyes stare vacantly at the table as Ben continues.

"Tyler made sure Charlie and I have a place to stay, and then he introduced us to people who could give us a job. So, now I and Charlie work in an abattoir. We have been working there since we came out from the prison. And the best part..." He chuckles as his eyes glimmer with happy tears. "Tyler gave me all the money that I would get if I was retrenched properly. I have more than enough now for my retirement." He glances at Charlie who is still playing with his chocolate drinks and marshmallow. "And for Charlie as well."

He falls into being melancholic for a brief before he jumps up merrily. "Plus, James, my current boss, has offered to transfer my work to Brisbane since he has a factory branch there. How can I complain about that? My life has turned amazing."

Then he laughs wholeheartedly. As if sensing the utter joy in his father's heart, Charlie joins in the laughter.

Amanda witnesses the father and son with a relieved smile, feeling the weight lifted from her chest. Ben and Charlie's lives turn out better than she expected, but what truly warms her whole body is discovering that Tyler is behind it all.

He is really a changed man.

The man whom two days ago, she felt the heat of his body against her. His soft caress, his lips against her skin, his dark deep eyes on her. The memory instantly sends a shiver down the spine. A warm tremble feeling floods her heart. She cannot deny that now she has seen him in a different light.

He is simply a beautiful man. Not because of his good look solely, but because of his change of heart that he has determinedly put into action.

"I am so happy for you, Ben," she whispers breathlessly.

"Thank you, Amanda. I owe you."

Amanda shakes her head. "No. You deserve it."

"So, have you seen Tyler since then?"

"Yyy-...No!" she curses herself for lying. But bringing up how far she has been with Tyler feels awkward at this stage. She even does not get a chance to think properly about how she breaks the news to Isla one day.

"I'm sure he will be thrilled to see you, Amanda."

Amanda bit her lips as Ben's eyes lit up with excitement. Quietly she takes a relieved sigh when the topic of conversation changes.

"So, I've shared a lot about myself. What about you? How old is your daughter now? How long will she be in Brisbane?"

Amanda sips her drink, then as she takes a deep breath, she begins to share what she has been up to for the past ten years. It amazes her that when she comes to the point of telling Ben about her divorce, her heart feels free, her lungs feel clear with fresh air, and she feels ...*happy*. There is no more bitterness when she tells Ben the reasons for the divorce. Unsure whether she's actually lying or not, but it's the first time she finally tells someone that she is accepting Sean and Tom of being together.

It is an inexplicable freedom.

Their talk lasts for about an hour. Before they part ways, they exchange contact numbers and promise to meet up again before Ben and Charlie move to Brisbane.

Amanda heads back to her car park, feeling a sense of lightness in her limbs. She drives home, humming to the songs on the radio, which is something that makes her giggle because she has not been doing it for such a long time. Upon arriving home, an idea to cook her favourite food risotto pops up. Seeing the sight of the kitchen, her mind flies to Tyler.

She has to think about how to begin a conversation with him one day. Tyler is right. They need to address what happened between them. She just has to formulate the right words, preparing herself before she contacts him.

While she is having her dinner, a gentle chime on her mobile phone nudges her to check her messages. She anticipates a message from Isla in their group chat confirming her safe landing in Brisbane. Scrolling down to her mobile phone message, the anticipated message appears, but what Isla writes afterwards makes her breath hitch.

Tyler's helicopter had an accident. He and the crew are not yet found.

The incoming messages start pouring in rapidly, with many responses from Hamish and Sean as well, feeding their curiosity about the accident. Isla explains that Tyler went for a meeting in Yarra Valley on the helicopter, and unfortunately, the chopper seemed to have lost control and might have landed in an unknown location. However, it had been a couple of hours since the accident, and no hopeful news received yet.

As if a ripple of hope in her heart that she just built up is immediately shattered, Amanda feels her lungs are constricted. The spoon slips from her hand to the floor, her body frozen in place, unmoved from her seat as if all her energy is drained. The vision of Tyler in her house, in her room, on her bed brings tears to her eyes.

She is too late.

How life can be so cruel sometimes?

As she is about to embark on her new life, a new hope, the unexpected person who has started to touch her heart, is snatched away from her. This cruel twist leaves her feeling unworthy of happiness, trapped in a world of bitterness and loneliness.

Tears streamed heavily down her cheek, she set aside her dinner. Walking through her house to the bedroom, an overwhelming sense of emptiness and coldness seeped into her heart. Embracing herself tightly, the feeling only brought back memories of when Sean was absent during their marriage. She is doomed to be alone, perhaps for eternity.

The sight of her bed only intensifies her heartache as the memory of the last morning she and Tyler spent together comes flooding back. It was a wonderful time they spent together and now she understands why it felt so right. Because he is not the old Tyler anymore. A new Tyler probably she has failed to recognise earlier, and now she misses it.

Lying down on her bed, and clinging tightly to the pillow, she wishes she could feel the heat of his body wrapped around her one more time. She sobs uncontrollably, burying her face in the pillow. As the night grows deeper, she lets herself drift off to sleep, dreaming of him.

Chapter Twenty Three

Her heart stopped for a moment at the sight of him. He appeared casually handsome, bright like an angel in his white, slightly unbuttoned long-sleeve shirt, revealing a hint of chest hair. His warm gaze never wavered as he slowly made his way towards her, navigating through the tall grass and wheat around them. His smile radiated warmth, sending a ripple to her heart. She returned the smile with pure joy in her heart, absolutely thrilled to see his presence. The inevitable happy cries choked on her throat as she eagerly ran towards him only to have him vanish before her.

Amanda's eyes snap open, a soft gasp escaping her lips.

It was just a dream.

But the ache in her heart tells her otherwise.

Tyler is truly gone.

Her heart is shattered. Brushing away the tears streaming down her face, she sinks into her pillow, yearning to be enveloped in sleep once more despite the morning light trickling in.

She has not slept since last night, haunted by the vision of him vanishing from her grasp. Waking up in tears in the dead of night, she mourns before drifting back into sleep. It was similar to when she just had her divorce. She knows one day she will be able to go through this, but at this time, she desires nothing more than to retreat from the world, grieving over her shattered dreams.

The sudden doorbell rings forcing her to lift her head from the pillow. Grumbling to herself, she suspects the uninvited visitor is probably a delivery man who has confused her house for the neighbours. She is not a keen online shopper, and not expecting any delivery for her. Meanwhile, her next neighbour is a young millennial couple who loves online shopping and receives deliveries almost every day.

Choosing to ignore the persistent doorbell, she rests her head back on the pillow. But the sound becomes more insistent, now accompanied by a male voice calling out her name and banging on the door. Recognising the familiar baritone voice of Sean, though she cannot figure out why her ex-husband is looking for her at this time, she jumps out of bed and drags her feet to the door. Once the door is widely opened, Sean stares at her dumbfoundedly.

Amanda knows she must look horrible. Messy hair, swollen red eyes, and still in her cotton pyjama, she does not give a damn care about what Sean thinks. Her current look is a true reflection of her devastation.

"Are you alright?" Sean finally manages to ask, his Adam's apple bobbing nervously.

Ignoring his question, she simply leaves the door open for him to enter the house and closes it behind him.

Sean is following her to the kitchen. It is probably the first time he steps into this house, the house that they used to live in together as a family, since the divorce. She notices his eyes are scanning around, checking out the interior makeover that she has done.

She has to admit that she has transformed the ambience of the house from what used to be his favourite's light and bright theme, to her cloudy and gloomy mood. The entire house has been repainted in a darker shade of grey, the curtains swapped out for heavy grey drapes, and the doors replaced with a dark grey hue. She has spared down the knick-knacks in the house significantly by donating most of them, and the furniture now mostly matches in a lighter grey shade. A crease is formed between his brows as he pursues his lips, restraining himself to comment.

Silently entertained by Sean's disdainful expression while admiring the house, Amanda frowns in contemplation of his true intentions for the visit. The only topic that they agree to talk mostly about the children. It triggers an apprehension within her as she suspects something is amiss.

She shoots her husband with a wary look. "Why are you here? Is everything alright with Hamish and Isla?"

Sean seems just being pulled back into the present. He blinks and quickly shakes his head. Reading his calm demeanour, Amanda quietly takes a relieved breath sensing nothing serious is happening.

"Nothing is wrong with Hamish and Isla," Sean confirms. "I'm here to..." He hesitantly looks at her. "...apologise."

Amanda is tilting her head, racking her brain to figure out the reason for Sean's apology. Their last meeting was in Hamish's house and it ended up unpleasantly. She has a feeling that Isla also has spoken to him following her daughter's apology at the airport. Her guess is correct as Sean continues to speak while placing his both hands in his pockets. It is a habit that Amanda recognises when her ex-husband is nervous.

"Isla filled me in about your past with Tyler." He takes a deep breath as his gaze falls to the floor. "I'm so sorry Amanda for what happened. I am so sorry I was not there for you. And I am sorry that..." He lifts his eyes at her for a brief before he looks at the floor again. "I am sorry that I have accused you of being unfaithful instead." He shakes his head. "I have been unfair to you."

His face is full of regrets and guilt. Knowing him since he was her high school sweetheart, Amanda acknowledges that his words are true from his heart. His apology extends beyond recent events, encompassing past failures as her husband. It is probably not the first time he utters a sincere apology to her, but only this time, and she cannot fathom why, her heart is finally touched.

She owes it to Tyler. He is a true example of someone who changes to be a better person. Sean is no different. He is also trying to be better, reaching out to her despite her cold and distant treatment, putting himself humbly before her, and extending the olive branch all the time, for the sake of their old friendship and their children. The irony lies in the fact that these men caused her bitterness. She, on the other hand, has turned into someone unhappy.

These transformations serve as a reminder that nobody is perfect, and everyone deserves a second chance.

Letting out a heavy sigh, she casually waves her hand. "It's okay, Sean. It's all in the past now." She is being honest with herself. The misunderstanding has ended, together with Tyler is gone from their life.

"Thank you, Amanda. I appreciate it." Sean gives her a sincere look with a faint relieved smile on his lips. "Isla mentioned that you advised her to leave her current job. I agree with you. We don't know what Tyler Fraser might do to her given his history."

Chuckling rather bitterly, Amanda shakes her head. "I think it does not matter anymore since he's gone anyway. Besides, Isla must know how to take care of herself. She probably encounters bad people in other places if she moves out from her current job."

Sean furrows his brow. "What do you mean he's gone? You mean Tyler is leaving Fraser & Co? Isla never mentioned that."

"Isn't he gone because of the accident?" Her voice is rather trembling as the reality begins to hit her harder. She has been crying for the whole night for Tyler, and being reminded over again that he has gone like slicing her heart. "The chopper accident yesterday? I thought they could not find him. I suppose that means..."

Her words trail off as Sean's lips part, his confused expression signalling that she may have overlooked something. Suddenly, realisation strikes her. Sean's look suggests she may have missed a crucial detail.

"Do you think he's dead?" asked Sean.

Unsure of how to respond, she nods weakly. Sean's lips slowly turn up into a smile. He tilts his head down to conceal his grin.

"'No. He's still alive. They found him."

Amanda is breathless. Sean's statement sounds positive. A ripple of hope swimming in her heart, but there is still a tiny doubt that she can fully trust it. His words linger in the air, echoing in her ear as she processes the information.

"Don't worry, Amanda. Though he's not gone yet, we will have a good talk with Isla about leaving his company. I think Isla is considering that, too. After Tyler's confession, she seems uncomfortable to work under the same roof with him."

"He's still alive?" she whispers, still in disbelief, mostly to herself as if she's trying to convince herself.

Sean nods his head affirmatively. "Yes, Isla forwards us the link to the news about his rescue. He suffers minor injuries, but I'm pretty sure it will not deter him to be working again."

Amanda had not been checking her mobile phone since Tyler's helicopter accident news broke. She was too quick to fall into her own sorrow. Rushing to her bedroom to get her mobile phone, she quickly scrolls the messages in their family group chat and opens the news link from Isla about Tyler's rescue. She returns to the living room where Sean is waiting while reading the article.

Tyler and the pilots have been found just before midnight. Everyone is found safe and sound, and being taken to the hospital for a check-up.

She is still trying to let the information sink into her brain. She lifts up her head to meet with Sean's furrowed brow.

"So, he's still alive," she quietly mutters.

Sean responds with a light chuckle, rather amused. "Well, I know he was a horrible man to you in the past. I know it's easy to just get him out of our life. But unfortunately, ..." He shrugs his shoulder. "He's still alive. I guess he will be around for a while."

Amanda's lips break into a small laugh. Not because of Sean's joke, but because of a sudden wave of relief that washes over her. Her palm is covering her parting lips, as she is breathless in a mixture of feelings of awe and bliss. The hope that she thought had been trashed seems to come alive again.

Perhaps she is not too late after all.

Tyler is still alive. That means she can go and find him, and they can sit down and talk about what they had, and how they will move forward. It could potentially be the happiness that both of them have been looking for.

Lost in her own thoughts with a wide grin on her face, she is oblivious that Sean has been observing her with a repressed smile.

"I thought this news would disappoint you, but you seem happy," Sean remarks.

Amanda lowers her face to hide her sheepish smile. "I am not the type of person who is rejoicing over someone's death."

Slightly grimacing, Sean laughs. "That's right. I don't think you mean that. Besides he looks like a nice guy now. Perhaps he's changed. Isla believes so, too. Otherwise, she would have quit the company a long time ago." Suddenly his gaze at her becomes severe. "And I think no one is blind to the way he looks at you. Tyler likes you."

The statement sends a thud to her chest, but Amanda keeps her face to be impassive. Tyler is a changed man. Amanda acknowledges that, too. And she cannot wait to let Tyler know that she is accepting the new him. Her heart is currently bursting with joy, eager to see him soon. She wants to ensure that he is truly still living on this earth. However, no one knows yet what has been developing between them, casting a certain apprehension over her heart as she contemplates Sean and her children's reaction if they find out.

Pursing her lips, Amanda restrains herself to say a word while Sean keeps staring at her as if waiting for her confession. But she arches her eyebrow, waiting for his next words.

Sean nervously rubs the back of his neck. "I may have drawn a wrong conclusion that night at Hamish's birthday party. But it's not only me who can see how both of you look at each other. I did not mean to upset you with the past you had. However, I suppose, he is a changed person now. It's clear he's into you."

Amanda is quietly taking a shuddering breath. Averting her gaze to the floor, her arms are crossing on her chest, hugging herself. Her heart is racing, her brain is whirling hard. She has no idea how she should respond.

"I guess whatever that happens now between you and Tyler, no one including myself, or Isla, or Hamish, has the right to judge," Sean continues. Amanda lifts her eyes to meet with the sincerity in her ex-husband's eyes. "We only wish that you find your own happiness with the right person, Amanda."

Amanda can feel a prick of tears in her eyes. Restraining herself from blinking to allow tears to roll down her cheek, she takes a deep breath.

"Thanks, Sean. I appreciate that," she quietly replies. "Did you speak with Isla about this as well?"

Sean nods his head with a solemn smile on his lips. "Yes, Amanda. She will be happy for you."

Amanda feels her whole body trembling. She quickly wipes away the tears that start rolling down her cheek. When Sean approaches her to pull her into his arm, she cannot contain her sobs anymore.

For what seems like an eternity, she let her tears make a small pool on Sean's shirt, letting him soothe her back, which reminds her of when they were still in high school and Sean consoled her when she was sad. They are not husband and wife anymore, but they can still be friends because they used to be good friends once, too. Hearing the blessings from him, as well as from her children is what she needs the most though probably she does not need to. It is the strong pillar she needs to finally grasp her own happiness that she has ignored for too long despite deserving it.

Chapter Twenty Four

The cry of seagulls and the soothing ebb of waves in the distance create a symphony of nature that delights Tyler's senses. He craves the wild beauty of the world around him, finding solace in its unpredictable rhythm. Reflecting on recent events leading up to Christmas, it is clear why he eagerly anticipates being in this tranquil place.

Standing on the balcony overlooking the peninsula, he leans on the rail, his gaze out at the vast blue water below the cliff. The sun's rays dance on the water, creating a sparkling spectacle. The boats and jets on the water appear to come to life, a clear sign that everyone is taking advantage of the perfect weather, including himself. He feels a surge of joy to be in this picturesque spot, away from the chaos of city life, just in time for the approaching Christmas in three days.

The helicopter accident over a week ago has heightened his appreciation for life. He almost lost his life once, and having another near-death experience only gives him another reminder of how he should lead his life better. The upcoming festive season is an additional excuse for him to leave his work early. Though in reality, he is not officially on holiday yet. He is pretty sure that there will be a couple of calls from work, but he believes Megan will do some magic for him to minimise it.

Nevertheless, he cannot ignore the call from his family, especially his father. The moment he arrives in this beach house this morning, his father promptly rings. As usual, their talk begins around work before it ends with his father's excitement to join their family Christmas party in this house.

The party is his idea. He has sent an ultimatum to Aaron and Kylie not to miss it, and he welcomes Janine to join in as well. Though he has not thought about what he will do to decorate the house, at least he will get help.

AMELIORATION: A CHANGE OF HEART

Megan has informed him that Margaret and John, the housekeepers will be coming today to assist him with the Christmas decorations. He is impressed with the couple's initiative to put up the white Christmas tree theme in the lounge room before his arrival. He cannot wait to work together with the - in their sixties - husband and wife, to transform the house into something magical.

However, amidst all the excitement, Tyler cannot ignore the fact that a piece of his heart is still missing.

Amanda.

They had not spoken since the day he left her house. He ponders whether she knew about his helicopter accident. Isla probably informed her, but there has been no word from her. Not that he is expecting one, but at least Isla sent him a text message, expressing relief that he was found and wishing him a speedy recovery. The message from Isla is enough to send a warm breeze in his heart. It is comforting to know she still values their friendship. He wishes he could get a similar message from Amanda, but probably he has put his hopes too high.

Amanda probably regrets what they had.

Letting out a deep sigh, he realises he must take action. He has to find a way to convince her. If not for the helicopter accident that landed him in the hospital bed for a week, he could have made it happen. And probably by now, he can have her in this house, celebrating Christmas time together.

Chuckling dryly to himself, he shakes his head to shake off his daydream. The sound of the doorbell manages to pull him through from falling into his unpleasant thoughts. Reaching the intercom near the entrance, assuming the coming visitors are Margaret and John, he presses the talk button.

"Hello there! Please come in!" Then he presses the open gate button.

While waiting for the housekeepers to enter the house, he decides to prepare some drinks for them. He whistles happily upon seeing the fridge stocked with plenty of alcoholic beverages and festive foods. Grabbing a couple of beers, he opens one for himself and gazes out to the vast blue sky view from the opened wide balcony folding door. For a couple of minutes, he falls into his own reverie, thinking about what Amanda is doing for Christma. Suddenly he realises how quiet his surroundings are, that even he can hear the sound of the clock ticking.

A realisation suddenly hit him that it had been a while since he opened the gate to let the housekeepers enter the house, however, it seems they still have not reached the entrance door yet. Living in one of the massive properties in Dromana Millionaire's Walk, the driveway stretched for about a kilometre, a distance easily covered by a car in two minutes. But time has gone by five minutes and there is no car in sight near the entrance.

Another thought strikes him, realizing he had been foolish to open the gate without verifying the visitors. Margaret and John should have been given access to the house as they are the housekeepers! How could he have been so careless to simply allow a stranger through the gate?

Getting himself on guard, Tyler quickly dashes into the billiard room and grabs a stick before heading to the door. Upon stepping outside, there is no sight of a car or any person in sight. Quietly cursing himself, he suspects the intruder may be lurking somewhere on the property. However, he questions why the trespasser would ring the bell and announce their arrival if they had ill intentions. Feeling amused at himself, he decides to venture further towards the main gate.

Then, he just remembers that he can check the visitor via CCTV. Slapping his own forehead with his palm, he is about to turn back to the house again, when suddenly his eyes capture a silhouette of a woman within a meter radius. His breath hitches when the figure approaches his way as he recognises it belongs to the only woman who has been haunting his mind.

Tyler blinks his eyes, questioning himself whether he is dreaming, or if the blazing thirty-degree heat has him hallucinating. If he is in the middle of the desert, her presence would be his oasis.

She approaches with a broken tired smile, wiping the sweat from her forehead with the back of her hand as she takes her wide-brim straw sunhat down. Her other hand is carrying a pot bright red Poinsettia plant and her cream woven straw handbag hangs from her shoulder, complimenting her white v-neckline summer dress. Her appearance is always breathtaking for him, but this particular moment makes him paralysed on his spot.

This is precisely what he has been longing for. Amanda is making her way towards him with her warm smile for him. Only for him. It is undeniably a beautiful dream that he does not want to be awakened from. Yet, as he glances around, the manicured French-style garden of the beach house appears oddly familiar. When she finally lands an arm's length away from him, her labouring breathing reminds him that this moment is real.

"Hi."

Tyler is unable to tear his eyes away from her as if he is awed by an angel before him. He is utterly speechless, still not fully convinced. Her wide smile gradually fades as she notices his lack of response. A sheepish apprehension smile takes over as she lowers her head for a brief before swallowing hard to look at him again.

"I am here to see how you are going. I am sorry for not giving you a heads-up beforehand."

Though her tone is full of hesitancy, her voice is a sweet melody. She is standing so close to him. If he stretches out his arm, surely he will touch her forearms and catch her into his arm. His lips part and close nervously, fearing she might vanish at his touch.

Noticing that his hand is already lifted mid-air, she pushes the pot plant to him.

"This is for you. I hope you like the flower. It will be perfect for your living room this Christmas."

His eyes drop to the pot plant as his hand takes the item from her hand. Their fingers inevitably brush in the process, sending a surge of electricity through his body. It jolts him awake that this is not a dream. She is physically here, before him, in such close proximity. He even can scent her subtle flowery fragrance that has been lingering in his memory from the last time he planted his lips on her skin. Lifting up his head, he is quietly grateful that she has not puffed out from his view.

"Thank you," he breathes. "I..." He shakes his head, feeling silly and relieved at the same time. "How did you get here?"

"By driving, of course. My car is parked outside."

He chuckles, feeling amused that he could not find his visitor earlier. "You could have driven your car all the way in."

A shade of blush creeps on her cheek. "Yeah, you're right. I did not expect your driveway to be this long." She fans herself with her hat. "I feel like I just completed a workout."

Feeling foolish for not noticing they are standing under the scorching thirty-degree sun without any shade, he watches as she looks as though she is about to melt. Driven by the desire to make her comfortable, his other free hand instinctively lands on her small back, guiding her towards the house. It is not until they step inside and are greeted by the welcoming cool breeze that he realises his actions. His hand lingers on her back, gently caressing her skin with his thumb. Probably she does not realise his small touch because of the heat, quietly he feels grateful that she is not shoving him away. When she turns to him, dejectedly he lowers down his hand slowly.

"Let me get you a drink." He rushes himself to open the fridge. The cool breeze emanating from within feels like a breath of fresh air. Quietly inhaling deeply, his brain is squeezing hard, thinking about what he has to do next to make her stay. This is probably his only chance. His eyes scan the contents of the fridge, but he struggles to decide which drink he should give her. Finally, he seizes the prominent 'Coke' can drink that catches his eye first, then twirls around, still in disbelief that the woman whom he cannot forget is on his property.

Amanda's back is on him as she gazes away to the opened alfresco door that captures the breathtaking view of the peninsula beach, the most stunning sight in the house. It makes him ponder what she is thinking at the moment. Is she here to see him, to finally talk about what they had? Is she going to bid goodbye to him instead, asking him to disappear from her life for good? He has been bracing himself for those heartbreaking words from Isla, and it would not be a shock if they come from Amanda. Taking a deep breath as his heart shrinks in an anticipated disappointment, he walks towards her and gives her the can drink.

Feeling the cold metal of the can against her forearm, she turns to him and quietly thanks him as she accepts it. His lips itch to ask why she is here, but he holds back, not wanting to push her. Moments pass in silence as they both gaze out into the distance.

"I heard about your helicopter accident from Isla." She breaks the quietude which somehow makes him cheer inside. "I'm so relieved to see that you're okay."

She gives him a sincere look. Gazing at the beautiful sparkle in her grey eyes, tempting him to give them a kiss. He licks his own lips while pretending to sip his drink.

"Thank you," he quietly replies, though his heart is rather screaming how he wants to demand an answer to why she did not visit him sooner in the hospital. But he reminds himself to be patient, especially with the unpleasant past they had. She has strong reason to keep him at bay.

"Are you feeling better now? I heard about your leg injuries," she asks. Her gentle voice sounds gentle with genuine concern.

He shrugs nonchalantly. "It's only a minor injury. I was limping for a couple of days, but I'm on the mend now."

She smiles timidly. "Good to hear."

Yet another silence envelops them. Her gaze is fixed on the ground as she nervously bites her own lips. He can see she is nervous, but it offers no insight into why she has come. Is her apprehension due to delivering the dreaded news he fears? It prompts him to ponder if he should take the initiative and break the silence first, in hopes of bringing peace to them both. Nevertheless, he concedes, his heart will not rest until he holds her in his arms once more

"Well, ..." Her voice breaks through, filling him with a glimmer of hope, though he is still in suspense about whether she will bring positive or good news about them. "I am here because you mentioned that we need to talk about us." She lifts her chin, a determination shines from her eyes. "I guess you're right. We need to talk about it. I've been doing a lot of thinking, and I..." A lump goes through her throat as she touches her temple slightly with a dry chuckle. "That morning was out of character for me. I am sorry for asking you to leave, but I needed time to process it. It's been a while since I had such a thing. I am not one to act impulsively. You were a different person before. So, I was not sure if it was wise for us to...."

Whether she notices it or not, he clenches his fist hard as if it will give him strength.

And yet, he may not actually require it.

Before she finishes her sentences, a commotion at the door interrupts them. Tyler quietly groans but he masks his annoyance by flashing his stiff smile as Margaret and John enter the living room. Tyler introduces the couple to Amanda, who appears slightly flustered but politely engages in a chit-chat with Margaret and John.

Margaret is probably more perceptive as she sheepishly apologises when she realises they have arrived at the wrong time.

"We can come back later," offers John.

"You don't have to," Amanda quickly stops him. Tyler restrains himself from rolling his eyes.

Margaret jumps in. "We will be at the back of the house, far enough away not to accidentally eavesdropping your conversation." She gives Tyler a meaningful glance but with a mischievous curve on her lips. "Just let us know when you're ready, Mr Fraser."

Then, off the couple goes, rather rushing and half running disappear from their sight. Tyler is unsure whether he should be thankful or annoyed when he has a chance to speak with them later. His eyes are back on Amanda, who is nervously still rooted in her spot, tightly hugging herself. How he wished he could pull her in his arms, assuring her that she could trust him. But he is not confident that he has done enough yet to gain her trust.

"They are a lovely couple. Are they the housekeepers of the house?"

He understands that her questions are meant to dispel her own apprehension.

"Yes, they are!" He replies with a loud exhale. " They are here to discuss my family's Christmas party that will be held here."

"Right." She nods her head but probably has interpreted his impatience in a wrong way. "I don't want to take up too much of your time, then."

"No! It's alright." He shakes his head, giving her a firm look, to make it clear he does not want her to leave just yet. "They can wait. What ....?" He swallows hard. "What did you want to tell me earlier?"

He actually hates to ask the question. The last sentence she said was not promising. But he still wants to hear the continuance of it, though it will probably be heartbreaking. He is prepared to understand what she wants him to do to prove himself.

"Well, I was going to say..." Her expression tightens as she nervously rubs her own forearms. "What we had that morning...." Her eyes dart around, avoiding his gaze until they suddenly fix on something behind him. He turns to see what has caught her attention.

On the wall next to the fridge hangs an A4 framed picture, featuring a single word. The word, written in white font on a black background, stands out boldly. Reading the motivational word, he smiles, knowing he personally selected and displayed it. This word has become his favourite, bringing a smile to his face every time he sees it.

Turning back at her, he can tell that the same word resonates with something deep within her. A gentle smile forms on her lips, and her expression softens. When her eyes finally land on him, he knows that the word has helped him to make her understand. Another glimmer of hope swimming through his heart.

"What do you want to say about that morning?" Half whispering, he asks, bracing himself for a potentially disappointing response.

Taking a shuddering breath, she replies quietly, "I will never forget that morning."

Immersed in her captivating grey eyes as she utters the words, Tyler feels a sudden surge of warmth in his chest. His lips part as his eyes search for an affirmation of her words from her facial expression, waiting in suspense if probably she will continue with negative sentences. But her gentle assuring smile sends a breeze of fresh breathing air, as their eyes speak for each other's hearts.

This is the moment that he has been longing for. She finally says something profoundly important to him. At least she is not regretting what they had. But he quickly reminds himself not to put his hopes too high as it does not mean she will accept him fully.

"What does this mean for us?" he asks.

"I don't know." She shakes her head weakly. "I ran into Ben."

The mentioned name of the man makes his head snap up as his eyes widen. "Ben? That Ben?"

She nods. "Yes, that Ben. Ben who held us hostage."

"How?"

Surely Tyler wants to know how. Since the morning he left her house, he immediately instructs Megan to reach out to anyone he introduced to Ben, who might have employed him. If it was not because of the helicopter accident, he might have had an answer by now.

"It was a coincidence. I met him while dropping off Isla at the airport."

"Right."

"He mentioned you."

His eyes search her, his mind is whirling hard as he debates whether the encounter will bring positive or negative outcomes now that she has met with the only man who could potentially help him prove himself.

He arches his eyebrow as his heart pounding hard. "And then?"

"Well..." She sheepishly lowers her eyes. "I guess you've changed. And you have proven yourself that you are a different person now. And I..." She lifts her eyes, gazing deeply at him which is enough to send a shiver throughout his body.

"And what?" His voice is hoarse, full of restrained desire. Like a magnet between them, he gravitates closer to her. His eyes bounce between her lips and eyes that consume his every being. He cannot wait to savour her, holding her in his arms. With every ounce of his strength, he restrains himself, waiting for the words from her lips that will be his breaking point.

"And I am considering that we should..."

Tyler is uncertain if he is breathing at this moment. Their faces are mere inches apart. Clenching his fist, he keeps reminding himself not to rush. Yet, her intoxicating scent is overwhelming, pushing him to the edge of his self-control. The suspense of this moment is excruciating, he cannot fathom it. However the moment a soft flesh brushes gently on his lips, a giddiness takes over as if he is flying.

The awaited word remains unspoken. Yet her gentle playful kiss provides more than enough solace. Every ounce of tension in his body melts away as her kiss deepens. Quietly sighing as he wraps her lithe body in his arm, pressing her hard against him, he feels like being transported to paradise.

His perseverance has finally paid off. The reward is priceless. It is not just about winning her heart, but also about earning her trust and her entirety.

His palms press on her cheek when they gasp for air after a long kiss, ensuring that this is not a dream. Unsure when their position changes as they have been carried out in their bliss, he finds himself staring at the picture on the wall instead. His eyes capture the word that has been his guiding force for the past ten years.

Amelioration.

AMELIORATION
To make better....more tolerable...more acceptable...

Did you love *Amelioration: A Change of Heart*? Then you should read *The 40 Year Old Virgin*[1] by L D Raylene!

[2]

Cassie is approaching forty years old. What has she achieved in her life?

Never have a boyfriend.

Never been kissed.

And clearly, that means she never had sex.

She has an average job and average life, and she blames herself for being a middle child.

When her sister plans for a wedding that falls on her 40th birthday, Cassie feels even more left out.

Since her sister-in-law tragically passed away in a car accident, Cassie always put her two gorgeous young nieces' needs ahead of her.

---

1. https://books2read.com/u/bxrd5d

2. https://books2read.com/u/bxrd5d

When her brother Kieran finally manages to get on his feet again, Cassie is encouraged to look into her own life.

Reminiscing the past to an old mate who she feels reciprocating her feelings, she thinks of building a romantic relationship with him. However, an almost kissing moment with him causes another havoc. She falls into another man's arm instead who hardly spoke with her.

One-night stands and casual sex are not in her life dictionary. And yet, she falls into one. And brokenhearted.

From the inner city slums of Jakarta, the favourite park in Melbourne city, to the beautiful small beach town in regional Victoria, this is a journey of a woman who stands hold of her principles against the modern perspective of a romantic relationship.

To finally find her perfect match.

Also by L D Raylene

A Little Amusement
An Amelia : A Modern Twist Pride and Prejudice
The 40 Year Old Virgin
Amelioration: A Change of Heart

About the Author

Based on The Big-Five Model (B5M) of five broad personality dimensions described by Dr John A. Johnson, the assessment test conducted in Raylene's workplace, she was identified with a high level of imagination. That means she perceived the real world as often too plain and ordinary, but it does not mean she is ignorant of things that happen around the world and how she is grateful for her life each second.Since then, Raylene has started expressing her fantasy through writing to create a richer, meaningful world apart from her daily job as a part-time office all-rounder, a baker, a mother of two energetic kids and a wife to her, unfortunately not a bookworm, but factual oriented husband.

Find Raylene at Instagram @ldraylene

www.ingramcontent.com/pod-product-compliance
Lightning Source LLC
Chambersburg PA
CBHW020246180626
46810CB00006B/2400